# SLICE OF GLORY

G. E. DABBS

This is a work of fiction. Names, characters, places, and incidents are products of the author's imagination or are used fictitiously and are not to be construed as real. Any resemblance to actual events, locations, organizations, or persons, living or dead, is entirely coincidental.

**World Castle Publishing, LLC**
Pensacola, Florida

Hardback ISBN: 9798246736012
Paperback ISBN: 9798891265141
eBook ISBN: 9798891265158
First Edition World Castle Publishing, LLC, March 2, 2026
http://www.worldcastlepublishing.com

Cover: Cover Designs by Karen
Editor: Karen Fuller

This writing is dedicated to the memories and contributions of the following great allegorical fiction/fantasy writers of our time:

C. S. Lewis
Charles Kingsley
E. Nesbit

# CHAPTER 1

Darkness reigned over the people of the mountain. Fear drove the compromises, the shame of the submission, the agony of betrayal, and a tiny ray of hope. The prophecy offered the only sparkle to motivate resistance, kept secret in hopes that one day, the four promised ones would appear, bring hope, and end the tyranny. So many fainted from that anticipation as if it were just a pipe dream and succumbed to the darkness. Still, a precious few held on, believing against all odds that the victors over the reign of terror lay in the hands of just four strangers.

---

Carson and Wayne rushed to the elevator just as the doors closed, stepping through the closing doors. They felt blessed now to stand in the elevator with two attractive teenage girls near the same age. After departing from a Beta Club Convention rock concert that the two twelfth graders found lacking in artistic merit, their desire to finish off the leftover pizza in the room proved more appealing. Running into two girls in the process provided a new turn of events, intriguing to both boys. There was a moment when the proximity left them all a little too thrown together.

When Carson noticed the girls were uncomfortable, he said, "We have an urge to raid the fridge and finish our leftover pizza from last night."

The blonde girl smiled and said, "Same here, only we are going for leftover Subway sandwiches."

The brunette girl said, "Yeah, it sounds like a good breakfast since we overslept and did not have time to eat anything."

The blonde said, "We stayed up all night because we did

not want the convention to end."

"We were drug out of bed by our sponsor this morning despite how much we wanted to sleep in," said the brunette.

The door opened after the elevator dinged the second time, and the four of them stepped into the hallway and turned right toward their respective rooms at the end of the hall.

Wayne still struggled with what to say next as they started down that hall.

"Wow, we are on the same floor," Carson said.

---

At that point, a sudden disaster was in the making in front of the hotel. A terrorist, with a hijacked fuel truck, sped toward the entrance of the enormous hotel. The al-Qaeda terrorist's eyes were wide open with excitement as he drove the fuel truck through the glass doors. The eighteen-wheeler jackknifed on impact with the cab, veering to the right. The fuel tank smashed into the lobby's central structure, spilling fuel and sparking an inferno. The explosion rocked the entire building. A mushroom of fire billowed through the entrance. The blast's force dislodged the elevator doors, sending the rolling flames up the open shaft. Flames gushed from every crack in the closed elevator doors, severely startling the four teenagers who had already stopped in shock as if the entire building suddenly felt the crescendo of a great earthquake from below. The force of the continued eruption rocked the building further, sending more flames rolling through the now-bulging elevator passageway.

The concussion and the heat immediately knocked the teenagers to the floor. Climbing back to their feet, they started a panicked rush toward the end of the hall. The floor rumbled with severe tremors. The intense heat filled the corridor behind them as the ignited fuel and floors below erupted beyond the elevator shaft. The four ran past the girls' room, knowing the heat and flames lapped at their heels.

Smoke and flames greeted them from the emergency stairs at the end of the hall.

Carson yelled at the girls, "My room is right here! Hurry!" He then pulled his room card out of his pocket and quickly swiped the card through the handle. The door hesitated, the light turned green, and then Wayne rattled the handle until it released. All four plunged into the room and immediately shut the door, hoping to ward off the heat and flames that were incinerating the hall just outside the room.

Panic embraced all four of them. Inhibitions escaped them now. The roar's crescendo rattled the structural integrity of the whole building and resembled that of napalm as it sucked away every molecule of oxygen and pulled at their last barrier of protection. Suction briefly pulled air from the room, then dark smoke billowed back through the space under the door.

The brunette opened the curtain and frantically waved for someone below to notice her. All attention focused on the entrance, where intense flames billowed as well.

Carson frantically shouted, "Quick! Help me stuff some towels under the door!" He sped into the bathroom, grabbed the towels off the metal shelf above the toilet, threw them into the toilet, and flushed. It immediately overflowed, but all the towels were wet simultaneously. He started removing the wet towels and threw them to Wayne and the two girls to stuff under the door in the now-smoke-filled room.

The blonde said, "The door is turning brown from the heat. We need to break the window and jump before we burn alive."

Carson brought wet washcloths dipped in the toilet to his three colleagues to cover their mouths and help them breathe.

Wayne picked up an oversized chair and threw it toward the window, and it bounced off, failing to break the glass. His efforts were heroic but futile. The thick, dark smoke grew worse, and much of it came from the door and walls that gradually changed in temperature and color.

Carson grabbed a mattress off the first bed, and the two girls joined him in using it to barricade the door from the heat and smoke. The door was already dark brown, and suddenly, flames burst forth from it as the paint ignited from the heat on the other side. That flame quickly ignited the mattress, producing a heavy, rolling cloud of smoke that filled the room with intense darkness.

The brunette said, "Get down on the floor! The air is always cleaner there during a fire!"

They lowered themselves to the floor. All but Wayne, who held his breath, and as he stood in the dark smoke, he made another gallant effort to throw the chair through the window. The smoke was so thick that it overwhelmed his second effort, making it weaker than the first. The chair bounced back off the glass again. He fell to the floor with his three companions and began to cough heavily.

They all continued to try to breathe with their mouths covered by the dark, soiled white washcloths as the heat climbed around them. Their faltering effort to suck up the last bits of air possibly hidden there offered little hope at this point. They coughed and choked as the smoke thickened even more around them, irritating their eyes. These were their last fleeting moments, and only thoughts and prayers lingered in their minds as all hope faded fast.

Suddenly, a lit passageway opened in the middle of the wall, and hands reached them and dragged them all from the dark, smoke-filled room. The bright doorway closed when all of them were safely beyond. The air cleared quickly. With a confused look around, the four were quickly aware that they were no longer in the hotel. There, people who were not your average hotel bellboys stood around them. The unusually brilliant clothing was of finer quality than this group could find at Walmart. They looked at each other, baffled by the new circumstances before them, but the main emphasis was on breathing again. The air seemed so much fresher than any they had previously breathed.

"This is astonishing. One moment, we are breathing our last breath, and now we are in a quiet, cool, dark place," the brunette said hesitantly.

"Hey! This looks like a tunnel," said Carson, regarding the light evident further down the passage.

The blonde said, "Yeah, but it doesn't look like the tunnels used in *Sliders*."

"Maybe we found a wormhole?" said the brunette, "Or should I say the wormhole came and got us?"

"Quickly leaving that room, I thought they pulled us into a *Stargate*. I just knew we were on our way to another world," said the blonde with amazement as she looked around at the dimly lit tunnel. Not that it was dark; something brighter glowed far in the distance, dwarfing the light where they stood.

"I will say I like the change," said Carson, "The air is so much nicer than that stuffy room filled with smoke."

"Perhaps we died back there in that smokiness," said the brunette with an air of breathlessness, "And now we are going to our eternal destiny."

"Cool! If we are dead, at least I can introduce myself. I'm Wayne, and over there with the smutty face is my best friend, the Carson dude," said Wayne, feeling more comfortable around the two young ladies now.

"I'm glad to meet you, Wayne. I'm Rhonda, and this is my sidekick, Roxie," said the blonde.

"Now that we know each other's name, let's follow this tunnel toward the bright light," said Carson, "Those angelic-looking dudes that certainly are not hotel bellhops seem impatiently waiting for us."

"Yeah, they do have their arms crossed for some reason,"

said Roxie, the brunette, "Let's see where they lead us, but I'm nervous."

"Yeah, I know what you mean. Is this where we stand before God?" asked Rhonda with a tone of insecurity in her voice.

Carson looked puzzled and said, "We are in a serious predicament. What will become of us now if we are dead? Do we go to Judgement Day? Will He be inviting or mad at us, dying so young?"

"Good question, but I don't feel like I'm dead," said Wayne, "I can look at Roxie here, and I still find her unusually attractive, and I thought you did not have those feelings after you have croaked."

Roxie looked at Wayne and said, "Yeah, we can be romantic to heaven's gate." She smiled, and the tone of her voice suggested she was only joking.

"Now, don't we make a cute couple?" asked Wayne, looking back with amazement.

Roxie changed the subject, "Look at the adorable flowers on the sides of the cave. It must be from the light that is getting brighter up ahead."

Carson appeared more focused on what was beyond. "Is that a dock up ahead of us?" he asked.

Wayne quickly said, "Yes, it must be—I smell the ocean. Look, there's a boat, too."

Rhonda looked onward as they all did at the wonder up ahead. She pointed toward the brightness and insisted, "Look, there's a boat, and beyond that, a bright, golden fortress with a gigantic dome!"

Roxie said, "A dome you can see through, and light shines into the heavens from it? That looks more like a giant force field that protects a huge, walled city."

In astonishment, Carson said, "Are we on another planet? Where has there ever been a city so huge and magnificent? The walls extend in both directions as far as I can see."

Rhonda said, "We are definitely not in Birmingham anymore, and with all of that smoke we left back there, I don't miss it. I do, however, fear Who we will see next."

Roxie said, "Could this be heaven? How come I don't see any angels floating around on clouds playing harps?"

Wayne said, "Even our escorts look like angels, where are their wings?"

Carson said, "Do boat drivers need wings? I don't think it matters at this point. We can be thankful they decided to drop by and rescue us, bringing us back with them. I thought we were parched peanuts back there."

"The sky is such a dark blue, and there is not a cloud or even a star in the sky. It is as if the walled city we are looking at provides the only light anywhere," Rhonda said with continued intrigue in her voice.

"Check out the water. There are no waves, and there is a mist that captures the light from the city but hangs so low above the surface," said Carson.

"I like this dock," said Roxie, motioning toward the structure where the boat awaited. "It has never experienced wear or tear from bad weather. Maybe someone just built it or something."

As they stepped on its surface and followed the silent guides to the boat that awaited them, Carson said, "The boat looks like a sleigh. Where do they keep the engine?"

Roxie said, "No, it's more like a tour boat or something. I've seen boats like this at amusement parks."

"This is a funny place," said a puzzled Rhonda, "I can't say I ever imagined anything like this as an afterlife. Wouldn't it be hilarious if we find this is an abduction by aliens?"

"This is by no means amusing, either as eternity or alien rescue," said Wayne in confusion, "I'm feeling uneasy about this whole affair." He looked to see if anyone had a response to his concern, but went on to gaze into the distance with the others.

Carson and his friends viewed the scenery around them with total amazement. They had just left the exit at the mouth of the tunnel, stepped through an open area, and walked across a dock where the most elegant of boats awaited them with several heavenly-looking people. The floating apparatus the four teens boarded, sleigh-like in design, seemed inviting to take them to that great destination. Beyond the boat stood an ever-approaching mighty fortress, with a clear, glass dome extending far into the heavens, and sat in a sea smooth as crystal or glass. The ship had no sails or propulsion devices, yet it moved from the dock with great speed and ease when they were all seated. The boat moved with no bumps or struggle, passing quietly through one foggy patch after another.

Roxie popped the big question. "Hey, outer space-type man, where are we going?"

The angelic being who stood before them as if to guard them said, "You know where we are going, but you know not why."

Carson said, "We're going to a city and have no clue why we are there, but I'm glad to be here. This place is puzzling but unique."

Wayne said, "Is it important that we don't know why?"

The angelic being said, "Because you are not dead." He smiled as if he knew the idea would blow their minds.

There was a moment of awe, with several mouths open in puzzlement and confusion, when Roxie said, "I thought we got away with that far too easily back in the smoke-filled room. We must be on another planet, right?"

Wayne said, "Yeah, dying hurts, and we just had a coughing spell, and then we're grabbed and pulled through this door of light that appeared in the wall. Now we are on Planet X!"

Carson said, "Did someone make a mistake or something?"

The angelic being said, "We hope not. We're not accustomed to mistakes at this level. Let's just say you are chosen because you are needed."

Wayne said, "Wow! We are chosen. Good time for it, too, or we would be crispy critters back there by now."

The angelic being said, "Your selection meets the needs for a special mission designed by the Creator. It is like the ancient prophet, Elijah, removed from the earth before experiencing death, only you're called on to enter another domain of creation to carry out a mission for the Creator."

"Cool! We are the chosen ones. We have a mission, but what can four teenagers from Alabama do?" asked Carson.

"Nothing by yourselves," said the angelic being.

"Would you look at that," said Roxie.

They all gazed with amazement at how close the golden city had become. From their vantage point, the great fortress walls extended left and right forever.

"That's incredible!" said Wayne with his mouth open.

"Yeah, by the brightness of that area in front of us, it must be a gate or something," Wayne said, "You don't suppose it's a docking station or something, do you?"

Carson quickly said, "Yes, and look at the gate, the walls around it, and the entrance."

They all gazed at the splendor before them. The white surfaces presented a magical effect, as if they contained all the colors of the rainbow yet remained incredibly white. That particular effect showed on the walls of the gate and all around the edges. It brightened the whole area around its opening with its reflective ability, as if prisms hid in its surface. Everything on the water seemed dark and empty compared to what dazzled their eyes at the gate and beyond. It held a pearly texture at every point and throughout the structure.

The ship sailed smoothly to the awaiting shore and stopped with little fanfare. The beach was immediately noticeable as the four stepped out of the boat.

"Check out the sand," Rhonda said, "It is tiny gold particles. It sparkles with the light." She reached and scooped up a handful and allowed the reflective particles to fall to the ground with no dust evident.

Roxie walked through the sandy beach toward the vast complex, only to stop and stare in awe at the splendor. She finally found words to say, "Just look at those steps and how they extend both ways as layers of a cool-looking foundation for this entire complex." She knelt at the first step and stared at the crystal-like green side of the stage, layered with gold on top.

"They are beautiful, and this step contains a solid green emerald surface."

"Is that a step with a red and white glass-like mixture? And that one looks like huge ruby blocks. There's one layer of rectangular diamonds. And the top step looks like golden crystals," said Rhonda in her excitement and mystification, "The architect who built this spared no expense."

Suddenly, in bold fashion, a strong voice came from above, "The Word says, 'Remove your shoes because you are standing on holy ground.'"

With a puzzled look, Wayne then agreed, "Looks like we are in a country where you can't wear shoes inside the house." They all sat down in the golden sand and began removing their sneakers.

Carson said, "We have something in common with Moses, dudes!"

Wayne's face glowed with a smile, and he said, "Yeah? We probably broke the Ten Commandments or something like he did." He knelt and removed his shoes as quickly as he could.

Carson said, "I suppose I won't need socks either." He

swiftly removed his shoes to reveal his rather large feet.

Roxie, after a glance around, pointed out some disturbing news. "The boat is gone, and our escorts as well."

"Guess they experience boredom looking at four teenagers gawking at a set of steps," said Wayne.

Carson suddenly became aware, as did the others, that a new heavenly creature stood at the top of the beautiful stairs. The creature wore a robe of incredible magnificence and splendor. Carson said, "Don't tell me; you're St. Peter?"

# CHAPTER 2

The heavenly being smiled and said, "No, Carson, Peter does not work the gates much, and if he did, he would work the gate of St. Peter, the Apostle."

Wayne ribbed Carson. "See there, smarty. Now, we are in trouble for calling people names. Not everybody wants or likes to be called St. Peter. Now you have eleven more guesses."

The heavenly creature in the lovely robe smiled again and said, "I've been called far worse things than St. Peter. I'm the archangel, Gabriel. I'll be your tour guide and instructor for your short training phase before departure for your mission. Please come up to the top of the steps, but no further."

All four teenagers climbed the stairs in amazement. They looked upon the famous angel with respect and admiration.

Gabriel halted the four at the top of the stairs. "It is written that no unclean thing shall ever enter into the gates of this mighty city."

Rhonda questioned with a look of surprise on her face. "You want us to go back to the beach and take a bath?"

"Rhonda, a bath in physical water would not be enough for the cleaning you seek. The cleanliness needed to enter these gates must be achieved by the confessing and purging of your iniquities." He stood before the four and gave further instructions. "You must kneel before Your Maker and Savior and, in silent prayer, confess your sins to purge yourself of uncleanliness. By doing so, you allow grace, a form of God's undeserved forgiveness, to purge your souls as is written."

The four knelt before the gate and closed their eyes. Each

said a prayer as if hidden in their closet to communicate directly with God and to be freed from their unconfessed sins.

Carson, the first to complete his prayer, said, "Amen." He climbed to his feet and also noticed his clothing had been changed. He looked at his sleeves and robe and saw the most beautiful outfit he had ever worn. He was speechless and in total awe.

Soon, all four stood in admiration of their new clothing.

Gabriel interrupted their awestruck wonder. "These are the wedding garments of the Master. Wear them with honor and respect to the Groom who has provided them for you. You may now enter by following me."

Gabriel stepped toward the gate, but the four slowly followed with eyes that soaked up every detail of wonder before them. He led them through the gate into a beautiful forest. A shimmering sidewalk of golden cobblestone bricks led through the woods. The trees were well-lit but not from above. It was as if the light came from everywhere, giving the whole forest illumination in a way that had no shadows or shade. Under the trees stood many men and women, and all walked around barefoot in the grass. While they strolled along, many picked leaves from those trees and ate them.

"Why are people eating leaves?" asked Wayne out of curiosity.

Gabriel said, "This is the area, like the gate, for those who enter through the Gate of Judas Iscariot. The leaves offer strength. Grace provided a means of salvation and eternity, but strength can be added and sometimes needed. Say you want to go bicycling across the country and not be used to it. Either you get in shape, or come here for strength from those leaves. Taste one."

Roxie reached and picked one of the plump leaves and bit into it. "Wow, no wonder they pick them. It tastes a little like

Spearmint, only better, and the leaves are so plump. The leaves are like energy drinks you eat instead of drink."

"They are here for the pleasure of eating and additional strength in that fashion, yes," said Gabriel.

Rhonda asked, "I can see children with adults. Does that mean their whole family died?"

"Not necessarily. Children may die, but they continue to age to maturity. Would it be fair for a two-month-old to stay two months old for eternity?"

Carson suddenly showed interest. He asked, "If that is so, my little brother, Joseph, who died when I was seven, is here and around ten years old now?"

"I would think so, Carson, and I know your next question. I'm sorry, you can't go and see him right now. We have more pressing matters pending," said Gabriel with a look that appeared to understand the disappointment in Carson's eyes. "I know your brother meant a lot to you, but that opportunity will come at its appointed time in your life."

"I suppose asking to see my granny is out of the question, too?" asked Rhonda as she snapped her fingers in disappointment. "I suppose we are to just follow this yellow brick road and see where it goes?"

The golden path followed many hills, and finally, in the distance, the elevation of the grounds took them toward a beautiful, bright city of buildings, and many reached into white, puffy clouds above. The sky was light blue, and no glass dome protected the enclosed environment's outer limits.

Their path took them to a street that seemed to climb the hills into the great distance. The shiny cobblestone walkway had the look of golden bricks, so shiny that you would think you could see through them. Each barefoot step upon them fogged up when the foot was removed. Before they stepped through the open gate into the community, they looked at the wall, which was also made of gold trimming. It was layered with the most beautiful marble decorations.

Roxie excitedly pointed toward the well-lit buildings, "Would you look at those streets? Even the pavement shines like golden glass without a crack or a pothole. And the buildings; there are no porches, overhangs, or shade devices."

"This place is incredible," said Carson, "Look at the surface we are walking on, so pure and smooth. I have never seen gold so polished and magnificent. I can also feel the warmth of the metal under my bare feet. I suppose the pavement here is warmer than the cobblestone earlier, which was cool and fogged up with our steps. We must be getting closer to the source of the warmth."

"Some of the bricks of the walls of the buildings are dazzlingly transparent in appearance, also. They are made of gold, so pure and so polished that they look like golden mirrors, and the mortar that holds them together is pure silver with no tarnish. Fort Knox has nothing on this place," Wayne said with wonder and amazement in his eyes, his smile, and the glow of his demeanor.

"Wow! Check out the vehicle that just appeared when that man approached the curb!" said Rhonda, who suddenly overcame her silence in wonder.

They all gazed at the vehicle as the man boarded, and it levitated past them, maybe six inches from the golden pavement.

Carson said, "I've got to get me one of those."

Again, Gabriel interrupted their wonder and amazement with a statement of their instructions. "Please step this way. We have work to do."

To have to walk away from the incredible visual splendor was very difficult. Even the atmosphere gave the four teens tranquility and a desire to stay forever, as if they felt they were at home. Gabriel cleared his throat as if he seemed a little impatient with his wait for them to follow his guidance. All four turned hesitantly to see a door open in front of them, leading into what appeared to be an all-white office interior.

When Carson looked around, he saw all the comforts he would ever want in an office, only on a much grander scale. At one end of the room, there appeared to be a marker board. Diagrammed on the board was a drawing of a type of jumpsuit, along with details of wings in the back, but not feathery in design.

They looked more transparent, like those on a dragonfly.

At each end of the marker board stood two more well-dressed figures in garments similar to Gabriel's. Glimpsing around the room, another figure stood in the opposite corner. Each was well-robed and, like Gabriel, wore swords as part of their attire.

The room's walls glowed as if made of living matter in its purest state. Still, with their eyes absorbing every detail of the office and a few final minutes of visual consumption of their surroundings, their attention moved to the gathering of the four well-robed angels in front of them.

Wayne, perhaps out of pure adventure and a little deviance, said, "Suppose I have an evil thought, like looking here at Roxie and thinking something like…" Suddenly, without a sound, no Wayne was in the seat beside them anymore. He had vanished instantly.

Gabriel smiled and said, "He's back on the beach and has returned to his jeans and T-shirt. Hopefully, he will know what to do and return soon."

About a minute later, Wayne appeared in front of his seat, kneeling. He got up and returned to the chair he had mysteriously vacated moments before. He also wiped away a couple of tears. He looked at the others and tried to diminish their thoughts.

"Don't ask and don't do that either. It's like being out of your Father's will and knowing it. I promise to respect this place and the clothing I wear from now on. For some reason, I was afraid I would see gnashing of teeth. Possibly, I made my confession quick enough to return before I could find out what gnashing of teeth meant." His voice had a humble tone, a bit of shame, and concern over his foolishness.

"Thank you, Wayne," said Gabriel, "That was a grand demonstration of the perfection of this place and the fragile condition of your human state. You are still alive. You did not die in that fire. You are all redeemed but still sinners, growing in faith. Before we go any further, let me introduce my fellow archangels to my left. The first is the Archangel Raphael, the second is the Archangel Michael, and the last is the Archangel Ariel. We are four of the archangels of the Most High. It is our job to equip and guide you toward your assigned tasks.

"It might sound stupid, but I want to call you a quartet. Do you get to sing together as a group, too?" Carson asked with a bit of color to his cheeks.

"Bless your soul. You must know it is part of our duties to praise the Most High, and we do many quartet specials. We would be glad to do one for you, but they last for weeks and sometimes months because of the worthiness of our Master," said Gabriel.

Carson smiled at the answer and awaited further instructions, realizing he had digressed from the subject.

"You are the chosen four for a great mission of hope to another world of God's creation. This world is upon your world, but not in the capacity you might imagine. This group of God's former followers crumbled in their relationship with their Maker, and many have joined forces with evil to bring a great shadow over their land. All have been consumed by this darkness, and the world as they know it is now a godless society where mankind has drifted into a domain of power and totalitarianism. You escaped death several hours ago in that hotel room and were given a second chance at life. To have that second chance, you must be clothed in righteousness by the One who sends you and carry a mission of hope to this wayward group of people. You will all be put at great risk and peril, but through faith and trust, you can achieve great things for the glory of the God you serve." He looked at the four with admiration in his eyes.

"Gabe, dude, this sounds like a lot of fun, but what if we choose not to do this?" Wayne asked.

"Well, we can just, what you would call, beam you back to the hotel room where we found you at the very instant you were retrieved," Gabriel said, "You would have to work things out from there. No help from here until after it's over."

"Dude, sounds like we have a great opportunity here, and I think I like how it sounds," Wayne said with a big grin.

"Where are we going?" asked Carson, "To the Middle East or something?"

"Far worse than the Middle East," said Gabriel with a concerned look, "You must go back to Alabama and the mountain country."

Roxie questioned this time. "Are we going to witness to the forest rangers or something?"

Gabriel smiled and said, "Well, this group of God's people is not human by your nature. They are a different species entirely, but with equal intelligence and created in the likeness of God, as you all are. They are located in the higher mountains of your state of Alabama and nowhere else in the world."

Rhonda spoke up from her silent perspective of confusion about the challenge. "How are we to reach this group of people?" she asked, puzzled.

"Well, again, you are picked because you all have the opportunity and flexibility to make things happen. You are not chosen because you are equipped; He will equip you, the chosen. Exoskeleton suit issues are next, as the diagram on the board in front of you illustrates. In addition to your physical makeup changes needed, these suits will give you the protection your activities will demand and the added abilities you must master as you need them," said Gabriel.

"Let me get this straight," said Carson, "We will get a hard-shell covering like a bug, and we will have to learn how to use it. Are we going to have wings like the diagram illustrates?"

"You are so right! You will have the shell and the wings only when you need them. You learn and gain perspective quickly, my good fellow. You will be placed near a group that should offer you sanctuary until you are ready for the world you are entering, providing you act quickly to find them," said Gabriel."

"What will be the first thing we will need to master concerning this exoskeleton we will get?" asked Wayne.

"You will have to learn to fly," said Gabriel.

"Cool, I always wanted to be able to fly. Here's my chance!" exclaimed Wayne with joy in his voice.

"Now, if you would, please step to the back of the briefing room and stand on the four pedestals before you," said Gabriel.

The four moved relatively quickly toward the short stool-like features next to the back wall. They all stood on their pedestals as if they waited for someone to beam them down to earth, as they had seen on*Star Trek*.

Carson looked around the room, noticing a red light surrounding him, and felt a sudden sting along his shoulder blades. When the light disappeared, he thought he had another layer of clothing that fit more snugly. Feeling himself, Carson felt that some kind of jumpsuit replaced his previous clothing. He moved his hands back to his sides and found a waist belt with several packets. Mounted on the right side was a sword in its sheath, attached to the belt. He looked at his partners and noticed they all had swords, but he was different: his was mounted on his right side, theirs on their left.

Gabriel said, "The swords are the gifts given to you by your favorite quartet. Their design and loyalty are strict to your use. They offer you the power of protection, and yours is mounted as though you are left-handed. I assume that is the correct status, Carson?"

"Yes. Sure. You guys are very thoughtful," said Carson.

"Perhaps we are. If we missed something, be sure to ask when you get there," Gabriel said, "You will each have a guardian angel dwelling with you, but invisible. He will be there, but you will never know of his presence or the spiritual warfare and work he does on your behalf. There will also be a voice that speaks to you in times of comfort and need. Listen to His voice. He will guide you and help you in times of trouble. You must listen and follow His guidance at all times. He is called the Comforter. At random times, I will meet directly with you, Carson, and the others, individually if permitted, but this mission is a need-to-know and as time requires. Too much information at one point would overwhelm all of you and prevent the mission from taking place. You can understand all languages through the modifications given to your exoskeletons. Your mission must begin at a landmark of your choosing. What would that be?"

Roxie quickly said, "A road sounds excellent. At least we will have a way around or catch a ride. You can always find your way back to where you started if you know where the road is. Is that a good choice?" She looked at Gabriel for his answer. There was a sudden uneasiness over the selection, but no changes were made.

Suddenly, the briefing room, with its grandeur of excellence, vanished before their eyes. All four stood, amazed, as their surroundings changed to reveal a large group of giant rocks and stones. To their right was a wall of tar-covered stones, many pressed together. Many giant trees stood around them. They were the biggest they had ever seen.

"Wow! Had no idea Alabama had Redwood Trees," said Rhonda.

"Cool. Check out the long black wall," Wayne said, venturing toward the thick layer of black stones. "It's slanted just enough for us to climb and get out of these boulders.

"Maybe we can see more from the top." Wayne climbed up. He turned to help the girls up and Carson, too. They stood upon a rough, blackish-gray sea of a surface that seemed to be at least a football field across. "Hey, look at this white stripe that runs along the edge of the structure. It sure is wide."

Carson looked and said, "If I am six feet tall, it has to be sixty feet wide.

Look up that way. It goes up that hill, and not only does it have white lines on each side, but it also has yellow lines in the middle. This is a gigantic highway!"

"Don't you think we should get off of it in case gigantic cars run on this gigantic road?" Rhonda asked with a worried sound in her voice.

"Like, those vibrations that are getting stronger and stronger," said Roxie, "Look! Here comes one. Run!"

Quickly, they moved back to the steep slope of the black wall or the edge of the pavement as it now appeared. Before they could climb entirely down, the car passed, and the concussion of the air from the vehicle knocked them back onto the boulder-sized gravel below. They continued to roll with the strong air current across the rocks and down another steep slope that appeared to be the most bottomless ravine anyone had ever seen. They rolled and tumbled to a sudden rise that presented them with a massive tree trunk and a tree that seemed to reach for miles into the sky.

"Wow, you girls chose a road as a starting point," Carson said out of sarcasm, "Good choice. Great landmark! We should be able to find that road any time we want."

Roxie said with emotion that expressed a bit of hurt for the first time. "Well, I love you, too."

Carson, dumbfounded by the remark, felt a sudden tug from inside that moved his thoughts from his bruises to the girls, who were pretty banged up, too. He suddenly thought he was too harsh in his cute remarks. "Look, Roxie, I'm sorry. I was just being sarcastic. I would have probably made the same choice, only you took the initiative by choosing it first."

Rhonda turned suddenly toward an approaching and fluttering of wings and shouted, "Look, a giant wasp!"

Each of the girls moved into the tree's root system while the black flying insect of giant proportions swooped toward Wayne.

Wayne was already against the tree, with nowhere to go. The gust of wind from its wings frightened them. They all watched in horror as the creature landed upon Wayne and grabbed him with its six legs. It flew slowly into the air and moved out across the ravine. As it flew into the distance, it appeared to try to sting Wayne with several attempts.

"That's no wasp. That's a mud dauber," Carson said. "It's taking Wayne to its nest. I have to follow it. It's already too far away to follow on foot. I'll never catch it that way." He glanced around and identified a large boulder that protruded from the bank on the opposite side of the street. It had a spray-painted peace sign in green and red texture. He made a mental note to find this point when he returned. He looked at the girls. "I have to leave. Hide, and I will try to rescue him and come back. Hide under something." He looked around to see giant leaves. "Get under one of those, and hurry!"

"Go before he is out of sight. I hope you can learn to fly fast," Rhonda said.

Listening to his inner voice, Carson leaped in faith off the side of the ravine. He plunged forward, and the ground seemed to head his way swiftly. Features extended from his back and shoulder blades, and a breeze came forth from them. His body lifted just before he reached the ground, sending giant leaf particles into the air and into his vision. He knocked the leaf shavings away and quickly avoided a collision with a tree.

He rushed forward in the direction he thought the mud dauber had flown. He searched in the distance and noted his vision was much keener than before. He detected a tiny movement and flew toward it at great speed. He flew across the ravine, up another rise, and then over the edge of some protruding rocks, only to find that the insect and his buddy, Wayne, were no longer visible.

After a quick search in several directions, he suddenly thought that he would not be in a travel posture if he were still in flight. Suddenly, the thoughts in his head that broke his concentration on his flight caused the flutter from his back to stop. Then, he felt air pass him by as he descended at incredible speed toward yet another ravine and a stream that flowed through it. Before he could start to fly again, he hit the water with a great splash. The water was deep, and the current swift. As he returned to the surface, he realized the flow was about to take him over a waterfall. He grabbed a soggy limb that extended from the water. It was covered with green slimy ropes. He struggled to maintain a hold on the stem, but as he slipped further down the branch into the waterfall's current, the limb extended out, and much of it reached beyond the water's surface. He could pull himself out of the current and place most of his weight on the branches. He found less slime on the smaller components as he climbed further out, away from the water.

Once out of the water and safe, he finally looked again for the dauber. He searched for a good five minutes, thinking that perhaps he would have to fly up high and over the subsequent rise to pursue further. As he glanced toward the bank and protruding rocks he had just flown over, he saw a mud dauber fly away from the underside of the extended rock formation. He wanted to quickly leap into the air and pursue the creature again, but with a tremendous letdown, he could see it did not carry his friend anymore.

He looked at the lower portion of the extended rock formation. There, he saw a mud dauber's nest with five mud tunnels. He turned on the branch, dove toward the water's surface, and his wings started to work again; he veered from the downward plunge and swooped upward toward the rock formation. He collided with a large patch of leaves on a tree branch but managed to push away as they gave way to his acceleration upward. He hoped that the mud nest would contain his friend, Wayne. He carefully observed his avenue of approach to ensure he was not about to fly into a group of daubers or any other giant predator that might wait for him, and his ignorance of the dangers before him.

Carson swooped carefully around the enormous rows of mud. He noted several had already been sealed. Quickly adjusting the location, he recognized the last as slightly shorter, with a clear opening at the end. He circled to ensure it was empty of company. He felt uneasy with the possibility that he might surprise the dauber, still busy with its prey, and inadvertently meet his doom. There would be little hope left if both boys were to end up paralyzed to become the eventual meal of the dauber larvae that would soon hatch.

He circled three more times to ensure his attention in search of the area around him did not take away from his continued flight or use of his wings. He made a wider circle on the last pass and turned sharply to fly into the opening at the end of the dauber tunnel of mud. He made a running stop just inside the dark mud tunnel. He tried to stand up but realized he was too tall to stand in the darkness. He stooped forward as he moved further into the opening. The passage was darker as he went further in. His eyes quickly adjusted to the dark environment. He looked toward the tunnel's far end and saw multiple spiders with their legs all coiled up. He found his closest friend, Wayne, in the middle of that group. He lay there, stretched out with the look of death upon him, his eyes still open.

"Wayne, wake up," he said, shaking his school buddy, "We've got to get out of here."

His efforts failed to stir Wayne. He looked closer at his friend; his heart raced with the thought that perhaps he was dead. He put his ear to Wayne's chest and listened. He could just faintly make out a shallow heartbeat. He realized the paralysis caused by the dauber's sting was to preserve its prey for several days, eventually making it a food source for the growing larvae. His fears grew with the thought of losing his sidekick since kindergarten.

Carson suddenly realized that the tunnel had become darker. He thought that perhaps the sun had just gone behind a cloud, but the deeper darkness also carried the sounds of movement at the entrance.

As he turned, he felt panic to see a giant mud dauber crawl into the passage. He questioned himself quickly about what to do. He thought that perhaps now would be a good time to pray. He backed toward his friend but then stepped forward toward the creature.

A voice in his mind suggested perhaps the sword he carried on his right hip was more than a decoration. Carson immediately grabbed the hilt to pull the blade from its scabbard. It made a metallic sound that even startled the insect before him. He spoke aloud as he moved toward the creature. "Prepare to die, you creature of mud and spiders!"

The dauber coiled in fear. "Please! Please have mercy, oh great one with the blade," it said while backing out of the tunnel, but stopped. The creature lowered itself to the bottom surface as a dog would when it pleads to get into the house.

"You speak?" asked Carson in amazement, "Is this just another ploy to make me a victim of your child's diet program for the coming weeks?"

"No! I mean, yes! I think not," said the dauber in its confusion as if it knew it approached possible death in just seconds. "I speak, but never has a Wasamanee understood me before. You must be the Promised One."

"Promised One?" asked Carson, "I'll take it that you were expecting me. Now, let's talk about how you put us here. We are not spiders."

"Please forgive me. I had nothing to do with the capture of your friend over there. My missus captured him and likes the taste of Wasamanee, your people."

"I'm not Wasamanee. I'm me, and I'm here for a great purpose," said Carson, "Your missus attacked us and took my friend, putting him in a lunch state. I'm in danger of the same trap, and you want mercy?"

"Yes, please," said the dauber, "I'm the male. I built the nest by collecting mud and bringing it here. My missus lays the eggs and collects food for them when they hatch. I also guard the nests. Please, I get all the dirty work. Don't kill me for that."

Carson still stood with his sword in both hands, prepared to charge and ram the blade into the face of the insect. He had already made the deduction, but there was not enough room to raise the sword and strike. He relaxed his stance for a moment. "If so, you must exit this tunnel to let me carry my friend away. In showing you this mercy, you owe me one."

"Thank you, oh, Great One," humbly said the mud dauber as it rose slowly and backed out of the tunnel. "I will be your servant on call. My mate will soon know. You carry a new weapon she should fear and never bother the Wasamanee again."

"That sounds like a good promise," he said to bluff, "Now

we must see that you live up to it. I know where you and your children live. My wrath will be tenfold if I must return looking for you again."

"You have my word, oh, great and mighty warrior," he said, bowing before Carson, "I will live up to my promise. I will look after you from afar. My people will also know of you and watch your back at every opportunity. There are many dangers in this land."

"Farewell, then, my newfound associate and ally type dude. I must now take my friend back to where he was captured by your missus," he said. He felt slightly more relaxed but still needed to return to the girls. "Be gone, then, so my departure will be made in haste."

The insect scurried out of the passageway and flew away into the distance. Carson observed, returned his sword to its scabbard, and then turned toward his dear friend. He took him by the shoulders, dragged him to the outer edge of the tunnel, and back into the brightness of the forest. He tried throwing his friend onto his shoulder in a fireman's carry, but found he would have to stand on his knees. Even then, his thoughts of the wings as obstructed presented technical difficulties in flight that might make his next take-off his last. Finally, He pulled Wayne to the edge of the tunnel, rolled him over onto his stomach, wrapped both arms around him, under his armpits, and lifted him so that he would drag his legs behind him.

Carson stepped to the edge and looked around the area for movement; he leaped forward to drag his friend with him. The plunge downward was sudden and awkward. Wayne's legs left the edge last to cause his flight to be a bit off-balance. His wings came forth and began their work. He barely missed the ground below and caused a bit of leaf disturbance as he cut the flight upward at the very last second.

The extra weight of his friend and his dangling legs caused

some unstable aerodynamics until the swing settled down. Finally, he gained some control and veered back toward the rise, with a dodge of a tree here and there and the next valley where, hopefully, the girls remained waiting for his return.

The climb over the rise was straightforward. Carson continued to look in all directions. His vision seemed amazingly keener than ever before. He flew quickly over the valley and reached the top of the subsequent rise. He veered upward to look around and saw the road ahead, noting that the traffic was clear.

He flew over the area, thinking it might be a good time to impress the girls. He spied out the boulder on the other side of the street, marked with the green and red peace sign. He picked out the tree trunk where he had left them just a few minutes before, only to notice, with great disappointment, that they no longer waited for him. He made another pass to search again, ensuring it was the right tree. He recalled he had told them to hide.

They were accomplished at that task. His next pass caught a sparkle on one of the rocks.

He landed on the enormous gravel along the edge of the giant road and sat his friend down. He reached for the sparkling object to find a bracelet. He picked it up, concluding that it was not broken, and left it there to mark the spot. His heart still raced. He looked around, hoping the girls might be hidden in the leaves. He called out, "Roxie! Rhonda! Where are you?"

His voice echoed through the valley below and the many trees. He began to calm down, though still frightened and worried over his failure to find the two girls waiting. He felt his strength suddenly dissipate. He looked at Wayne and noticed his eyes were still open. He reached and closed them. His exhaustion suddenly overwhelmed him, pulling him into significant fatigue. He felt his energy level drained in paramount proportions. He thought that if he did not sit down or stretch out immediately, he would collapse into sleep where he stood. He pulled his friend toward the tree trunk, attempting to kick the enormous oak leaves as if they would just move out of the way. He realized they were much heavier than expected, and it was easier to pull his friend under one for cover. With one last look around, he noted no sight of danger and lay his head down. It was as if he had played Sony PlayStation II for three days and nights straight, and now it was nap time. He could wait no longer.

# CHAPTER 3

Rhonda watched with disbelief as Carson leaped down into the ravine. She was amazed at the wings that suddenly extended from his back as if they were there all along. She watched him swoop deep into the gorge and back up the other side. She glanced upward and could still see the mud dauber as it crested the subsequent rise. She feared Carson would not be able to catch up with the insect. She looked over at Roxie, who proved equally astonished by the sudden flow of events that struck them in the last few minutes.

Roxie spoke first. "Where did he learn to fly like that?" she asked as he crested the ridge and disappeared into the distance.

"Maybe he was so desperate to save Wayne that learning to fly was all he could do," said Rhonda, "Does that mean we can fly, too?"

"Yeah! You go first," Roxie said.

"I don't think so," said Rhonda, "Do you see wings on my back?"

"No, but neither did I see them on Carson's back before he leaped," Roxie said, "He found them when he needed them."

Suddenly, there was a rustle in the leaves beyond the white oak tree right next to a giant acorn resembling a tank on a water tower. Out from under a leaf came a vast, black ant, proportionately large, and it was as surprised to see them as they were to see it.

Roxie was the first to pull her sword. Rhonda followed suit. They both stood with their blades in defiance of the menacing insect that saw them as the latest menu selection for forest dining.

With the sudden emergence of two flashing steel swords, the ant panicked and fled back into the leaves.

"Did you see that big creature skedaddle?" asked Rhonda.

"We scared it off in a hurry. That was one big Carpenter Ant, wasn't it? Does this mean we are bad or what?"

"Sure, wished we could have been as effective when we dealt with the wasp that grabbed Wayne earlier," Roxie said.

"Yes, and how?" said Rhonda. "By the way, that was not a wasp. It was a dirt dauber. If a wasp had stung him, there would be no need to chase. The dauber has a weak poison that does not affect humans."

"Maybe not regular-size humans, but we're tiny compared with that creature."

"Yeah, it looks like we are tiny, miniature versions of ourselves," said Rhonda, "Could this world we are here to help be as tiny as we are? Is this a world within our world?"

"Either that or we are on a planet of giants. Would that mean we are the ones that are normal size?" asked Roxie.

"Wait! I hear a noise in the leaves again," Rhonda said as she pointed toward the leaves and reached for her sword.

"Do you think we can keep scaring it away until Carson and Wayne get back?" asked Roxie as she brandished her sword.

Out of the leaves came not one but several ants. They poured out of the foliage. The young women stepped back and drew their swords to do battle. They could fight the ants or retreat onto the pavement and try to cross the road, hoping to avoid large oncoming automobiles and the wind concussions that would come with them. Even the idea of the traffic threats had a ring of better outcomes than being pinched and stung to death by the ants surrounding them as they stood back-to-back.

The circle of ants grew thicker and darker. A few climbed over the front row as if they could wall off the girls' every escape. Their pinchers opened and closed just a foot or so from their waists.

Out of fear, they held their pose to strike.

Their confusion swayed the two young women from taking the ants on to kill as many as they could before they died, or not trying to tick them off all at once. At this point, a scream of many male voices cried out from Roxie's side of the ant circle. The voices got louder, and the ants seemed distracted in their encirclement. Just as quickly as the ants surrounded them, they made a quick exodus back into the leaves.

From just beyond, the ants in front of Roxie charged a crowd of men who wore thick clothing and brandished short blades.

The men raced past the two young women to hound the ants deep into the leaves.

Two men stopped before them, and one said in a deep voice, "You will come with us."

Rhonda looked at Roxie to see her gaze back as if to seek her decision on what to do. "I don't think so, Buster. I have to stay here," she said, "We have to wait on our friends."

"Yeah! They've gone to get some food from McDonald's down the street," she said, "about a hundred of them."

"You will come with me," he said with a voice of authority, "Your two friends, on return, can expect the same hospitality. If you wait here, the carpenter ants, you noted, will return with numbers even our men cannot handle. We mean you no harm. We offer you sanctuary."

"How can we trust you?" asked Rhonda.

"What choice do you have?" asked the man, "You are sitting in the open, and many dangers will not give you a second chance. Come with us now."

"Where are we going if we choose to do so?" asked Roxie as she glanced back at Rhonda to see if she agreed.

"You must go to our cave for your safety," said the stocky

man in a thick leather dress.

"Show us the way, but we demand the freedom to come and go freely," said Rhonda.

"So be it, now hurry," said the man, motioning, and they began to walk in his direction.

A few men returned and joined their movement, carrying several of the ants. Each ant had ten to fifteen men under it who heaved it on their shoulders with great effort, despite the leg movements that were still obvious. Many of their blades showed damage as if they had done battle, and their wooden frailty suffered in the attack. However, the juices that seeped from the ants suggested their use proved effective against the outer skeletons of the now incapacitated insects.

Roxie said with urgency in her voice, "We do have two friends coming back expecting to find us."

With a voice of assurance, the stocky man said, "We will have lookouts posted above for your two friends. We have already watched their departure from our observation points, high in the trees, and we have seen your promises to wait for them. We wish only to protect you. We also sense you are not here to oppose us or bring harm. You are too clumsy and ill-prepared to invade and conquer our mighty people with just four two-year-olds."

"I'm not a two-year-old," Roxie told Rhonda, as if the comment had left her deeply puzzled.

"Don't worry about it right now," said Rhonda, "Let's see what protection he is going to provide."

Roxie and Rhonda followed the men who wore rough brown leather cloak-like dresses that reached almost to the ground and were altered only by the waist strap that suspended their weapons like a holster. They moved along a path that took them under leaves, around roots, and over thin logs resembling gigantic pine needles. Soon, they approached a cave partially hidden from frontal view by root obstructions. The small army of strangely robed men entered the cave to find guards on either side of the entrance, which opened from the narrow passageway into a dark, large area below.

They followed the descent down into the cavity, barely able to see anything until their eyes adjusted from the sunlight outside to the sparse torch-lit room below.

When she looked upward at the dark ceiling, Rhonda punched Roxie to make her look too. "Do you see that?" she asked as she gazed upward at a wasp nest that covered most of the ceiling with structural damage toward the middle, where perhaps another nest once extended.

"Yeah! Are we in a giant yellow jacket nest or something?" asks Roxie with amazement.

"Yellow Jackets?" asked Rhonda, "Where do you get that idea?"

"It's obvious. We are tiny, and yellow jackets burrow into the ground and make their nests in tunnels like these," said Roxie.

"We are supposed to be on earth, and I guess you are right. We're unusually tiny because I recall no land or country with these giant proportions anywhere in Alabama. Of course, I've never been to South Alabama," said Rhonda.

"Duh! That car that zoomed past us at our arrival gave a serious clue to our definite miniature status," said Roxie.

"Yeah, I can see the nest in a cave could fit the yellow jacket classification," said Rhonda, "But, how do you know the nest is not a bumblebee hive or something like that?"

"The individual holes for the yellow jacket larvae would have to be much larger for bees," said Roxie.

The bulky man with the leather robe spoke in amazement at their insight. "It seems you may not be familiar with our culture and traditions of cave-dwelling. Your people do not settle in the old nest holes of our arch-enemy, the yellow, winged warriors?" asked the man, quickly removing his leather cloak to reveal a suit of armor with a great mixture of yellow and black, which could explain his bulkiness.

"That's an awesome armor suit you wear, mister," said Roxie.

"Thanks, but all of our soldiers wear this armor. By the way, I have not told you my name," said the man, "It is Captain Maxim, at your service."

"Well, Captain Maxim, it is a privilege to meet you, and we hope to serve with you," said Rhonda. "I am Rhonda, and this is my friend, Roxie."

"I am pleased to make your acquaintance. Now tell me, how do you get your armor to change from brown to that of the yellow and black that we wear?" asked Capt. Maxim.

Roxie and Rhonda looked at each other, suddenly aware that their outfits now had the color and makeup of the captain's armor. "The lighting here is dim, but now that my eyes have adjusted, this is the first time I have noticed the color change of our armor suits," said Rhonda.

"Well, if I had any insight, I would say these suits we wear are chameleon in nature and change to match what is around us," said Roxie.

"Perhaps you are right," said Rhonda, "Watch me while I approach the rows of paper nests that line the room's corners." She stepped away from them toward the three-row nests at the corners and walls for storage.

"You are right. Now you are gray in color, and your feet have a brown color to just past your ankles," said Roxie, "How do you do that? It's astonishing."

"You have excellent armor. Where do you come from?" asked Capt. Maxim, "You act like you have never been to a Wasamanee Nesting village?"

"What's on my knee?" asked Roxie.

"Wasamanee, yes, that is the name of my people," the

captain said, "We live in caves like this one throughout the lands as far as you can see or fly, as your friend examined earlier."

"You don't fly?" asked Roxie in the fashion of a tease, "I thought everybody flew these days."

"We're not gifted with wings as your friend who flew away to chase a mud dauber earlier," said the captain, "His wings did not show until he needed them. I assume you have wings hidden like that, too."

"Yeah, we both have a fine set of wings just ready to take off at a moment's notice," said Rhonda, "Got a picture you want to be hung on that wall? I can buzz right up and hang it way out of reach."

"Why didn't you fly away when the ants found your location?" asked the captain, who sensed an effort to pull his leg.

"Well, we wanted to get a good look at them because they are amazing creatures," said Roxie as she backpedaled a little, "Besides, I have this sword I was getting ready to use on them just at the right moment to catch their reaction for shock appeal." She pulled her sword from its hilt and held it up in front. She looked at the other men in armor who came toward them, obviously to look in admiration at the dazzling blade.

"Perhaps you do have a mighty weapon, but even then, the number of ants would hardly slow in their quest for you to join them for lunch over a single blade," said the captain. "That is a fine instrument of battle. From what creature did you get this device?"

"It wasn't taken from a creature; my Master's highest servant equipped me with it," said Rhonda in a boastful tone, but avoided a revelation of too much detail of their source.

"Could I please hold this instrument of peace?" asked the captain.

Roxie hesitated, glanced at Rhonda for her reaction, and then extended her sword outward to allow the captain to reach for the handle. The blade vanished when the weapon changed hands, leaving only the hilt.

Roxie said, "Oops! Guess it does not like you, or there's a trace of poor quality in its design."

The captain looked the handle over and felt the metal of the guard. He then gave it back to Roxie. "Here, it won't help in battle if it vanishes when needed."

The blade reappeared when the weapon left the captain's hand and returned to Roxie. "Now, that is a weapon made for me only," said Roxie.

"May I touch the blade?" asked the captain. His hand reached for the blade. It remained intact. Suddenly, he felt its sharp edge, just slightly, and a red line appeared as if he had cut himself. "That is a mighty blade. I barely touched its edge, and it stung as it broke my skin. Perhaps you could have wielded a mighty battle with the carpenter ants when they returned for you, even without our rescue."

"I'm glad you came anyway," said Rhonda, "You've been so open and friendly to us, even though we are strangers. I hope I have not developed a false sense of security and trust, but I feel inside like a voice has assured me that you are the ones we need to see."

Another man approached the captain, gave an odd salute, and whispered something. The captain suddenly looked at the young woman and said, "Your two friends have returned, and we must send scouts out to bring them into our shelter before something happens to them. They appear defenseless."

Several men passed them as they threw on brown cloaks and headed toward the guarded opening. They moved quickly and were gone in a moment.

Roxie and Rhonda started to move to catch up and follow them, but decided the soldiers' movement was urgent. They did not want to tag along as the men rushed to rescue their friends.

Suddenly, uneasiness surged similarly to that of their arrival. Now, the fear of their two friends' return for them and freaking out over their early departure lingered in their minds.

"What have we done, leaving them out there with no markings or clues of where we are?" asked Rhonda.

"Well, while we were being persuaded to come down here, I dropped my bracelet, hoping they would find it, to give them a clue to where we were to reduce their apprehension," said Roxie.

"Did you see the salute the soldier gave to his captain?" asked Rhonda.

"Yeah, it was the international sign language symbol for stupid," said Roxie, "Should I tell them?"

"No. There are some stones we need to leave unturned," said Rhonda as they continued to look around the cave area while they eagerly awaited the arrival of their friends.

Shortly after the men departed, they returned with the two boys suspended, each on a large brown sheet, with six men stretching the four corners and the middle to support their makeshift stretchers.

Rhonda and Roxie watched as the two stretchers passed them. Rhonda took in a deep breath as she gazed in horror at Wayne. She exclaimed in disbelief, "He's so pale. He looks almost blue. That cannot be good at this point."

Roxie asked, "Did Carson get stung by the mud thingy, too?"

No one answered. The girls followed the men down further into a cooling chamber. In rows on rows, yellow jacket nests were cut in half. They resembled cubicles with shavings in the middle, serving as beds for the many occupants who lived in this collection of tunnels and caves. Carson and Wayne were placed in separate half nests and examined by several men to decide what to do.

The last man to examine Carson smiled and turned to

Rhonda to give his diagnosis. He said, "He's exhausted. There is no sign of a sting and no symptoms. Seemingly, he has not eaten for a long time, and it caught up with him."

Rhonda looked at the man and back at Carson. She asked, "Do you suppose his flight drained his energy level or something? I'm sure he ate breakfast earlier or planned to eat pizza in its place."

"There's no problem. We will just give Carson a dose of Nectarade, and he will be on his feet in no time."

"Nectar as in sugar water?" asked Rhonda. "He has small containers on his belt that may be the same substance." She reached and snapped one of the containers from his belt. She sampled the liquid to see what it was. She decided it was a rich, high-sugar liquid. The man held him up, and she poured the liquid into Carson's mouth. He choked and coughed but began to drink the juice in his semiconscious state. He consumed the remaining fluid and was allowed to rest and let his digestive system restore his energy.

"Let's take a look at your other friend," the man said and led Rhonda out of the paper chamber and left to the next half-nest to find Wayne, still blue, with Roxie and a couple of others who aided. He opened one of Wayne's eyes and held a piece of wood above him, which he had taken from his pocket and which glowed from a fungus or something. He also raised Wayne upward and examined a swollen portion on the back of his head.

"At least there is no stinger," said Roxie as she viewed from the corner of the half-nest at the deeper end of the bed. She knelt and watched with worry in her eyes, too.

"No, there will be no stinger when it comes to the Mud Dauber," the man said, "The Dauber uses his stinger to conquer his prey and defend himself. It can sting repeatedly. He also uses it to gather spiders and small insects to feed his young larvae. If it had been a honeybee sting, we would find its stinger because it is barbed to stay and slowly continues to add more poison, causing its victim to feel increasing pain and want to flee the area, trying to escape the cause of the discomfort."

"You wear the yellow jacket armor. Does the yellow jacket leave a stinger when it inflicts its venom?" asked Rhonda.

"No, they have a smooth, sharp stinger like the Dauber," said the man as he took one of Wayne's containers from his belt and opened it to pour it into Wayne's mouth. "We use the yellow jacket stingers as weapons. The swords we make still contain some of the poison, which is an excellent weapon for taking down our prey."

The Daubers hate us because we find their stingers are great weapons, too, and instead of inflicting pain, they can cripple our prey and preserve it for more than one day, avoiding spoilage. With both types of stingers, we just stab and squeeze, and the internal poison does its bidding."

"Your prey," asked Roxie, "Pray tell, what do you eat to stay alive?"

"We eat yellow jackets, bees, wasps, and spiders. Anything we can penetrate with our weapons, we bring home for meals and use their shells for making furniture, weapons, and cooking utensils.

"Bugs? You eat bugs?" asked Rhonda as if this repulsed her.

"Doesn't everybody?" asked the man, who was either a doctor or a nurse.

"No. I never ate one. I hope I don't have to, either," said Roxie. She looked over at Rhonda and sensed worry in her eyes as if concerned over their sudden awareness of their future diets in this world.

"I've inhaled a couple of flies while playing soccer, but never made a meal out of one," said Rhonda.

"How do they taste?" Roxie asked to humor Rhonda.

"Do you eat flies, also?" Rhonda asked.

"We don't eat flies. They carry too much sickness with them. They always appear to be crawling with tiny parasites that we don't want to bring into our homes," the man said.

"I can see that or imagine that anyway," said Roxie, "Could those tiny parasites be bacteria that you can see?"

"It does sound like it, Roxie," Rhonda said.

"Call them what you want, but they make you sick by destroying from the inside, and few live long to talk about it," said the man as he began to feed the third container to Wayne.

"Will Wayne get better, or will he stay paralyzed forever?" asked Roxie with a tone of worry in her voice.

"He's sick, and sleep will control him for several days. He will be force-fed for some time, and then the poison in his blood will eventually weaken as he regains strength from the new foods fed to him. He will be weak for at least a week or so, but he is alive and no longer fears the dauber larvae before the poison wears off or starving to death first."

"Well, looks like we are your guests for a few days. What's for lunch?" asked Roxie, with a smile. "I'm so hungry, I could eat a bug."

"I think I'll try one of these belt packets that sound much better than insects," said Rhonda.

"No, save those; we may need those for Wayne," Roxie said. "Come on, eating bugs can't be all that bad. I hear they are loaded with protein," she said as she continued to look at Rhonda while she replaced the empty containers on Wayne's belt.

"The containers refilled when placed back on the belt. I think Wayne will have to take his chances with his own," Roxie said, as she opened her first container and consumed the first bottle of nourishment she had enjoyed in what seemed like days. She noted the puzzled look in Rhonda's eyes and pointed to the first container on Wayne's belt, which was almost wholly refilled.

"Well, maybe one would help me feel better if you insist," said Rhonda.

They kept the secret from the Wasamanee men in their yellow-and-black armor suits, who had gathered around the cubicles and quietly discussed Wayne's condition.

# CHAPTER 4

Carson opened his eyes to see a dimly lit, gray-walled room with the roof absent and the darkest brown clouds above the open ceiling. His movement alerted Roxie, who rushed to his side. She looked at him and smiled. He looked back, smiled, and said, "I must be in heaven."

"No, you're in the other direction," she said as if to humor. "You are underground. Did you like the mud daubers? We are now in a yellow jacket nest."

He suddenly rose and looked again at the room around him, with an awareness that the walls did look like the inside of a wasp nest.

He looked at her differently and asked, "How did I get here, and why weren't you waiting for us when we returned from fighting the dauber?"

"Calm down," she said. "We are safe, and no yellow jackets are alive in this cave."

Carson seemed relieved until three men in yellow and black walked by. He raised himself alarmingly to the point where the men had already passed. "What was that passing by just then?"

Roxie smiled and said, "Just some guys our same size that kill yellow jackets for a living and eat them. They use their outer shells for armor. It's what's for supper."

"You've got to be kidding," said Carson as he rose and dusted the shavings off his back.

"Are you strong enough to walk around?" asked Roxie.

"Sure. I feel great. Don't know why I fell asleep back

at the roadside, but I feel fine now, other than this sticky stuff around my mouth and a serious urge for a trip to the little boy's room," he said with an attempt to wipe away what he felt was uncomfortable.

"We poured some juices down you earlier to help you regain your strength," she said assuredly, "Looks like the next time you go flying, you need to keep something in your stomach. It's been a long time since breakfast, and your flying consumes a lot of calories, from what I can tell."

"I'll keep that in mind the next time some bug grabs one of us and flies off into the sunset," he said sarcastically.

"Since you are back to your normal strength and sarcastic manner, let me show you what they have in the next room," Roxie said. She walked through the shavings and stepped over the retainer at the edge of the half-nest bed. "Rhonda, look who's up and wants to go down to the next lower chamber and see the milking machine they have down there."

"Great to see you up and about, Carson," Rhonda said as she rose from her watch beside Wayne. "Our little Wayne, here, will be fine. He has opened his eyes several times but has not answered any questions. He's starting to get some color back. Those bottles of sugar water seem to be giving him his strength back, too."

Carson stood in front of the half nest to observe his best friend. "I sure thought I had lost him to that mud dauber. He really could swing and make flying difficult. I was lucky I didn't crash and have to walk back. He sure looks great now that he is in good hands."

After Carson's pit stop, they proceeded down a well-traveled clay path that led past many half-nest beds. The ceiling above appeared to be a large rock, giving a clue as to why the half-nests could be left open without worrying about any moisture that could cause seepage to reach the sleeping quarters.

As they passed through the open bay area of the cave, they came to a small hole-like doorway. They entered the passage with Carson in the lead, while in the other room, they could hear yells and a considerable struggle beyond the opening. Carson jumped away from the entrance and almost knocked Rhonda and Roxie down in the process. "What in the world is that black monster they are roping?" he asked.

"It's a giant Black Widow Spider," said Roxie, "Cool, huh?"

"A Black Widow Spider?" he asked, "They have poison, twenty-five times as strong as a Pigmy Rattlesnake." Let's not return to that room; it might get loose, and I don't want to do the kicking chicken."

"Kicking Chicken?" asked Roxie, "What do you mean by that?"

"That is a description of the muscle spasms you have from being bitten by one of those, and it can last two days to two weeks."

"Wow, you're a walking encyclopedia, but no, we are not going to miss this," said Rhonda as she pushed Carson back toward the opening where the spider was last seen struggling with several men.

"OK, but remember, I warned you," Carson said as he reentered the lower room slowly. He observed the spider and the fact that multiple ropes or cables extended in both directions and were manned by what appeared to be hundreds of yellow-jacket-suited men. Behind the spider was a long, stem-like spool of thread, which was being rotated as if to spool more of the silver line from behind the spider.

"This is called milking the spider," said Roxie.

"They have surgically modified the spider so that it produces its silk without the glands that produce the sticky stuff that catches bugs on them. They rope the spider and toss the eight-legged creature into the air, and the arthropod starts spinning silk, thinking the spider can catch hold of something to gain stability."

"The silk is as hard as steel and a vital part of the economy for the Wasamanee People," Rhonda said, "They feed the spider. She stays captive until winter. She produces their marketable silk, and they export to other cultures around them."

"They split the silk by unraveling the inward substances of the fibers and use it to sew, hold things together, and construct obstructions to passages that may be entered by other creatures, and even make clothing from it."

"How'd you learn all of this in such a short time?" asked Carson.

"Short time? You slept all day and night to wake this morning," Roxie said, "You looked like you needed rest, so we left you alone and checked things out. If you venture down to the next chamber, you will find tunnels going in many directions, and one leads to a water table."

"It's like a giant, underground lake. People go there to wash their clothes, armor, and bodies," said Rhonda, "They even have an area isolated for women and men to bathe separately. I don't like bathing in a large tub of super cold water with other women, but it is a nice, refreshing spill if you like cleanliness."

"I suppose you are hinting I need a bath?" asked Carson, "All right, I'm game. I don't suppose they have any decent soap?"

"Nope, they make their soap from the ash of burnt oak and insect fats. It's rough on the skin, but you'll be clean and odor-free when you are through," said Rhonda, "I would not recommend getting it in your eyes."

Soon, the spider was exhausted and secured, and they passed through the area to a well-traveled tunnel passage that led downward in what would seem to be too dark to enter. Their eyes adjusted well to the darkness, enabling them to see quite well.

They approached a large, open area, and humidity dominated the air. In the distance, they saw many women dressed in silvery gowns as they worked busily on laundry. They pulled armor suits off their men to reveal softer clothing below. Beyond a curtained bathing area, with two doors that the men were destined to enter once their protective gear was removed, awaited them.

"I suppose I must go through the door where the men are going?" Carson asked, "What if I went into the other room?" He said with a smile.

"Do, and we find we have to stay in cages until Wayne fully recovers, then we get released into the wild with no help or assistance," said Roxie.

"Point well taken," said Carson as he reached for the men's bath section door. "Look at the structure of these curtains. They are like solid steel woven cables."

"No, Carson," said Rhonda, "That curtain is made of black widow spider webbing. It is woven together to make solid steel-like silk curtains that won't rust or deteriorate."

Carson entered the bathing area unescorted, and others were busy with their baths. With no intention to stare, Carson saw that all were just as he was in structure and, naked, were just as human as the next person. Carson tried to remove his armor suit but found it was attached to the skin. He stepped into the shallow pool. Carson then reached for water, splashed his hands, and felt the cold liquid pass through his suit. He saw several bars of soap on a pedestal in the middle of the area, with a large log that glowed, mounted in the middle, and filled the room with light. Carson lathered his hands, then his covered arms, and saw the soap penetrate his clothing as if it were not there. He went deeper into the water and began to wash.

One of the men with curly black hair asked, "Hey, fellow. Do you always bathe while still wearing your clothes? Where do you come from, boy?"

Carson turned his head toward the man in an effort not to look directly at anything but his face. "Yeah, my zipper is broken, and this is the best I can do right now."

"Wow! How'd you get your clothes to disappear like that?" asked the man, looking in amazement at Carson.

"What?" asked a puzzled Carson. He looked down at his now naked body and realized his clothing had changed to the appearance of those around in the water. "Well, I'm just really fast at getting undressed. It doesn't play to blink around me."

He realized his special suit was invisible and had gone to enable him to bathe. He quickly lathered and rinsed as fast as he could. The other men dressed and left the room quickly, and he remained by himself to finish his bath. Thoughts about his imminent departure from the bathing room worried him even more.

"The girls did this on purpose. I just know it," he said as he looked around to spy what appeared to be a fabric-like towel and recalled that other men had dried off with them, so he had a cover method.

Shortly, Carson stuck his head out of the doorway, looked around, and came through the passageway wrapped in the rough towel. As he approached the two girls waiting for him, he noticed his invisible suit changed into the yellow-and-black armor the girls wore. "This outfit is going to take some getting used to."

"We thought so, too," said Roxie with a smile still, "I could not find a towel when I took my morning bath. I was lucky. Rhonda tossed me hers when she got her yellow-and-black back outside the bathing area. This place is a trip."

"You should see their gold mine," said Rhonda, "They have their economy and trade routes with other groups and a central government. They even have a mandatory religious service once a week at noon, and that time is today."

"Yeah, they will sound an alarm just before getting

everybody to gather for that worship service," said Roxie.

"Who is their god?" asked Carson.

"Don't know yet; this will be our first service, too," said Rhonda.

"The worship service is mandatory," said Roxie, "There's an altar in every chamber. You can see it in the far area, covered with that black cloth."

"Wouldn't it be great to find they worship the same God we do?" asked Carson, "But why would we be here if that was so?"

"Doesn't sound like they have separation of church and state because worship is mandated," said Roxie, "Having to go takes all of the fun out of it."

The three walked through many tunnels and visited many chambers before noon.

They noticed the covered altar in every chamber. They saw the gold nuggets that were fished from the underground stream. They were amazed at the types of webs taken from different spiders and caterpillars. Some were produced there. Others purchased in trades with other colonies. There was even a tiny smelting chamber where charcoal was used and vented, and where several metals, particularly aluminum, were smelted.

Living quarters were found in several small caves where families lived, and children played. Makeshift furniture, often made from metals, wood fibers, and insect parts, decorated the areas. Some items were manufactured there, but many were purchased with their gold ore. Stores were present, but the products were nothing compared to what these three had grown accustomed to in their society. There were also storefront windows, though not as flat or as thick, since the plastic came from plastic drink bottles, often giving the windows a bulge instead of being flat like glass.

At noon, the horns blew, and people started moving to the

sides of the factory room, where several men and women were setting up tables under construction. The crowd moved to the open area below the altar. There were no pews or chairs, so they would stand to endure the ceremony.

Carson stood in the back with the two girls. His thoughts reflected on their last activities before they toured this facility. They had visited Wayne earlier, but he still had not regained consciousness. They fed him his liquid lunch and cleaned him up as best they could, hoping the cold water would arouse him, but still, he slowly breathed on, maybe a bit faster than yesterday. His color seemed a bit better than on his initial arrival. His eyes opened, but gazed into the distance without real awareness of their presence.

"Look!" Roxie said as one of the yellow-and-black armored soldiers reached for the covering that subdued the altar when not in use. Once the cover was removed, it revealed a golden statue of a man in what appeared to be noble attire; everyone in the chamber fell to their knees, bowing to the statue, except Carson, Rhonda, and Roxie.

Roxie said in a low voice, "We know what the gold mine is for now. We can't bow to this. Not and do the mission we are here for, but what about Wayne?"

"Just keep quiet," said Carson, "We are in the back of the group, and no one is looking."

The quiet worship continued for about 15 minutes, with a few interruptions from the congregation's chants. The three stood with the hope that no one would glance their way. The chants continued, and for some reason, none of them could understand the words. For the first time, their ability to understand all languages failed. The chants and the time seemed to last forever, but it did allow them to look at the statue from a distance. The image of a man before them was a winged creature with thin wings like a dragonfly, extending to both sides of his body. His robe reached to his feet, with a belt holding a weapon like their sword, curved and with a woven handguard. He wore a crown-like hat that gave the impression that he was a ruler. His hair was long and curly. His face was ruddy, partially covered by a mustache and goatee. His face was severe and mean, as if you could see the evil presence. Around his neck was a stole wrapped around his back and extended over his left and right shoulders to his waist with tassels at both ends, with an obvious hole in the back for his wings to extend.

After the ceremony, everyone began to rise, some stiffly. Carson made a point of dusting his clothing off, as did most people once they were back on their feet. He looked to see Roxie and Rhonda, who did the same.

Roxie asked Carson, "Do you think we got away with it?"

"That guard is looking at us funny," said Carson, "He's coming over here. Oh, boy!"

His face flushed red as the guard's approach increased his heart rate. He was also the same individual who pulled the cover off the statue and put it back on while everybody rose.

"You will come with me," said the guard in an assertive voice.

Rhonda and Roxie looked at each other and back at Carson, but said nothing, as if they watched Carson say, run, or draw swords or something.

"Shall we follow the gentleman?" asked Carson, and all three followed the guard toward the upper chamber near where Wayne slept. He whispered to Roxie, "At least we are not in cuffs."

They continued until the guard indicated they were to enter a side tunnel that led in a new direction they had not explored. The path continued until the brighter light of an open door was noted on the tunnel's left. The guard stopped and motioned with his hands for them to enter.

Carson allowed the two girls to go first and followed them into the small chamber, where several men sat at the other end. Some were older, with much gray hair. They all took their seats on the odd empty stools before them.

# CHAPTER 5

Carson stood at his stool with Roxie on his left and Rhonda on his right. Before him, on the opposite end of the long table, was a larger chair that was empty but obviously of some importance. Eight men, four on each side, stood and glared at the three. They were not clothed in black-and-yellow armor like the man-warriors outside the room. They were all dressed in purple robes with very thick fibers and tassel decorations. He also noticed that perhaps they might all have the yellow and black armor underneath those robes. Carson's worst worry occurred next. He also noticed that his and the girls' suits had turned purple.

This caused some embarrassment and worried him that it might give this counsel the idea that they dared to be equal with them. Suddenly, the eight men rose to the position of attention, their eyes forward and their bodies rigid at the arrival of their leader. An elderly gentleman appeared through the passageway to their left. He stood more petite than the other eight. He was also clothed in purple and yellow tassels. He crossed the room to the other end of the table and stood before the most prominent chair. He motioned with his head, and the eight men took their seats. Carson and the girls did the same.

All nine men now looked at the three visitors, dressed in purple clothing similar to theirs, only in color, not in robe styling, but purple just the same. The refined gentleman of mature age cleared his throat, and all faced him to hear what he had to say. "Guests, you have been invited into our quarters for your protection. We have studied you and find you and your armament quite intriguing. You are all quite young and indicate you are not military representatives of our emperor. That was very evident when you did not participate in the worship service of our Holy Emperor at noon. No servant of the mighty emperor would dare defy his proclamation of worship and demonstration of loyalty. What do you have to say for yourselves?"

Carson rose to his feet because he felt he could communicate better that way and answered, "Sir, it has been a great learning experience to be your guest. I apologize for defying your emperor's guidance, but we are of a higher order who cannot and will not bow to a graven image or statue as if it were a god. Our stay here has been greatly accommodating, and we are deeply grateful for this incredible hospitality. We hope to meet your emperor and all your people soon. We are not of the emperor's people and come as ambassadors to your land on a mission of great importance and secrecy."

Still seated, the gentleman responded to Carson's introduction with a stern look at Carson and said, "You are bold to defy the emperor's commands to worship him. You must know that the penalty is death."

Out of shock and confusion, Carson said, "Sir, surely you do not wish to treat ambassadors with death penalties. We represent a great and mighty people, far greater and stronger than any of the emperor's forces. We came to make peace and bring change for the better. We worship the God of the Most High. To bow to anything less would make Him sore with us and compromise our mission of hope."

The eight men quickly looked toward their leader and whispered among themselves after this revelation. "Young man, we have not served the God of the Most High in many cycles. That religion is banned by the emperor. You must realize how serious a situation you put yourself in. When the worship time approaches tomorrow and from now on, you must report to this office before the horn is blown and stay here until it is over.

This open, public defiance will be tragic if allowed to continue, and it is my civil duty to either protect you from your lack of understanding of our laws or enforce the law by providing the penalties demanded by our emperor."

"Thank you, sir, for providing us with a way to remain with you while our friend recovers from his injuries," said Carson, "May the Grace of God go with you and your people for what you do for us."

"We offer you aid only because you need it. We do not, however, condone violations of our emperor's laws. Your boldness is unique but dangerous in these times. When you and your friends can travel, we will assist in your departure and safe passage to allies of your persuasion, but until then, you must be careful of what you do and say," the gentleman said. "As far as you are concerned, this meeting never occurred, and we never had this conversation."

"I am Shalan, chairman of the Rule Enforcement Counsel. We are all of one accord in this meeting. We hope to learn about your weapons and clothing, but you must not risk your freedom and hope for life by publicly breaking the laws of the land. This room was the only place in the colony that did not have the emperor's statue. It is a neutral zone. It is a place of peace and negotiation. We put all our lives at significant risk by giving you this second chance. Don't let it go to waste."

"We thank you again, kind sir," said Carson, "May we depart your company at this time?"

"Yes, you may go, but keep your women quiet," he said, "Women are to be seen and not heard. Their task is to raise children, not to be warriors. We are already puzzled by their wearing of armor instead of the robes of our wives."

"Sir, these ladies are not my women," Carson said as he glanced at the two girls who had been amazingly quiet throughout the meeting. "They are my fellow warriors chosen for this mission by our great leader and guide."

"Another puzzling thing you bring into our colony."

"Perhaps your departure from our colony will be soon before you start ideas that don't belong here," he said, "You may leave the room now and continue to see about your sleeping friend. He will be ready to leave in a week. We will provide an escort and guide to our allies who distrust the emperor, where your views and practices can be better served."

"Thanks again, and have a lovely day," said Carson as he turned toward the door, and the girls rose to their feet to follow him, moved into the hall, and turned toward the sleeping quarters of the big rock to further see about Wayne.

---

It was a week before Wayne was on his feet again, as predicted. It took him three days to regain consciousness and use his limbs. He was delighted when he could stand with support to make trips to the latrine to take care of his personal needs. Food had become a constant liquid diet, high in sugars and few solid foods, but they found they adjusted well to the provisions. A portion of exceptional food taken from a yellow jacket's larvae was provided to give them a scent that would drive away other stinging insects, including the mud dauber. It would only linger with them for a few days and was available only during warmer temperatures, so they appreciated any additional defense they could find.

During the long wait for Wayne to regain his strength, the Chief of the Guard allowed sword drills and practice sessions out of curiosity and fascination over their unique swords. The art of using the whittled stingers taken from yellow jackets and bees proved to be a powerful weapon in one-on-one battles. It was not necessary to kill the other individual. Often, a quick stab with the stinger to any exposed portion of the body and the individual was crippled by the excruciating pain from the injected poison.

The stealth weaponry involved using the stinger taken from the mud dauber. This weapon was familiar only to the Wasamanee people and was their favorite weapon in scout missions. The amount of poison in the weapon could be varied to render a victim incoherent for a considerable amount of time, suitable for their mission. However, the stinger swords were no match against the swords worn by Carson, Wayne, Roxie, and Rhonda. They were also drilled against each other using those weapons and were greatly cheered by the warriors. The art, the incredible strength of the weapons' blades, and the training used were most impressive. They moved beyond the dual methods of a small dagger and the straight sword for engagements where you blocked the gouge by the opposition and used the stinger blade to stab and inject the poison.

The metal blades were more effective by slicing right through the stinger blade to render it useless and spraying the poison contents toward the owner to instill fear of its effect. Authentic swordsmanship was exhibited and practiced repeatedly by all four. A wooden post was brought forth to test the strength and sharpness of the blade against solid objects with considerable thickness. The edges could pass through the center as if the post were not there. They expected the blade to chip away chunks but not to go right through it as if it were butter or, in this world, larvae sauce. (Sounds yucky, but it is high in protein).

That evening, the Chief of the Guard confided in Carson that they were in grave danger. He said he felt that there was a significant risk that the emperor had already been informed of their presence. He feared the emperor had sent spirits into their area, which had detected their presence and sent word back to headquarters. The idea that they were of his royal guard had diminished as it became apparent that they were from another empire. "Our guards are on watch, and you must be prepared for a hasty retreat from this colony at a moment's notice. We have an escape route, and I will go with you to guide you to the point of a quick departure." He also pointed out that their weapons were like those developed and produced by the Tree People group that he would take them to when they departed this location.

After the briefing, Carson informed Wayne, Roxie, and Rhonda to be prepared to move on short notice to their next quest. After a debate on the issue, they agreed that an early morning departure could prevent any cutoff or conflict with the party sent by the emperor to capture them for interrogation. This was discussed with the Chief of the Guard, and he agreed to take them to the departure point.

Their exit from the Wasamanee Village was early the following day. Their hasty withdrawal from the area went unnoticed because they all traveled lightly. The Chief carried a backpack, as did four of his soldiers. It was assumed they were prepared for a long trip, and food might be necessary.

Carson and Wayne walked behind the girls as they made their way toward what appeared to be a root cut away to make the passage. They reached the wooden front and observed that one of the Chief's guards touched the surface in a strange, square pattern, opening a pattern-shaped door. All were motioned to quickly enter. As Carson passed through to bring up the rear, the guard who opened the passage immediately stepped in before the route closed and put them in the dark. The guard then opened a side purse to reveal its glowing contents. Unlike the many lamps, which held several glowing pieces of fungus wood in most of the quarters ' chambers. Each person was given a segment, and once their eyes adjusted to the darkness, the glow enabled them to see each other faintly and allowed them to travel through the dark passageway.

The avenue proved very narrow with a low ceiling, which often required them to stoop to the point of almost a crawl. Roxie was the first to try walking without the crawl posture and struck her head. Carson quickly caught her as she winced in pain from her collision with the splinter protruding from the top of the wooden tunnel ceiling.

Carson held his glow stick close to her face and could tell the splinter had scratched her. He reached into his belt to retrieve a handkerchief to stop the flow of blood from the scratch just into Roxie's hairline.

Roxie's first reaction was to take the handkerchief, but aware Carson could see more of what had happened, she let him touch up the wound and check for splinters that might remain in the injury.

"It is just a scratch, and I see no more splinters," he said. He also noted her eyes as he made the assurance. They seemed to melt his heart. He suddenly became aware of where they were and that everybody continued up the tunnel without them. "We need to hurry up. It is not bleeding anymore. You'll be fine. Just keep your head down and crawl as best you can."

"Thanks, Carson," she said with a faint smile. "You make a cool medic. We'd better catch up before they make an unexpected turn without us."

They both scurried up the path, almost on all fours, and soon caught up with the others.

Carson continued to think of the unique look that Roxie had given him. It was the kind of look a guy would only wish for from a girl his age who noticed him and allowed it to show for the first time.

Soon, they all gathered at the end of the wood tunnel, to what appeared to be the hollow of a tree. The cavity was wide enough to fit a gymnasium. Along the rotting walls, many holes were scattered among the lower divisions of the hollow opening. Scattered along the borders were several light-brown protrusions. Those protrusions all extended upward.

The Chief noted that everybody was present. "I assume we enjoyed our little wooden tunnel," he said as he smiled and looked toward Roxie as if he noted traces of blood on her forehead. "I hope you were not injured too seriously back there."

"I'm fine. " It hurt more than it injured," Roxie said, embarrassed. "Carson helped me out." It was just a couple of minor scratches."

"Glad it was not worse," the Chief said, "If you look around, you will see many mud trails. We will be traveling through one of those soon. There are many trails, but only one leads to our destiny. We will also have to contend with low ceilings since most of the tunnels were constructed by termites a while back. Walk lightly and keep low. We have quite a climb ahead of us. Keep your fungus light sticks handy because we will pass through several dark areas."

Carson looked up at the opening at the top of the hollow tree. He could see the blue sky with traces of stratocumulus clouds. Experience told him it meant a chance of rain in the near future. He could also tell it was early morning because the sky was a bit darker blue than it would be later in the day. He noticed the guard missing who brought up the rear at their initial start until Roxie collided with the splintered ceiling. He was again assigned to bring up the rear of the climbers' trail as they entered the select mud tunnel. He pondered what happened to the missing guard when Roxie was injured, and they stopped to treat the injury. He also noted that the path was much smaller than the mud dauber. It was also thinner and allowed light to pass through the mud walls as they climbed higher and higher. It gave an eerie, dark red look but allowed them to see better while they crawled. Several times, the mud tunnel took detours into the tree's wood, perhaps to bypass intersections with other mud tunnels or obstructions such as knots in the wood or poor support areas.

After what seemed like an hour of an uphill struggle and

reaching the point of total exhaustion, the group passed into an open area, much narrower than the original starting point. A hole in the side of the tree, just short of the break-off opening at the top, had a long cable extending from the other end of the wall. Mounted to the line were several leaf cutaways suspended from a rope from the thread to a peg. Extending from the peg were six cords: four to the front, rear, left, and right, and the other two toward the center.

"What are those things?" asked Rhonda, out of pure curiosity that had to be answered.

One of the guards smiled and replied, "Those are our leaf gliders."

"Wow! I can see that, but they've never looked that big before," said Wayne, "What are they for?"

The Chief stepped up to explain the purpose of collecting around fifteen leaves. "As you can see, they are all tied to spider web cables twisted into a stronger cord to support weight. The leaf gliders are pushed down the cable, and you must stand in the middle, holding two of the straps that support it. There is a peg visible, which is your quick release in case you slide down the cable, is suddenly interrupted by a hungry bird or creature of some sort, and there are many."

"Doesn't that leaf have a flight pattern of a falling leaf and may even roll over and over?" asked Carson.

"Yes, it does," said the chief, "You must stay in the middle and shift your weight to surf the air down to your landing point. Your weight will not cause it to fall much faster than its normal descent. All you must do is pull the peg, and away you go. It's a lot of fun. We do it all the time. The only problem is recovering our leaves, because we removed the ropes and just cut a new one from this tree's branches instead of hauling the original leaf back up here through the tunnel. It is a great thrill ride, but a long haul back up here. You must remember this when you launch. You must hang on to the strap once it is released and observe your surroundings through the holes cut in the floor or around you as you glide downward."

"Hah! That sounds like fun," said Wayne, "Will this ride take us to the next colony?"

"I wish it did, but we have a ten-day journey ahead of us through dangerous territory," said the chief, "This flight on the leaf gliders with the wind right will take five days off the trip at the most."

"What is that?" asked Rhonda, pointing to the approach of two long antennas.

They peered over the edge, a concept left alone with the fear of heights in most of the world; a cockroach crawled up the edge of the drop-off, its head extended and its antennas waving back and forth.

# CHAPTER 6

Carson drew his sword, looked at the chief, and grinned, "Shall I?"

The chief looked back at Carson and said, "It's you or die. Make it count and earn your spurs."

Carson walked toward the cockroach that gazed at them at the brim of the ledge where they all stood. He pulled his sword simultaneously to make himself evident in front of the cockroach. Its head was four times Carson's width, and it tilted its head and antennae (actually the insect's smelling device) over the group. Carson swung the sword to slice the left antenna off, hoping the insect would flee because of the injury. With great speed, it climbed above them and moved its rear to Carson's left, and its front legs groped for the object of its recent pain. The girls and Wayne stepped back toward the mud trail and prepared to make a sudden plunge down the passageway.

The colossal insect climbed up over Carson menacingly, and he thought surely it was a more enormous creature that dared slice off his antenna. The incredible size of the beast seemed to intimidate them far more than when it just peeked up at them, with only its head and antenna visible.

Carson realized his opportune time, swung his blade, and removed the front leg on the lower side of the roach, then the second, and then the third leg. He stepped back, rushed toward the roach's midsection, struck it with a flying kick, and pushed it over the edge. At this point, he realized his feet had long left the ground, and the wind from his wings held him in the air.

The roach moved over the edge and fell. Its middle leg

caught Carson suddenly, and he found himself in a descent in the grasp of one clawed leg. The wind of the fall told him he accelerated quickly in the plunge.

Carson swung his sword one last time to cut the hold and send the cockroach downward. He watched as it opened its wings with a toss of the remaining piece of claw hooked to his clothing away from his body. Carson sputtered during his flight attempt but regained altitude and returned to his original point of departure.

He flew up, over, and downward to land on the ledge with a quick shuffle of his feet. He bent over in a bow as they applauded.

"You had us worried there, Carson," said Rhonda, "Fine swordsmanship, but cutting off his head would have been more effective."

"Sure, I could have, but wasn't my approach much more challenging and dramatic?" asked Carson.

"Yeah, but you made an enemy today," said the chief, "Those creatures will be here when we return and with friends."

"Then we'd better get moving," said Rhonda, "Roaches, give me the willies."

"Especially those bigger than a bus," said Roxie.

"Wait!" exclaimed the chief, "We must send a scout to the opening to ensure we are not being observed. The quieter and stealthier we depart, the safer the journey will be.

One of the warriors crept out on the edge of the wooden structure and moved quickly across. He held on to splinters and jagged protrusions to reach the opening where the silk cable extended into the distance. He pulled out a looking glass and carefully examined the areas below, with great concern and time.

"Is that a one-eyed binocular?" asked Rhonda.

"One-eyed binoculars, now that's a concept," said Wayne as he looked back at Rhonda to see her puzzled expression. "I suppose it was called a looking glass until two were put together to add depth to the view to determine distance better."

"My question is, do you have glass here?" asked Roxie.

"Glass? Yes, we do," the chief said, "You don't have glass in your colony?"

"Sure, we have glass," said Carson, "We melt sand, skim off the floating debris, and take the clear stuff and mold it into lenses or blow air into its middle to make glass containers."

"Well, so do we. It is too expensive, but we have it," the chief said, "We have to buy it from the Tree People, and they ask a lot of gold for such items."

"Sounds like you could use some of their technology to make your own," said Rhonda.

"Well, even if we had the proper setup to melt sand, it is rare this high up in the mountains," said the chief, "There used to be an abundance of glass as litter from the giants, but they have switched to softer containers, and the supplies have diminished greatly. Besides, to burn this close to giants can bring unwanted curiosity."

"We have giants in the land, too?" asked Roxie.

"I suppose that huge car that drove by just after we arrived would be a good clue to that possibility," said Rhonda.

"The giants are not the issue here," said the chief, "Our issue is the many emperor's warriors that are on the lookout and monitor the compliance of our people to their rule."

"Is he some kind of dictator?" asked Carson.

"Dictator, emperor, ruler of darkness, call him what you wish, but he is a ruthless man that wants total control and pushes his authority on all people," said the chief, "We thought you were from the emperor when you first arrived, so we gave great respect and hospitality but were puzzled by your lack of survival skills in the wilderness. Word was sent to the emperor to see if he had sent some of his cadets our way on a training mission.

He sent word back last night to hold you until his security could arrive to take you prisoner. I decided to take you away before they arrived. That is why we must scout the area before our departure."

"We do appreciate your concern for our safety and the risk you have taken," said Carson.

"Yes, there are things worth taking a risk for," said the chief, "I overheard Roxie praying quietly for both of you when you were stretched out and unconscious. I have not seen that kind of faith in my lifetime, and the fact that you prayed for them often speaks volumes. No one is allowed to pray to God. Just praying to the great emperor, who considers himself the god of all gods, is allowed in this empire."

"Maybe you do understand why we are here more than you know," said Roxie, looking at the chief in admiration.

The lookout whistled to them and then gave a series of hand signals that the chief quickly understood. "We must be going soon. The emperor's forces have already arrived, transported by lizards, and are now entering the colony. There will be a search. It is time for us to flee undetected while we still can. His lookouts will be watching, too," said the chief.

"Then let's be on our way as quickly as possible," said Carson.

"We must have the sun at a certain angle in the sky to avoid being seen," he said, "It is almost time. Let me explain how we will leave this tree and ride the wind to our release point. You must pull the release pin at the same spot that the person in front of you does. It is also important to man your glider as it floats downward. You must stand on the leaf, hold to the middle straps, and try to keep the leaf balanced." The chief stepped from the first leaf to the next with the movement of his hands down the cable of twisted spider web chords. He reached the last leaf glider, turned to speak to them, and demonstrated how to hold on to the strap with his legs straddled to have a foot on each side of the two central straps.

The remaining group members moved around the ledge to the inward extension of the limb that supported the cable. They prepared to mount the next leaves strapped to the line.

"Now, when you see me release or the person in front of you release, try to do it at the same point. We may be scattered across the terrain a little. The closer you are to the same release point, the greater the chance of landing at or near where I land. Once you arrive on the ground, whistle, and we will hopefully all move toward each other. I'll give a two-whistle sound, and I will know which way you are coming from by yours," said the chief. "The last point is how to launch. If you look at the cable, it is very rough for the first few arm lengths, and then it becomes smooth as glass. You just jerk the cable toward the smooth area, and once it is reached, you will find that speed will take care of everything. Also, if you look in the distance, you will see a rise that you will crest, then another rise. A rock extension is from the opposite side of the far slope on the other ridge. That will be our rallying point if we are split up. Try to get there by dark. If you drift too far away from each other, my whistle will not bring us together. I'm going first to be able to monitor each of your arrivals and check out the area for intruders."

Rhonda, Wayne, Roxie, Carson, and the three other guards climbed onto their mounts, which swayed and shifted as they cautiously walked across them, out of fear of a fall. Carson looked at the leaf's veiny surface and its oval shape. The leaf looked intimidating, indicating grave concerns about the first-ever windsurf. They watched as the chief scooted the strap a little at a time until it reached the smooth part of the cable, and suddenly, he was off and sailed into the distance on the downward slope of the thread.

Rhonda worked her strap next. She turned away from

her view of the chief to get her body weight into the jerks on the cable. Precariously, the girl scooted down the rope in what appeared to be six to eight-inch movements. She reached the smooth part of the cable, and off she went. The leaf began to turn around, and she no longer faced them. She seemed to struggle with the wind as it turned the glider. She put some effort into halting the rotation once she faced the direction she was headed and, hopefully, could see the chief in the distance.

Wayne was next and had made some effort to do the same thing when Rhonda started her movement. He scooted in more forcefully, but, being taller, he used his weight very effectively to move his strap to the smooth point, and away he went.

He spun four times before he could stop the rotation and view the direction of his descent down the cable.

He seemed to be in a strain with both legs that struggled to push against the turn in the wind.

Roxie was next and began to jerk on her strap. She expressed some frustration that it was not as easy as it appeared. Her height was a factor, so she didn't have as much jerk on the strap to move the seed down the cable.

"Reach higher on the strap," Carson said while moving forward on his strap to try to stay close to Roxie. He reached out to help her move the belt forward. He feared they were about to fall behind with the time taken by Rhonda's efforts.

Roxie pulled higher on the strap and gave it another jerk, only to find it moved a small amount. She reached a foot from the slick part of the cable when Carson's glider bumped into Roxie's.

Carson moved his glider sideways, used the side rope to venture out to Roxie's glider, and stepped onto hers. This effort moved her glider, but it still appeared to be stuck. He pulled his strap in hopes of reaching almost to Roxie's strap. He then reached out to hers to give it the last push to get it over the rough area, and with the push, he also inadvertently knocked out the release peg while off balance. The strap made a quick slipping sound, and he knew instantly that Roxie was headed downward. He grabbed her arm just as the leaf she stood on disappeared from under her. She swung wildly in Carson's grasp. Her weight plunged downward even with Carson's tight hold on her wrist. With him extended from the left side of his glider with one arm and extended downward, Roxie swung under his glider. This range of motion caused the leaf to swing one way, then back toward the cable's reach. This caused the final rough area of the line to slip by. Immediately, the glider descended the smooth rope with Carson stretched to hold on to Roxie, who dangled just beyond the edge of his leaf glider. The leaf started to spin in the wind. He focused on his hold on her and tried to get her to get a foot on the edge, but the area around them spun faster and faster. Carson pulled Roxie up onto the surface of the glider, closer to him, and she threw her arms around his waist, and he held the collar of her shirt.

"Pull your pin," came a voice from somewhere in the spin.

Carson, in his confusion, had missed his drop point. With Roxie having a severe hold on him, he reached for the pin and pulled. The pin offered resistance from the twist of the spin, but with a stronger yank, the hook popped out. With an attempt to grab the strap to hold on as they descended, he found he had missed it completely. Roxie screamed and held even tighter. He watched the glider flutter away from his feet and spin into the distance as they plunged downward. Carson wrapped his legs around her tightly. He knew right away that he was in for another flying lesson, but this time, he was dizzy from the rotation of their fall. His wings came forth and began to slow their descent.

"Hang on, Roxie," he said to assure her, "I've got you, and we will reach the ground very soon."

"I'm not in a rush to reach the ground," she said, "Just stop the fall."

The descent continued, but not as fast. The movement began to stabilize and move in a single, confused, rotated direction. He looked around. He hoped to see his partners, but noticed, more than anything, the continued swirl of motion in his vision, which confused his sense of direction. In the corner of his eye, he thought he saw the rock formation that the chief had pointed out earlier. Before he could adjust to that direction, he inadvertently collided with some pine needles that altered his flight pattern. He swayed a bit, and Roxie held tightly at his waist. The first collision with pine needles naturally led to another crash with the next branch. Suddenly, he found a fork in the pine tree branch, and they both stopped. Roxie, however, jerked forward with her hair slightly entangled in the bark, but the branch fork caught Carson at chest level. She bounced off the lower part of the branch and stopped Carson from losing what sudden hold he had on the fork. His wings stopped and disappeared.

"That hurt, Carson," Roxie said, sounding out of breath. "Are you okay up there?"

"I'm sorry. I've got a good hold on this branch. Are you okay down there?" Carson asked without answering her question.

"I assume the answer is yes," she said in reply, "I'm holding on still, and your death grip around me with your legs seems to be holding out pretty good. Don't you suppose you could stop this branch from swinging up and down? Adding that to my dizziness, I think I will be sick."

"Oh, please don't do that," he said, "That could get mighty slippery."

"No problem, I can toss my cookies to the left," she said, sounding slightly green.

"I'm not worried about my shoes one bit," he said to assure her, "Yours is a lot further down than mine, and the wind and sway of this branch. Just hold on to everything you can."

"I'll try. I think the dizziness is going away some," Roxie

said, "Now I feel that being replaced with fear of heights. Do you see how far up we are?"

"Roxie, you can fly," said Carson, "Now would be a good time to test your wings."

"Yeah, and if I can't figure out how to use them before we reach the next set of branches below, we bounce right back up this way or may just plunge downward until we reach the ground below," she said, "Is there a way you can pull me upward?"

"Roxie, I would in a heartbeat if I could," he said, "I have a branch under each armpit and a beautiful woman dangling below that I can't even see with her arms wrapped around me and my legs around her."

"Sounds like you're having fun," she said with a change in her tone of voice, "I wish I were having as much fun dangling down here. I would love to see your eyes again, even if you did knock my pin out and cause my ride to slip away, but thanks for catching me."

"I didn't want to lose you, Roxie," said Carson, "I think it is nice having you around. Besides, I don't want to spend the rest of my life remembering the girl who disappeared."

"Yeah, I would have gotten away, but I would come looking for you," she said, "You would not like me when I'm mad."

"Your anger could never match my rage toward me if I had lost you back there," he said, "Besides, if I had missed you, I would have flown down to catch you if your wings failed to stop your fall."

"Wow, a hero no matter what happens," she said humorously but with a sincere tone. "I'm sorry. That was a wrong choice of words when I'm in this predicament. You're my hero, but we must get down from here."

"Yes! Are you feeling better now?" he asked, "Has the dizziness subsided yet?"

"Sure, it cleared up pretty quick once this leaf stopped bouncing around," she said, "Getting stabilized was the key factor if you consider hanging on to a man by his waist and hoping his pants don't come loose."

You don't have to worry about these suits ever having a droop to them," he said, "Even if they would droop, I'll never do it. I try to be better than that."

"Good for you," she said, "Now, for getting us out of this tree and onto solid ground, I think I can see the rock formation on that slope we are supposed to use for a rallying point."

"I'm glad because I can't see anything from up here but pine needles and bark," Carson said.

"Do you think I can catch the next branch down if you turn me loose?" asked Roxie.

"I would rather you use those wings you were given and fly before you get there," he said, "How far down are the next branches?"

"They look to be about a hundred feet, but who can judge distance as big as everything is around here?" she said. "How much longer do you think you can hold on?"

"If it protects you, as long as it takes," he said.

"Well, lover boy, I'm about to let go," she said, "You let go when I do, and I will see if my wings work. If not, I'll hit those limbs below and probably bow the branch down, and when it comes back up, come flying right past you like a big jump off a diving board."

"That sounds scary. Are you sure you are ready?" Carson asked.

"Well, staying like this, holding on until we are both exhausted, will only make us too weak to try when we fall," she said.

"Good point. I'm ready when you are," Carson said. "Remember to think and focus on flight and where you want to go." Don't let your attention on flying stop. Your wings will stop working, and you will drop. I had that problem before I rescued Wayne. I got a sudden swimming lesson in a cold, fast-moving stream just beyond those trees."

"I'm ready to let go; I can feel I'm beginning to slip," she said as her grip around him gave way, "Goodbye, Carson; I hope we meet again below and airborne; if not, may God help us."

May God help us anyway," said Carson, and he felt the arms leave him and his legs give way. Her hands clawed at his feet as she fell downward. His heart raced, and he immediately pushed away from the branch and plunged downward in hopes of catching her before she met any branches."

"Going somewhere, big fellow?" asked a voice that hovered in mid-air halfway down.

Carson left his downward plunge, swept through some big pine needles, and started climbing back up to where she hovered as if she had done it all her life. "It seems you have a flight gift." He flew up next to her and reached for her hand.

Roxie reached out her hand as if she knew he wanted to hold hers. "It's God's gift to you at this point. You should have seen the shock in your eyes when you flew by."

"Well, you flying there, all by yourself, just happens to be the prettiest sight I have seen in a long time," Carson said, "I ran into those branches below, looking back in amazement. Shall we fly over to that reference point at the top of the ridge now, before we lose focus and start another downward plunge?"

Carson flew out and upward toward the distant bank. He suggested they both keep their eyes peeled to hopefully see their friends as they ascended the ridge and arrived on top of the rock in about two minutes. Their touchdowns were beautiful, with only a few steps to gain control upon arrival. They immediately began a visual search of the valley below with hopes of visual contact with the rest of the party. They listened for the whistle signal but heard nothing. They soon gave up the investigation from their lookout point because of the risks involved. They figured their friends were well hidden for a reason. They set out for a more isolated point on the rock formation for concealment and cover.

"Will you look at the view? I can see everything from up here. I think I can pick out the tree we came from and see the opening where the cable extended," he said, "I wish we had the looking glass to pick out our friends as they climb the hill. There's the ridge between us. Just below us is the very ravine I swam in a couple of weeks ago, and there's a stream as big as a river. The mud daubers have several nests on the other side, and we want to keep a close eye in that direction."

What are we to watch for?" she asked, "How much more danger can we find?"

The chief said we would meet much danger," he said, "How about you sit back-to-back with me? We will both keep watch until our friends arrive." He turned his back to her, and she backed up to him. His back against her was heavier, but her warmth comforted him as they relaxed in the late morning sunlight. It was the first time that day that they both could settle down.

This time, Roxie reached around, found his hand, and held it tightly. "You're a good man, Carson," she said, "I hope we live long enough to get to know each other better."

"May God be with us for many years," Carson said.

They both spent a good bit of the day in anticipation, hoping to hear their friends' arrival. Maybe even a whistle or something to give them a clue that the party was close.

They waited until noon while they baked in the spring sunshine on the rock. They consumed the first liquid rations they of how long their supply would last.

Soon, the sun began reaching the other end of their

horizon. It would not be long before they would see the stretched shadows of the setting sun.

Thunderheads were also forming in the distance beyond the ridge they sat upon.

Carson, while he looked around, strained to see any sign of their friends. He also noticed the honeysuckles that grew just beyond the edge of the rocks. Many blooms seemed to just open up before them.

He gave the area a good look around. He led Roxie over to the vine and climbed up to the yellow/white blooms.

He pulled his sword with one hand and whacked off four blooms, which flew down to Roxie. She gazed on with curiosity and perhaps was flattered by his picking of the flowers for her. He climbed back down, then stood beside her and the flowers. He gave another terrain sweep to ensure he could see no dangers approaching and hear no indications of unknowns approaching.

"That is mighty sweet of you to pick me flowers, but for the death of me, I forgot to pack a flower vase," she said with a grin and perhaps a blush on her cheeks.

"These are honeysuckles, sweetheart," Carson said with a grin in return, "Their purpose is to offer us our dinner. Allow me."

Carson stepped up to the first flower, equal to about twenty of his body lengths. He pulled his sword and chopped a fragment from the bloom above the flower's stem near the base in two small chops. It opened up to expose the inner pistil. He climbed up to straddle the flower, reached into the hole, and returned with two handfuls of leaks. He leaned forward and sipped the liquid he had scooped out of the cavity.

"Is it any good?" she asked curiously, "Should I climb up there, too, or can you pass me some so that I can have a taste?

"Oh, it's good. The best I ever had," Carson said, "Tell you what. I'll scoop out some and try to pour it into your cupped hands, and you can try some, too."

"You have washed your hands, haven't you?" she asked.

"Yeah, and where is a sink to wash up?" he asked. "Your hands are no cleaner than mine. We share germs now, right?"

"If I must do so to get to know you better, I'll try it," she said, humoring him further. She held her hands in the overlapped, cupped fashion she had just seen Carson use.

Carson reached in and scooped out another dripping handful. Carefully, he moved his cupped hands over to where Roxie waited. He gently opened the clasp of his two hands to slowly allow a trickle of the fluid to escape. Roxie moved her hands under the gentle flow and tried to avoid the splash of the liquid on her face as it splattered. She attempted to catch it. Roxie could catch about half of it and wore more than she caught. She sipped the liquid, and her eyes brightened in surprise at the incredible taste.

"It tastes sweeter and more refined than sugar water. Now, if we just had some Kool-Aid or some tea bags," she said in amazement. She drank all the fluid and said, "I'll cut my next helping, thank you. Nice of you to try, but I will never get this sticky mess off of me." She climbed up on the next honeysuckle with her sword and carefully cut a circle into the flower's stem. She reached in and scooped out her liquid handfuls.

They both continued to feast on their find, hardly noticing the sudden breeze that came upon them, other than the fact that the flower also seemed to rock a little.

"You seem to be enjoying yourself," came a voice from the adjacent part of the rock.

Both were startled and caught entirely off their guard.

Carson immediately reached for his sword, but did not remove his weapon as Roxie did.

"So, we meet again, my dear friend," said Carson as he spoke to the mud dauber that had arrived so stealthily moments before. He stated "friend" as an assurance to Roxie that she might not need her weapon.

"Yes, we meet again. I wished the circumstances were better. Your party met an ambush upon reaching the ground. You two are the only ones not captured or badly injured in battle."

"There was a battle?" asked Roxie, "Where is Rhonda?"

"Yeah, where is Wayne?" asked Carson.

"They were taken prisoner as soon as they crash-landed. Their weapons were taken from them, and they were hauled off by the flying warriors of the dark realm," he said, "The other four were severely assaulted and left to die of their wounds. I saw you here earlier and thought you might like to see the last of the still-alive wounded."

The mud dauber lowered his two middle legs to the surface of the rock to reveal the black and yellow armor of the chief, who had led them in their escape from the tree.

They both jumped from their flower stems and rushed to the chief, who seemed shocked. "It's okay, Chief. This mud dauber is my friend. He rescued you and brought you to us," said Carson as Roxie raised his head and supported it with her lap.

The chief blinked and looked at Carson, and Roxie, and then in fear at the remarkable insect perched over him. The dauber slowly moved to the side to remove the intimidation of his appearance from the seriously injured warrior. He seemed to show a tear. "I'm sorry," he said as he struggled with his words, as if in severe pain and having serious difficulty breathing. "I tried to get you away, but they knew what I was doing. They captured your two friends and killed my guards. They left me to die. I thought the worst when this creature came down, made some noises, and carried me away. I felt he was going to sting me, and I would be larva food in a couple of days."

"Chief, you need to stop talking. You are hurt pretty bad,"

said Roxie.

"No, you must hear what I have to...say," he said, "You must continue your escape. Your friends will be carried to the emperor... He will know you are still out here. He will search the area on foot, thinking you are wandering about. He has no idea you have made it this far. You must flee from here and go to the lake below the mountain. One end...has giants, and when it is warm, they play in the water. You must find the opposite end of the lake and go to the trees there to wait for our allies to find you. The Tree People will find you there. You won't find them."

"We will take you with us," said Carson, "We can't leave you here."

"Go...I will be ant food before the setting of the sun," the chief said after a few short breaths. "You must run before it is too late... I feel you were sent to us to free us from this bondage of hate... I see love in the four of you, and you two must go forth for the other two...and save us all."

"I will have my friend, the mud dauber, fly you back to your camp," said Carson.

"No, I am considered a traitor to my people at this point...I may have brought great bloodshed to my colony for fleeing with you... I cannot return. I feel the darkness coming upon me...you must go on and get help from...the Tree...People."

"You still may greatly help us," said Roxie, "We will take you with us."

Suddenly, as if he had been struck again, he said, "No...it is...too...late. You are my people's...only hope. I feel it in my... heart." His eyes became empty. His stiffness was replaced by the limpness of death.

Carson watched in disbelief. He had never seen someone die. His heart raced, rendering him helpless. He watched Roxie reach and close his empty eyes.

The two had a quiet resolve, and the mud dauber hung

low. Their heads hung low as they realized they had lost their strongest ally.

"He is right. You must leave now or find yourselves prisoners like your friends," said the mud dauber. "Go and with Godspeed. I will make him a mud hut under this rock and enclose his body as a monument of his service to your cause," the mud dauber said. "You will find him preserved when you return from your great mission, Oh, Promised One."

The mud dauber flew away quickly. He disappeared under the rock, and in a matter of minutes, he flew away again. He circled the top of the hill, presumably toward the stream beyond, to make mud for the entombment of the body of the chief.

# CHAPTER 7

"Wow! Now you're the Promised One," said Roxie with a smile. "You've moved up quickly in this world. I would think he would include all of us and say, Promised Two or Promised Four."

"All right, flattery will get you nowhere. If the dauber assumes I'm some kind of Promised One, it's to our advantage, right?" asked Carson.

"Maybe, but on the other hand, at least we know where to go now," she said, "What's the plan?"

"Considering where the lake is located, we should fly," he said. "We should eat before leaving so we won't wimp out before getting there."

They hurriedly consumed more of the liquid from the honeysuckle cuts. After an attempt to wipe off some of the sticky nectar that dripped from his hands, Carson contemplated their flight plan from their current location. "If we are going to fly, and soon, I suggest a leap from this rock, make a left turn, and fly over the ridge. If we get a tailwind, we could make it to the lake by dark."

"Sounds cool," she said, but added mischievously, "We can also find a fork in a branch to crash into if we need a break."

"Well, I suggest we use a simple treetop on a high ridge," he said with a smile.

With a slight hesitation, they leaped off the end of the rock formation. They fell for a noticeably short distance before the wind of their wings engaged. They reached out to hold each other's hands. Whether for comfort or to keep up with each other, it did not matter. The two held tightly, each clutched the other's arm between the elbow and wrist. Carson's arm was slightly forward, indicating that he was the leader.

The air currents were awkward and rather brisk at times. The wind was more of a frequent gust that knocked them to their left and forced them to adjust often to compensate. After they crested a couple of ridges, they could see the lake far below, beyond the steep descent of the mountainside. They were halfway there.

The highest tree on the ridge was a Red Oak. He pulled at Roxie to circle. They landed in its top branches.

"Did you see the dark clouds forming back that way?" asked Carson as he pointed toward their right.

Roxie answered, "Yeah, it looks like an approaching storm is the cause of the strong winds. We are in for soaking if we don't hurry."

"Considering our current size, one drop of rain could wash us away. We'd better find shelter."

"Okay, what do you have in mind?" Roxie asked as she pulled out a liquid energy pack from her belt in concert with Carson.

"On the other side of the lake, I see some green buildings. They could offer us shelter from the storm and for the night."

"Well, let's get going, but let me lead this time," said Roxie. She reached for his arm and sprang forth before he could disagree.

The wings lifted and carried them forth much quicker this time. The wind became more robust. It became more challenging to stay on course. With Roxie in the flight's lead, Carson could keep a better watch on the intimidating darkness of the approaching storm. He saw the torrential downpour as it moved to beat them to their destination. The setting sun, which had already crested the horizon to their left front, also reduced their visibility. The darkness approached fast, either by the storm front or the sunset.

He said, "Hurry, Roxie, hurry!" They reached the lake, and then a sudden updraft hit them as they approached the water. In the middle of the lake was an open pier with a diving board and a ladder. There was no overhead cover. The green buildings contained restrooms, changing rooms, and a covered picnic area, all awaiting just beyond the water's edge. This was a park.

Roxie led their flight and veered toward the covered picnic tables. She aimed them for the sanctuary of the roof's overhang as the first drops came by like giant high-speed silver spaceships and splashed on the ground below.

Suddenly, Carson altered their course to jerk them sharply to his right, while Roxie barely got grazed by a giant raindrop. She was soaked but managed to stay in flight and only lost some altitude. They went only a short distance before Carson pushed toward Roxie's direction and took a glance of his own as the next raindrop passed them. Shortly, they reached the protection of the roof of the covered picnic area through a sudden series of pelting splashes. Speed proved the only thing that kept them from being swept away by the vast raindrops. As soon as they got under the overhang, the bottom fell out. Darkness was upon them. The winds gusted even stronger than before. The only light remaining radiated from the streetlamps scattered along the shore.

Their flight slowed and took a U-turn under the roof because Roxie had already visualized water blown across the picnic tables below them. She selected, instead, the support beams of the ceiling above them to seek shelter. To gain altitude in their current wet condition was a challenge, yet they made it to the top surface of the dusty four-by-four beam that ran parallel to the surface below. Both landed with several steps before they gained stability. It was not a total escape. Wind gusts still forced them to go to their hands and knees to hold on to the surface cracks and crawl toward the corner pillar, hoping it would block away some of the forceful pulls of the air currents. They reached the point where the beam and the post met and wrapped themselves into the splinters of the lower board to ensure the wind would not knock them off their foothold. The darkness was upon them, and winds gusted even stronger than before to blow rainwater into the area of refuge they had finally reached.

Even though Roxie was soaked and intimidated by the storm's vicious assault on their hideaway, she said, "I'm glad I led you to this spot instead of the trees. We could have been washed off a tree and treading water."

"You led us to it? It was my suggestion," said Carson.

"Take credit if you want, but we planned well," she said, "I saw an outside light flicker on, and there goes another. It is good to be back in civilization."

"Yeah, I even see a phone over there. Want to call your mom?" asked Carson.

"Gosh, yes! Hey Mom! Thought you would like to know I was playing in the rain and did not burn up in that hotel. They would be searching the country."

"Besides, it would take about three hundred of us to pick up the receiver," said Carson, as he smiled back at her, as he sat down, placed his back to the green post, and tried to wring some of the water out of his shirt.

"Thank God we were allowed to reach shelter before the floods came."

"Someone is looking after us," said Carson, "If I had not stopped to chat on that tree, we could have made it here much sooner."

"It was a good idea to stop. " It is hard to chat while flying and concentrating on wing performance," Roxie said. "I remember you telling me that when you got distracted while rescuing Wayne, you dropped to the stream below." We did fine. It's just getting cold, and I'm soaked."

"We are in for a cold night," he said, "We need to find a

crack in this wall and get out of the wind."

"Yeah, you crawl into a crack. I'm not fond of dark places to hide because spiders like those places," Roxie said, sitting down next to him on his left side as if she tried to escape the cold winds by using Carson as a barrier.

"This place is a park area for lake swimming. It looks so familiar. It reminds me of Cheaha State Park. I used to swim there as a child," Carson said, "My dad had me jump off the platform in the middle of the lake, telling me he would catch me, but he missed. Thought I was going to drown. My dad was sneaky, trying to teach me to swim the hard way."

"I took swimming lessons," said Roxie. "My parents wanted me to know how to swim and be safe in the water."

"Guess you had a swimming pool, too, huh?" asked Carson inquisitively.

"No, we just had the public pool. We always wanted a pool, but my dad never settled down and bought a house," she said, "Renting and having to move is such a drag."

"Yeah, I remember moving a few times growing up," Carson said, "My dad got a government job at Anniston Army Depot. Then he moved us to the sticks. We were close to where he grew up."

"Bet you couldn't go shopping whenever you wanted to, right?" she asked.

"You could, but the drive to town was too time-consuming," he said, "I did love the nature walks and watching my dog chase and dig up ground squirrels."

"Sounds like you are right at home here," she said.

"Yeah, you can tell. Nothing like a bug's eye view of the world, wondering why I am here," he said.

"I know why we are here. We are here to help these people with their problems. Four people have died trying to help us escape. Our two best friends are captives of an enemy we know little about. Maybe the Tree People will give us more information about the enemy. According to the chief, the Tree People are not submissive to the emperor's control like the Wasamanee People," she said.

"Those people were scared to death. They had a standing army of every male," he said, "Were they guarding their people or enforcing the authority of the emperor?"

"I think they were like warrior bees, ready to defend their colony against any harm," she said. "They are good people, but too submissive to their terrible rulers. I find it hard to believe my praying would endanger us. I also can't believe that the chief lost his life trying to protect us. May I move a little closer to you?" Roxie asked. "I'm freezing."

Carson looked at her beside him and could see she was trembling. He was cold and allowed her to scoot under his arm. Not knowing where to put his hand, she reached for it and pulled it toward her stomach. "Any time you want to be close to me, feel free to snuggle away," he said with pride, "I'm here for you."

She looked at him, smiled, and said, "Thanks. You are such a fun person to be around and a perfect gentleman."

"I always respect your wishes," he said.

They sat quietly, with a close-up view of the heavy rain and the sudden flashes of lightning that accompanied the thunderstorm, which raged on for what seemed like all night. Before long, Carson could hear her heavy breathing and knew she was asleep. He helped her to lie down. With an effort to block the wind, he moved so that his back was behind her. His height allowed him to shelter her rather well.

He felt awkward in his effort to stay on his side. He had never been this close to a female. The warm softness and tenderness of her touch were mesmerizing. Falling asleep took a long time; his distrust of the surroundings kept his eyes open late into the night.

The following day began with the birds that chirped in the distance. The early rays of sunshine rose above the great mountain, reflected off the water, and the wet surface of the table below, where they spent the night. Carson woke, turning his head to see Roxie's dark brown, tangled hair. Even though it was an uncombed mess from being wet, he found her beauty intriguing. Carson could dwell on her features, but knew duty called. He needed to check out the safety of their situation. In the initial movement toward that objective, Carson slept awkwardly and began to massage a bit of a crick in his neck. He gently slipped away from Roxie without waking her.

He felt slightly disappointed in leaving her, but felt viewing the area as soon as possible might be in their best interests.

Carson stepped out into the sunshine. He soaked up the rays in the cold morning breeze.

The day before had been very cloudy. It was the first time he had seen a blue sky in a couple of weeks, at the start of a beautiful day. The sun glistened on the lake. The sun rose above the mountain in the distance. It was Mount Cheaha, the tallest mountain in the state of Alabama. He could also see the park hotel. He had relatives who worked at the hotel, and it would do him a lot of good in his situation.

Suddenly, there was a flutter. Carson turned to see a mass of blue closing in on him. He immediately jumped back and drew his sword. He yelled, "Who goes there?"

A giant bird landed and hopped a few steps toward him, then tilted its head. "It speaks?" asked the bird, "Shall I taste it and see if I like it?"

"No, I'm not to be eaten. You must leave my friend and me alone," said Carson as he brandished his sword. "I am a friend of all birds, exquisite male bluebirds especially."

"You mean there are more tasty morsels chattering around here?" questioned the bird, "I have never had an insect talk to me before I have it for breakfast."

"I'm not an insect; I'm a human, just small for my size," he said as he walked toward the bird. "Would you like to feel my sting? I would hate to injure your wings or legs and cripple you when we could be friends."

"Friends with humans," the bird chirped while it tilted its head to one side in a puzzled fashion. "Never!"

"We are here looking for the Tree People," said Carson as he tried to reason or change the subject from mealtime."

"The Tree People? You are not one of them; they are light green," said the bird, "You are dark green, like the painted wood we stand on."

Carson looked down to see that his suit had changed to resemble the wooden structure below his feet. Thinking quickly, "You can't eat me; I'm the Promised One."

"I'll say, and I have promised myself that I will eat you," the bird said as he moved closer to him.

"Do you eat the Tree People?" asked Carson.

"No, they have stingers like you hold in your hand," said the bird.

"Then why do you tease as if you are unafraid of this blade?" asked Carson.

"Because you speak my language so well, and never has a Tree Person dared to chat with me before," said the bird, "You intrigue me."

"Intrigued or not, I'm not going to let you make a meal out of me," said Carson.

"I have found making you worry about the possibility most enjoyable," teased the bird.

"If I am not to be your meal, then give me directions to the Tree People," he said, "We have urgent business with them."

"You won't find them. They will find you," the bird chirped, "If you venture into the thicket beyond the far bank's first spur, they will suddenly and overwhelmingly greet you both. If you survive, you may find them to be very hospitable."

"Thanks for your assistance," said Carson.

"Perhaps you should wake your mate before she gets surprised by some of my friends or perhaps my enemies," said the bird, and then the bird, with great ease, fluttered into the air.

Carson turned to see a trapdoor spider crawl toward Roxie. His heart suddenly raced. He still held the sword ready in defense, so he charged forward as he leaped from grain to grain, never having imagined a piece of wood would have such a rough, uneven surface. Roxie slept away, totally oblivious to the dangerous situation. Carson leaped forward. He sliced with his sword through the neck of the spider. With such a small sword, Carson thought his slice could only nick the creature and turn it away from Roxie and toward himself. As he sliced, it was as if his blade became longer. It pierced the entire throat of the giant spider with a complete decapitation and sent the body into total confusion. Carson collided with the wall and bounced back to the surface, keeping the blade pointed at the severely injured spider.

Roxie, suddenly startled from her sleep by the high-pitched squeals of the spider so close to her, screamed with panic when she saw the arthropod. She rose to her feet and backed against the wall. When she saw that the injured spider was no longer a threat, she asked, "Where do you get these playmates?"

"They just keep crawling out of the woodwork, maybe from one of those dark cavities you were afraid to sleep in last night," he said with concern. "Let's have a quick liquid breakfast and fly to the other side of the lake. We have a greeting party waiting for us."

"Greeting party?" she asked, "Do they know we are coming?"

"No. We will be greeted by an attack of little green men," he said.

"Little green men? You must have drunk too much of that honeysuckle juice yesterday," she said.

"Well, believe it or not, let's fly over and see," he said. They both broke out a container of liquid energy and drank their fill.

"I'm ready when you are," she said.

"Great! Let's try our luck this time with a takeoff from a good jump off from a four-by-four rather than leaping off rocks."

They casually walked to the edge of the green board, which not only had many grain patterns but also was covered with dust and clutter from its existence as an area rarely cleaned or dusted. There, they leaped off, and their wings kicked in. Their flight took them from the water's edge across the lake in beautiful form. In the distance, they could see four dragonflies.

"This way," yelled Carson, with continued focus on his flight, "Those winged creatures eat mosquitoes, and guess what we look like?"

Roxie followed close behind him, but still caused him to glance back several times in worry. One of the dragonflies caught sight of them and began to pursue aggressively. They flew a zigzag pattern as an evasive maneuver. The dragonfly gained on them. Their flight took them past the spur, and then they veered to the left over the water that extended into the draw. They both flew toward the thicket where the bank met the water, and the two ridges closed to elevate above the waterline. The dragonfly's pursuit could be heard, hot on their tails. When they crashed into the thicket, the dragonfly turned and flew onward in search of another food source.

Carson and Roxie found themselves tangled in the thick vines and green leaves. They could smell the honeysuckles and knew the vines would lead to the ground. Once they reached the wet surface of the rotunda, they found themselves up to their waists in muck. They waded forward as they both tried to reach the only clearing with some elevation. They stood and gazed around them with hopes of some sign of the Tree People and no more predator-type insects that seemed everywhere.

Carson felt uneasy and warned, "Roxie, on my command, pull your sword and stand ready to fight."

"Certainly, we are going to cut us a vine and play Tarzan, right?" she asked with no concept of the peril upon them.

Suddenly, as if by magic, thirty green men bearing swords like their own appeared out of the green surroundings. Roxie and Carson stood firm, almost back-to-back, as the circle of green men moved toward them with a threat to attack.

# CHAPTER 8

"Brandish your sword!" yelled Carson. His blade made a swish sound, and he held it directly before him, ready to battle.

"I'm ready," said Roxie with a bold voice that magnified the fact that she had pulled her sword also. "Shall we attack now or wait to see the whites of their eyes?"

Upon sight of the swords, the green men stopped dead. They stood motionless as if terrified of the two blade-wielding teenagers. Suddenly, all the green men lay down their swords and knelt before them. They began to chant. "Forgive us, Oh, Promised One, please forgive us."

"It's okay. It's okay. Get off your knees! Do not worship us!" said Carson as he stepped toward them while he put away his sword.

"The Promised One is humble just as the prophecies predicted," said one green man. Then they all said, in unison, "Please forgive us, Oh, Promised One."

"Quiet!" yelled Roxie. You could hear a pin drop.

"Nice touch," said Carson, "I was thinking the same thing, but as the Promised One, I have to mind my manners."

Roxie made a sly frown toward Carson, then said, "Now, take us to your leader."

"Yes, do as she says," said Carson, "She did not get a good night's sleep, and boy, she is cranky."

Roxie looked at him as if she were cranky. "Watch it, Buster; I haven't had a good wash this morning either, so I can be quite a stinker," she said with a slight grin back at him.

"Alright! Where's that leader we were speaking of?" asked

Carson.

The most decorative of the green men, who looked a bit like a mature human but with green feathers instead of clothing, made a unique request: "May we bear our swords for the journey?"

"Yes, take up your swords; we may need your fighting skills," said Carson.

"You must show us your mighty weapons when you reach a safe haven, oh, great warrior," said the same green warrior, "We have never seen a weapon more skillfully made than that of our own."

"I will have to think about that," said Carson.

"The chief of the Wasamanee people sent us to you," said Roxie, "May he rest in peace. We are sorry to inform you that he was killed helping us escape."

The spokesman of the green elf-like creatures turned in sudden shock with his mouth open. He said, "We have lost a great ally in the underground struggle against the emperor. He will be sorely missed. Yes, may he rest in peace."

The group moved to the trunk of a massive oak tree. Its roots extended downward in multiple directions. Carson followed, thinking about whether he would spend the night underground again.

His eyes roamed the area to look for a hidden cave entrance. To his surprise, the first Tree Man stepped right into the side of the tree trunk and vanished as if he passed right through the bark. Another followed, and so on, until Roxie reached the bark before them. She glanced back at Carson, stepped, and disappeared into the tree.

Carson reached out his hand and felt bark. He hesitated momentarily, then felt the Tree Man behind him gently push him forward. Carson passed through the bark and entered a well-lit set of stairs with handrails on each side. He could hear the others' footsteps as they continued up the stairway. He looked back to see the door he had just entered and saw the last Tree People step through. The doorway looked like tree bark from the outside and almost transparent glass from the inside.

Carson rushed up the stairs and quickly caught up with Roxie. He felt slightly insecure about the fact that he had allowed her to slip out of his sight even for a moment. Roxie chattered with fascination about the passage's makeup, the modern design, and the elegance of the wall carvings along the way. "Welcome to the most elegant hotel on Mount Cheaha, my dear," he humored her for a response.

"Yeah! Darn if this isn't beautiful. It is inside a tree, next to a lake, where people go, hang out, and swim all summer. They have no idea what is in front of them just across the lake," she said.

"We are inside a tree. I'll never look at an Oak tree the same again," said Carson.

"Many Oaks are hollow in the middle like the tree we departed from yesterday on the maple seed pods," said Roxie, "Perhaps they were hollowed by the Tree People."

"Or maybe termites like the tree we crawled through yesterday," Carson said.

They both continued up the long, spiraling staircase. Carson lost interest in the wood carvings and became more aware of this young lady, whom he had only met a couple of weeks ago. His heart ached for her in ways he never imagined possible. Carson thought of telling her how he felt. He wondered if it would embarrass them both and strain their friendship. He had better just wait. He resolved it would be best to know how Roxie felt first.

Carson and Roxie looked on with amazement as they continued up the staircase. It was as if they had moved from the most primitive society to the contemporary. Everything glowed as if it had lights built into it. The warmth was even more present as they reached the first exit door to what Carson assumed was the first floor. The spiral stairs continued their progress up several additional feet. Finally, it reached the last entry. The green people ahead of them opened and entered a passageway. The two followed, entering an open area that appeared to have a glass dome. The dome was made of the same transparent bark. The crown was round, with extensions extending in several directions toward the tops of the tree branches. Doors to those avenues piqued their curiosity. At the other end of the passages were thick leaf patches like a squirrel's nest. The walls were supported with glass artwork and trestles.

They were guided to a well-lit enclosed area with several padded chairs in a circle. In one of the chairs sat a green man who appeared to be very ancient. Upon their entrance, the door quickly closed behind them.

"You may be seated," said the gentleman.

"Thank you," said Roxie with a sudden look of excitement. "A padded seat!" She rushed to sink into its luxury. "How wonderful it feels to sit on something soft."

"Yeah, like, really cool," said Carson, "The Wasamanee needs to hire some of your upholstery people."

"I hope you are comfortable because you will be with me for some time," said the gentleman. He sat before them in a green body suit. His skin appeared to be made of scales, like a reptilian creature. Suddenly, the green man reached up and peeled off his green face to reveal his more human features. He then removed his gloves, revealing human hands. Carson glanced toward Roxie and found her dressed in the same style. "I see you have found our clothing fashion suitable for your tastes," said the gentleman.

Carson looked down to find he was clothed in the same getup. "We are very adaptive to those around us and the environment," said Carson, "I'm not sure how it works, but it works well."

"I see you need to learn to control it better," said the gentleman, "By the way, I'm Johannes, your guide for your mission here."

"Glad to meet you, sir," Carson and Roxie said in unison and smiled at each other.

Carson asked, "How do we control these suits you talk about?"

"I know where you got the suits and who you are," said Johannes, "We've been expecting you for a long time. You are prophesied as the promised four of hope."

"We have been called the Promised One by others," said Carson, "Please tell us more."

"The prophecy tells us that four strangers will come. They will be strangers to our world, and our ways must be taught to them. They will be young. There will be two warriors and two servants," he said.

"Well, I guess we are two of your Promised Ones. Unfortunately, the other two have been captured by your emperor," said Carson.

"Yes, the two servants were captured," said Johannes. You two are the warriors."

Roxie grinned and looked at Carson. Carson returned her look with a mild blush. "I'm glad we are together in this, Carson," she said as she reached and patted his hand.

"Thanks, Roxie," he said quietly and gently. "I'm glad, too."

"You two have a serious fondness for each other, but remember, you are here on a mission," Johannes said, "My world depends on you. If you fail, we will have to wait for another. My race can't afford to wait any longer."

"Carson, he is right, true love waits," she said, "We must work as a team and develop our skills to be successful in our mission."

"Roxie's right; you must develop those skills quickly. You must gain and master control of the weapons and protection you have been given. They have many purposes," Johannes said, "You must learn to use your suit to your best advantage. Most of what you do with it is instinctive. What you see is what you get. There's much more to learn."

"You mean we can choose the nature of our appearance?" asked Roxie.

"There is a way to choose, and I will teach you how," said Johannes, "Carson, describe how Roxie was dressed at the street-crossing in front of the hotel a couple of weeks ago."

"Wow, you knew about that?... Ah, I think I can remember. Let me see, she was wearing a blouse," Carson struggled to remember.

What color was the blouse?

"It was pink with an embroidered flower pattern," said Roxie, "I also had on a denim skirt."

"I think I can picture that in my mind," said Carson as he appeared to ponder the view.

"You certainly can," said Roxie with a teasing grin as she looked at Carson to return from his mental picture of her. "You look marvelous in that pink blouse and skirt."

Carson looked down at his clothing and found it was no longer reptilian. He now wore a pink blouse and a faded denim skirt, with his hairy legs sticking out. "How can this be?" asked Carson with sudden shame of his disposition.

"Your mind can control your appearance," Johannes said, "You have been given a great gift. You must master it and use it to its full potential. Now, think of what clear water looks like. Think of the water's surface and then look beyond the surface to see the bottom. Do not lock eyes on what is beneath the surface, but focus on the clear water's transparency before you."

Both focused on their attempts to follow the instructions. Roxie's reptilian appearance became wavy and almost transparent. Carson's pink blouse and blue denim skirt vanished, and he became almost entirely transparent with only the motions of bent light through a clear, watery appearance.

"You both learn quickly," said Johannes, "You must be brilliant in your world."

"We are supposed to be," Carson said, "We are both in the Honor Society at our schools."

"Allow me to tell you about our people," he said.

"We are a particular race. We have a purpose, like your concept of angels. We were assigned to protect the Wasamanee and several other similar groups. We are their secret guardians. Like angels, we were to be unseen by the naked eye, influence the right decisions, and be their guides."

"You mean this place is like heaven?" asked Roxie.

"No, it is far from heaven. It is a spiritual sanctuary for us. To the outsiders, it appears to be only a tree," said Johannes.

"If you have such great powers and knowledge in your abilities, why are we here?" asked Roxie.

"We may have powers and knowledge of them, but unfortunately, we have compromised our nature and purpose," said Johannes.

"How?" asked Carson.

"Our secrets were discovered by an evil group practicing the dark arts. They found our hiding places. They burned many of our tree homes to eliminate our sanctuaries and our influence," he said, "We were eternal beings. We could live forever. We have been here since the beginning of time. Some of us even rode upon the ark with Noah. We found a solution to the forces destroying us and reached a truce. We agreed to make weapons to equip their armies if they would stop. They left us alone until they needed more swords and flying suits for their troops. They continue to conquer others and force their dominion upon them."

"Can't you use your powers to take back what is yours and conquer them?" asked Roxie.

"We had powers of great strength, but our fears and lack of faith have been diminished. We have begun to age. We are growing old, just as the Wasamanee People are. Our only hope is the prophecy and its gift of the promised seed that will take away this evil and its power over us," Johannes said, "We have become old men and women with no hope of a future. We traded our gifts from the Most High for a peace treaty with tyranny."

"What is the seed of which you speak?" asked Roxie.

"The seed is not with you; it is carried by one of the two servants in captivity," Johannes said.

"Does that mean they have captured your great hope?" asked Carson, "Might we go and rescue them?"

"No, if you charge in now, you will be defeated. While their weapons are inferior to your mighty swords, their numbers would be overwhelming. When you drew your swords below the tree, they glowed mightily. Our guards also had their swords drawn, but when yours appeared, theirs glowed with mighty power again. Apparently, you bring the energy from the Most High with you.

Of course, we wonder if this power will transpire to all of the weapons we have made or just those possessing the forces of good?"

"How are our swords a sign of the might of the Most High?" asked Roxie.

"Your blades have magical qualities that our weapons no longer possess. May I see your sword?" he asked.

Carson pulled his sword, holding it upright so Johannes could reach for the handle and take it from him. The instant the sword left Carson's hand, Johannes held only the grip. The blade vanished. "See, your weapons are designed and loyal only to their masters. Our weapons were that way once, but we redesigned them so anyone could use them. I could take my partner's sword and fight with two swords. Redesigning them was a mistake. Many of our Tree People perished when our first tree fortress was burned. The emperor's men sifted through the ashes and found our swords and the flying suits. They continued to burn more of our sanctuaries to acquire more weapons. The only way to get them to stop was to make weapons for them. When you pulled your sword on the grounds below in self-defense, causing our weapons to glow with power, our hope became a reality again." He returned the sword handle to Carson, and admiration showed in his eyes as the mighty blade reappeared.

"Sir, I am beginning to feel like we are doing the right thing, going the right way, and I finally feel we can do what we were sent to do," said Carson with more confidence.

"Should we just charge forth and battle with them?" asked Roxie with eyes full of questions.

"No, you were not sent to battle," he said, "We are blessed to have you with us, but we must do our part. It is of great concern that you do not bear the seed. It is in the hands of those who seek to destroy it. We must develop a plan and don't have much time."

"How is it possible for Wayne and Rhonda to possess the seed?" asked Roxie, "Is Rhonda pregnant?"

"No, she is not pregnant," Johannes said, "Her virtue is vital to the gift she will bring. She possesses the seed that will fertilize and become the deliverer."

"Sounds like we will be here for a long time," said Carson.

"Perhaps," said Johannes, "We must prepare for a mighty battle. They know you are here. They have your friends. If they do not kill them, they will hunt you down to ensure total victory. We must prepare."

"Must we fight?" Roxie asked, "Is there no other way?"

"Freedom is never cheap. Once surrendered, it must be reclaimed with blood. You should know that from the history of your own people's violence to preserve freedom."

"Doesn't violence beget violence?" asked Roxie.

"Yes, you are right," said Johannes, "While we do not rush to battle, we do not run from it. None of us may live to see its end, but just the same, victory must be achieved, or this world will be ruled by darkness forever."

"Can a woman fight in this war?" asked Roxie.

"Yes, if it is willed by the Almighty. You have been chosen by the Most High as a warrior with a weapon and a suit of armor. No greater honor can be bestowed upon a soul. Now, let us see if a dinner is prepared to celebrate your arrival. Afterward, we will begin your training," said Johannes as he guided his guests toward their dining quarters.

Even though Carson and Roxie were anxious to begin their training, they were extremely concerned about the whereabouts of their two friends, Rhonda and Wayne.

# CHAPTER 9

*While Carson and Roxie settled down to their new objectives, concern still riddled them about the whereabouts of their two friends. To identify their predicament, this story must return to the point of departure to gain the complete picture. Recall that Rhonda and Wayne were the first of the four to move out on the cable to ride their leaf glider to the depths below.*

Rhonda gave the last jerk on her rope, and her leaf glider slid down the smooth cable. She watched as Wayne quickly followed with his leaf, but the wind caused her leaf to begin to rotate. Rhonda caught a glimpse of the chief further down the cable. She focused on him as she rotated with the leaf in the wind. Rhonda also noted the leaf's rotation accelerated. She had forgotten to use her feet to stop the spin and to keep it straight, and now it twisted the rope she held precariously. It took everything she had to just slow it down.

She saw, through the viewport in the floor of the leaf glider, the ridge pass underneath her. In the distance, she could see the rock formation on the next ledge and a stream below, despite the rotation of her foothold. She heard a twang and looked toward the chief to see him descending from the cable. He seemed to have pulled his pin just beyond the stream below. She figured he aimed for the side of the next ridge. She reached what she thought was the release point and seized the pin. She pulled. It would not come loose due to the cable twist. She pulled harder, and it came loose suddenly.

Downward, her glider plunged in that same rapid spin. She lost her balance and fell to the right side of the leaf. The weight on that side compromised the balance, and she slipped entirely off the glider, but held on to the cable with one hand, then finally with two. The leaf became a type of parachute as she continued her descent. The spin confused her perception. She dangled from one side, and that caused the rotation to be erratic. The wind whistled through her hair, and she held tightly to the cable but still dangled from her ready-made parachute in its counterclockwise rotation. She lost all awareness of the chief's location and of Wayne, who followed. She focused everything on her grip on the cable, hoping for a smooth landing below.

The wind did not carry her far. The earlier wind effects were due to movement rather than the actual stir of air currents around the ridges below. She watched as the leaves of the ground approached at a speed more accelerated than she felt was safe. The impact was unpredictable because the surface gave way like she had touched down on an old trampoline. It caused her to release her hold with the hope of a short fall into soft leaves. Instead, she broke through the surface and landed on the next brown leaf with a slight give as if equipped with springs.

Rhonda rose up from the surface of the leaf and the roof of the other leaf above her that had the gaping hole where she had just broken through. Everything was still in a spin. She fell several times as she tried to walk to the most prominent visible opening that still rotated to her left. She finally started to crawl toward the entrance. She also listened for a whistle but heard nothing. She felt sick in her stomach but hoped it would go away shortly and tried hard not to vomit, but some things have a way of their own. She decided not to crawl through that and get sick again as she moved back toward her entry point.

After a minute or two, she felt able to stand up. She walked across the springy leaf surface. It had some unstable give to it, but she managed to make it out of the shadow of the leaf above and stepped out into the opening that included a downhill slope. Her thoughts were on finding the chief and the rest of the group. She looked below toward the stream that appeared more like a small river. She turned to look up the ridge. As she did, she caught just a glimpse of the approaching horror of a sudden tackle by a stranger. She was struck in the midsection and fell backward into the leaves.

"I've got one," yelled the rough-looking character with black leather clothing. "This one's a girl."

"Good, that makes two of them," came another voice, as two men in similar outfits that showed traces of purple mixed in the black struggled toward her from high above. The two men struggled with their hold of a second person between them, whom Rhonda quickly identified as Wayne. They came up to the person who held Rhonda to the ground.

The man in the black leather stood up and pulled Rhonda from behind with both arms. "It looks like we found us a sweetie! Where do you suppose she got the emperor's raiders' uniform? You don't suppose she can fly and turn invisible, too, do you?"

"I doubt it, but maybe we should keep a tight hold and a close eye on them just in case," said the other captor.

Rhonda suddenly became aware of her outfit, now identical to the soldiers who held Wayne. She reached for her sword, but his grip on her arm held her back.

The soldier who restrained her spun her around, grabbed her sword, and yanked it from its sheath. The surprise on his face gave a clue to the fact that he held in his hand the sword handle, but the blade had already vanished. "It looks like she's wearing a costume and even has a fake sword."

He flung the sword handle toward the stream, and it splashed into the water and disappeared.

"This fellow had a blade handle, too. I figure he intended to scare the Wasamanee into the perception that perhaps he's a member of the emperor's guard. I think he's trying to move into our territory," said the soldier as he still held Wayne's right arm.

In the distance, there was a soft whistle with three other sounds like bird calls. Rhonda knew it was the others and looked at Wayne to see if he had noticed. Unfortunately, the three men also knew the signals were a clue to the approach of help for the two captives. Wayne was immediately tripped to the ground. His hands were tied with rope from one of the soldiers' belts. Rhonda felt the tug of her arms and the ropes tightly applied to her wrists as well.

The three quietly pulled their weapons. Swords that looked almost identical to the ones that Rhonda and Wayne were issued. Their wishes now were that they had pulled their swords quick enough to defend themselves from the capture. One of the soldiers made a whistling sound that resembled a Bobwhite. Others were heard in the distance along the ravine, but closer. An oak leaf was pulled over Wayne and Rhonda for concealment.

"When they attack, roll down the hill," Wayne said. "Make for the water."

"Sure, but how do you swim with your hands tied?" asked Rhonda.

"Never mind, just roll, now," said Wayne as the approach of footsteps was upon them. "Ambush!" yelled Wayne as he began to roll toward Rhonda.

Rhonda was slow to start her movement, but realized Wayne would roll over her if she did not move; she started her descent toward the water. The roll took them out from under the leaf with the visual of the three black and yellow guards. The three leaped out at the three soldiers, with their wooden stinger blades brandished for action. The fight started, three on three, and there seemed to be a ray of hope.

"Stop rolling so I can cut your ropes," came another voice, obviously, the chief.

Rhonda stopped her progress to look back at the chief

when she saw an approaching soldier.

"Look out!" was all she could say before the soldier ran his sword through the chief, and he tumbled over them and rolled toward the water. The fight was technically over, and the three guards were dead. Below, Rhonda could see the chief struggling to get back to his feet. He still held his sword but was mortally wounded.

"I'll take him out," said one of the three soldiers. "You get the two before they slip away."

He moved down the slope toward the wounded chief with his sword ready to add the final touches to the already severely wounded man.

Suddenly, out of the sky flew a mud dauber, which landed directly over the chief. It reached down and plucked up the chief to pull him to its stomach as its wings thrust him back upward into the sky. It flew not toward the rock where they were to meet but toward a series of mud dabber tunnels on the bottom of the stone protrusions on the other side of the ravine. It crawled into the open tunnel and remained there, out of sight.

"Let's get these two out of here before that thing returns for seconds. We are Slim Pickens right now if we just sit here and chat," said the oldest of the three soldiers.

"That's an idea, but I was looking forward to seeing how well my cold steel matches up to its stinger," said one of the other two soldiers. "Glib, are you up to a duel with a dirt dabber?"

"Yeah, it will fly right out at us, and we can take it down in one stroke," Glib said, "Chances are, it will fly around and catch us unaware and pick us off one by one until we are all paralyzed lunches for its little children."

"See. Now, as I said, let's get moving back to headquarters," said the leader, "If we are lucky, we can fly out of here and not even be noticed by the main unit. We, scouts, can do our job and await the troops' movements. We can return these two and put them up for auction. This little sweetie will bring a nice lump of cash, as young and tender as she looks."

"Shoot, I was thinking I would keep her for myself," said Glib, "What do you say, Geese? Want to share a new plaything?"

"I'm not at liberty," said Geese, "The boss seems to have claims to her already."

"Boss, let us have some fun with her first," said Glib.

"I'm not letting you spoil this young lady," said the boss, "She'll bring a pretty penny, and you'll get none of the change for helping if you keep getting ideas, and I can't trust you anymore."

"Perhaps we can cut up this boy for swordplay?" said Geese, "My blade was just warming up with the first three."

"What and leave evidence that the scouts have taken captives that were not Wasamanee?" asked the Boss, "We take them both back to sell. He's young and will make a fine slave at the auction, too, just not as high priced as this little chick." He reached and pinched her on the fanny.

Rhonda turned toward him with a look of anger and hurt. She tried to hold back the urge to allow tears to fill her eyes.

"You see that look she gave you, Boss?" said Glib.

"She's a spitfire. Better watch out. Those ropes may not hold her with that kind of anger."

"She'll just have to do. Tie her feet and get ready to carry them back to headquarters," said the boss.

"All the way back?" asked Geese, "I'm carrying the sweetheart. Glib, you get the boy." He grabbed the girl around the waist, his wings let loose with a gush of air, and they were both airborne quickly.

With a sour look, Glib grabbed Wayne, eyed the boss, and took off after him.

The boss followed and quickly caught up alongside.

Rhonda dangled from the rough character beside him, with his hairy arm wrapped around her midsection. She watched as the terrain passed under her. She could also see Wayne below, held by the other creep, and the boss tagged along, presumably to ensure they flew no detours.

They continued their flight nonstop along the steep slope of the highest mountain in the area. A building could be seen to their right, then a cut through the woods that was cleared down the hill to protect the power lines that ran up the slope. An observation tower and a television tower were also visible on top of the highest point of the mountain. After a long flight, hampered by wind gusts that seemed to leap at them from the top of the hill, they flew to an outstretch of huge rocks at the end of the upper segment of the mountain. Above the rock was a human-constructed platform with giant tourists that appeared to gaze and point into the distance. On the rocks were several large spray-paint graffiti pieces. The first inclination in Rhonda's visualization was that their flight path led right to a boulder that sat to the right of the viewer's platform. As they closed in on one of the seams at the bottom of the rock, it became apparent that there was enough space between the stones to allow them to fly into it. The first picture of the crack inside was totally dark, but as Rhonda's eyes adjusted, she could make out many holes in the rocks and saw people walking in and out of them. Many were dressed in black and purple leather suits like their captors. Others were dressed in various colors, some wearing poncho-type outfits with thick thread weaves, as if made from the clothing of much more prominent people.

They continued to fly past the many openings in the rock formation and downward through a long tunnel to an even greater entrance, like a great cavern. Some stalactites hung from the ceilings, and some stalagmites reached up to meet their dripping tips. There was much water at the bottom of the cavern, and there seemed to be many boats visible with people who wore strange outfits. People used long-handled paddles to thrust the flotation devices forward. A person also manned a rudder to supposedly guide the boat in their chosen direction. The rudder operator swayed the rudder quickly back and forth, perhaps to cause additional acceleration.

The flight continued until an island was sighted at the far end of the cavern. The three soldiers flew quickly toward a well-lit area that appeared to have jail cells, as evidenced by the wooden or metal bars that secured the windows on the front of the building. All five flew toward an open area before the barred windowed facility. Rhonda was dropped to the ground as the soldier who carried her made a running stop on the surface.

"You stupid fool, are you trying to damage the goods before the delivery?" growled the boss as he landed beside them and pointed to the girl, who had scuffed her face with the rough landing, still with her arms tied behind her.

"Didn't see you helping much during the flight," said Glib, "They do get heavy after a flight like that. Lucky, I'm a big soldier, like a little extra spending money, and can handle such trips, or you would be hauling them yourself."

The boss pulled a white cloth from his pocket and wiped some of the blood from Rhonda's cheek.

"Now, what have we here?" asked a strange voice in the background.

"Warden, we have some special guests for you to keep for us for a week, and then we will sell them off the auction block with your usual cut, of course," said the boss, who recognized the intruder's voice.

"I see they need some mending if that is what the extra week is for," the warden said, "Why do you always beat them up like that?"

"Rough landing," said Glib, "It's Geese's fault; he was flying lead and came in too fast."

"Blame me," said Geese, "I was holding on to the babe and

lost focus while she wiggled.

Do you see the scratches on my arm?"

"How can she scratch you? Her hands are tied?" asked the boss.

"Well, I thought I would pat her on the fanny, and she had other ideas," said Geese, "I almost dropped her when those claws dug into me while I held her with my other arm. She's a regular vixen, she is."

"Glib, you have any trouble like that with the boy?" asked the boss.

"Oh, no! I just dropped him on top of Geese just before I landed," said Glib, "He cushioned his fall quite nicely, I might add."

"It would have been better for our profits if it had been reversed," said the boss. "I'll take the price out of your wages soon enough.

"Now that you have discussed the condition of the merchandise," said the warden, "Why not put them up for sale at today's auction and save the expense of a week of boarding?"

"Well, we were the flying scouts for a company of the emperor's foot soldiers, and we found these," said the boss, "We don't want to do anything in haste. The emperor may want them for questioning, so we need to hang on to them briefly for those important purposes."

"Found something the emperor might desire," said the warden, "Chances are, he does not know you have found them?"

"Warden, you are wise beyond your years," said the boss, "We were looking for four suspicious characters, and these two did not fit their description. The suspects who were feared to flee were dressed in Wasamanee armor. These two had the emperor's wardrobe down to the tee. Spies, I suspect, and we shall make fine slaves of them for a good profit for us all and for the betterment of the emperor."

"Sounds like you have a plan for everything," said the warden, "I hold the booty, and you fly back and continue your mission as scouts around the marching army of the emperor."

"Warden, you know me too well," said the boss, "And you know we must return to those essential duties right away."

"Take excellent care of my precious sweetheart. She's worth a fortune to me with her refined looks, delicate figure, and youthful spunk. Do not let her get the best of your wits and escape."

"Haven't lost one yet," said the warden. "You'd better be off before the captain of the scouts finds you missing and charges you with being AWOL."

"That we must do," said the boss. They all turned and flew into the distance, disappearing into the cave's darkness, overwhelmed by the brightness of the opening at the other end.

The warden turned to the two who still lay on the ground, pulled out a knife from a sheath on his belt, and cut the ropes that tied their feet. He then pulled both to their feet by their arms that were still tied behind their backs.

"I'll remove your other ties when you reach your lovely accommodations," he told Rhonda and Wayne, "I'll even give you two your own personal cell. I do expect you to behave yourselves. I'll have guards constantly checking you. I know how boys and girls want to play, but we will have none of that here." He continued to explain to them as they made their way into the building.

They proceeded down a hall with open-barred cells, and most were filled with people who resembled Wasamanee People minus the armor of the Wasamanee guard. Rhonda looked at the many girls, usually held in separate cells from the male compartments. She thought of what was to become of them in this slave trade. Would they be sold as servants? Handmaids? Sexual toys for those of questionable morals?

At the end of the hall, the warden stopped and unlocked a cell door. This will be your paradise for the time being. "You'll stay together because I don't want anything happening to you," said the warden, "You two seem to be a pair. That golden hair is unique. Are you brother and sister?"

"Yes!" blurted Rhonda before Wayne could answer, "We've been brother and sister most of our lives?"

"Well, then I can rest easy with you two in the same room beyond the auction tomorrow when we clean out the current population at the big sale," he said as he removed the ropes from their wrists. "I expect you two to behave yourselves, no matter your relationship."

"Yes, sir," said Wayne, "I will not only behave, but I will also fight to protect her."

"Oh, got some fire in the old belly, young fellow," he said, "That must be in the hair color. What tribe do you come from?"

"The Jacksonville Gamecocks," said Rhonda, "We're ambassadors sent to visit the Wasamanee here, and if we don't make it back to our people with word soon, we will be sorely missed, and big search parties will come."

"Wow, search parties," said the warden. "It sounds like we will get more yellow-haired servants to sell at the auction block."

"Who would buy teenagers at an auction today?" asked Wayne.

"Many kinds of people buy their labor here. The scum of the earth, for example. They come upon a little money and want a good time to celebrate by buying a plaything. Sometimes even the wealthy come around for clean-cut individuals who will make servants for their palaces," said the warden, "I figure your sister will sell for the highest bid on the block next week. She may even be bought by the emperor himself. He likes pretty, young things. We will be cleaning her up a bit. She will get medical attention shortly for her scratches. I want her healed up and ready when auction day comes around."

"Thanks, you've been very informative," said Rhonda begrudgingly.

"Where are our wonderful accommodations?" asked Wayne, "You know, like restrooms."

"That bucket over there," the warden smiled, "It's the best one in the house. It doesn't leak like most of them."

"How do we use it without being seen by the other?" asked Rhonda.

"The other will have to turn his head," said the warden, "Brothers and sisters aren't interested in seeing each other during activities like that, now, are we?"

"I'll be on my honor, but that is a bit more than I am used to," said Wayne. "But I've never been to the restroom before in front of anyone other than my mother."

"Your modesty will just have to be stretched a bit, my good man," said the warden.

"What about baths?" asked Rhonda.

"Bathing is a special activity just before your auction day," said the warden, "We will come and get you. Take you to a room where you will remove all clothing. You will then be scrubbed down and given a once-over. After that, we will give you brand-new clothes to wear to the auction. If you are to bring a good price at the auction as a servant for the wealthy, you will need to look the part. Missy, you will be dressed in white, and your hair will be pretty. You will be our first yellow-haired bride to be sold. You will have to tell us how to get to the Jacksonville Gamecocks so we can find more treasures for my sales department."

"I'd be glad to tell you where you can go," Wayne contemptuously said.

"Yeah, we will give directions, but to get there, you have to ride a bird," said Rhonda, instead glaring at Wayne, "There's quite a distance to fly; even winged warriors would have trouble with that distance."

"Sure, bring us paper and something to write with, and we will draw you a map," humored Wayne as he moved away in conversation from what he contemptuously inferred for the warden previously as a place to go.

"Well, I'll leave you two to get acquainted with your new luxury quarters," said the warden as he locked the cell door and walked away.

"Lovely, being in the Honor Society really takes you places, doesn't it?" said Rhonda.

"Quit so. Sounds like next week, we get hosed down, de-lived, and get a whole new wardrobe," said Wayne, "I'm more worried about what they will do to you than me."

"The situation doesn't look good," said Rhonda, "Going a whole week without a bath is going to stink. Do you think Carson and Roxie will be able to find us in time?"

"I sure hope they saw how we were captured," said Wayne, "But if they had seen it happen, certainly they would have come to our rescue. They had to be in the area somewhere. Why were they not found?"

"Maybe they hid better than we did or were told by Chief to stay back and let them handle the rescue," said Rhonda.

"With the three of our protective warriors dead and Chief carried away for food by the mud dauber, we are not in a good situation," said Wayne, "Do you figure we were followed by Carson and Roxie if they both could fly?"

"Carson could probably, but Roxie's like me; she has never tried to use her wings," she said, "Carson had to jump off a steep slope to get airborne. The possibility of leaping toward the stream may have given Roxie flight potential. Still, then again, with her insecurities, she may not have been successful, and that would have sent Carson on another rescue mission to save her from getting washed down to some local reservoir."

"Well, all we can do is hope," said Wayne, "And pray. It does seem like we do not do that enough."

"Check out this mattress. It must be made of wax. It looks like it was shaped for a man's body by the gives at certain points," said Rhonda, "And we don't have a blanket either."

"Well, this being a cave, the temperature will remain pretty constant," said Wayne, "The problem will be that the temperatures always remain in the lower sixties. It might be something we can bring up to the guard. If we are to sell for a big profit, we must be kept warm and healthy. If not, we may have to think of warm overcoats to handle the chill at night."

The cell got quiet as they both stretched out on their wax mattresses and, for the first time, gazed up at their poorly lit room. The one lantern, suspended from the ceiling in the middle of the passageway between the cells, provided the only light. Across the corridor stood another cell with a couple of what appeared to be Wasamanee men, perhaps a little older than Wayne but captives just the same. They proved fascinated by Rhonda's presence, but behaved decently when it came to personal business that Rhonda was timid about. Wayne made a point of standing near the bars, and the two men in the other cell were nice enough not to look as well.

The next day was livelier. Many guards came by and carried captives from their cells.

Female screams were heard as they were dragged from their cells to the door just beyond Wayne and Rhonda's beautiful quarters. They were returned, dressed in more excellent clothing, but still had wet hair from the cleansing procedures used by the guards. Even the Wasamanee men in the cell across from them left and returned in better attire. Around noon, the guards carried two out at a time until the whole floor was quiet and empty, leaving only Wayne and Rhonda.

The following week dragged on. There was little difference

between daytime and nighttime in the cave and even less in the dungeon. None of the rays that crept in through the few cracks evident in the cave walls during daylight hours made it to the cells. The hope of a sudden appearance of Carson or Roxie through the high, barred window near the ceiling or perhaps through the window in the cell across from theirs faded fast. The anxiety began to grow as auction day approached. Toward the end of that wait, new arrivals began to fill the cells. Two girls were placed in a cell across from them. Both girls went to their wax mattresses and cried for a long time. The sobs were obviously caused by their grief and struggle with their own plights. Rhonda tried to get them to talk, but they were unresponsive. They appeared to be withdrawing from reality to escape the situation that haunted them.

Suddenly, the cell door rattled as a guard unlocked it. It caught both of them asleep and totally startled by the intrusion. The guard quickly shackled them at the wrists and the ankles. They were instructed to come. They left the cell block through the same door the guards used last week. They were escorted to another facility that appeared more petite than the previous building, and the water that surrounded the island carried a fishy scent in the air as they passed between the two buildings.

The door to the smaller building was opened. There were several bench-like places to sit along the sides of the hall. Wayne was instructed to go into the small room to the left, and Rhonda entered the room on the right. Once she was in the room, the guard said, "Bathe now, and put on these clothes when you are through. Knock when you are dressed. Allow me to remove the chains so your changing will be easier. There is no way of escape, so drop that from your mind. This door is the only way out."

Rhonda stood in the room, looking around, and saw a white dress. It was rather neat with serious embroideries. It would perhaps make a lovely bride's dress, were it not for the fabric's thickness. To her front was a large wooden tub. She also noticed a bar of soap. She reached into the water to find it quite cold. "Well, you can't have everything," she said as she looked at the water and thought of the desire to be undressed. The outfit she wore vanished. She was amazed at her own mastery of her special suit. It had been over a week since she left the Wasamanee and took her last bath. Getting clean would make the chill of cold water worth the tolerance.

She dipped into the water, which almost took her breath away. To get in quickly was the only way to handle the sudden shock. The water seemed a little warmer after a few minutes. She stood up to use the primitive soap. She lathered quickly and lowered herself again into the chilly water to rinse. She wet her hair, hoping the soap would not harm its body, but that issue might be to her advantage. She lathered her hair and leaned forward into the water to rinse it. She then stood up and stepped out of the tub. There was no towel to dry off with. She had no comb for her tangled hair, like the ones provided at the public baths of the Wasamanee. She combed it as best she could with her fingers.

Next, she proceeded to put on the dress. She looked at her body and thought of a soft undergarment, and her body was quickly covered by a silk slip, just like the one her mother wore in that other life that seemed so far away. She picked up the dress, unbuttoned the back, and slipped it over her head. It seemed to fit and was rough on the skin but warmer than her last outfit for the cool cave temperatures. As many young ladies do, she had often dreamed of her wedding day. At this point, she had no pleasure in this apparel. She knew she was prepared to step out into the meat market shortly. This was an auction that would sell her to the highest bidder. Her fears grew with anticipation, dreams of the cavalry coming with her friends to their rescue, and her prayers went forth in her mind, sounding more desperate.

As she reached to knock on the door to tell the guard she was dressed, a still, small voice spoke to her. It was not a voice that could be heard with human ears. It was a voice deep in the center of one's soul. It said, "Rest, my child. I am with you always. Hold your head high today because you will be delivered in ways you do not understand. Cling to your brother, so that he may go with you in your new direction." The voice stopped. She breathed more heavily, and her heart raced as comfort and assurance flowed through her veins. Hope was in the air.

She knocked on the door. The guard let her step into the hall. Wayne was in a red and black mixed-pattern jacket, almost Spanish in design. His new slacks also contained embroidery of Spanish design. He smiled and whispered, "Wait till they find the suit still hanging in the bathroom. I just looked it over, and I have an identical outfit."

They figured to be led back to the cell. They were both surprised. The guards, instead, took them to the next room down the hall to meet a couple of older women. Both captives were instructed to sit down.

They quickly combed the tangles from Wayne's and Rhonda's hair. More time was spent on Rhonda, including rolling it. She got a workover. Rhonda saw Wayne get up and walk around as he watched the two ladies fuss over Rhonda's beautiful blonde hair. They waited an hour for it to dry and for the curlers to be removed. Rhonda could see the admiration in Wayne's eyes as he looked at her. There was no joy in his facial expression. He looked as if he felt he might never see her again after today. It was as if he knew she was about to leave him forever, and he would be alone in a world gone crazy.

The two handmaids stood in front of Rhonda and bragged about her appearance. They told her she would make some man a beautiful bride. They stated she was indeed to wed one of the wealthiest men in the Emperor's Realm. This was far from an opportunity to date in high school or even a prom occasion. Had she not had the voice that spoke to her, she would have been a nervous wreck. She smiled reassuringly at Wayne to let him know everything was fine.

The door opened, and the guard entered to see why the two ladies were fussy. They immediately saw the beautiful work the ladies had done on Rhonda's hair. They moved forward and reattached the shackles to Wayne's feet and hands. They also placed them on Rhonda's hands, but had her raise one leg from her long dress at a time to expose one ankle rather than lift her skirt. There was an air of respect for her beauty, and they regarded her dignity very much at this point.

They were then escorted back to their cells. As they passed through the gap between the two buildings, voices and even a few catcalls could be heard. The men for the auction had already begun to assemble. They returned to their cell to wait for the next move. Several others were seen as they returned, primarily dressed in outfits similar to what they had worn previously. The girls, however, all seemed dressed nicely and in unique dresses.

No other girl, however, was dressed in a white wedding gown. There had to be something going on that baffled Rhonda, yet it gave her a peaceful but uneasy feeling that things would work out fine with a few catches.

Soon, their evening meal was served, and again, it was soup. Neither asked what was in it. No more surprises today. Wayne did not make the remark with this meal that it was probably cock roach again. That suggestion the day before had spoiled Rhonda's appetite. Wayne only said the food tasted like Alaskan crab legs, only they were dark brown instead of pink and white. He suggested it was a nice vegetable soup this time, as if he knew she needed her strength.

# CHAPTER 10

The door into the hallway between the cells opened again. In stepped the warden. His face glowed with great delight when he feasted his eyes upon Rhonda. He said, "Little lady, you look adorable. I would claim you for myself if I were not in this for the money."

"Now you have said a mouthful," said Wayne in a fashion that partially agreed with the warden in recognition of Rhonda's beauty and the sarcasm hinted at in his tone. Rhonda's look made him wish he could eat his words.

"When do we go meet the buyers?" asked Rhonda.

"That will be soon enough," said the warden, "Let me tell you. The emperor's right-hand man, the prime minister, is here today. He's a widower, having recently lost his wife tragically. He has been to several auctions, but has never found a girl to suit him. I feel that today, he will join in on the bids for the prettiest girl I have ever put on the auction block. You will make me proud and quite wealthy today, young lady."

The cell door reopened, and the warden stepped aside to allow the guards to place the shackles on Wayne and Rhonda again. They were escorted through the same door toward the washroom quarters, down through its hall to the other end of the building. Once out of that door, they were led to another building, then up some stairs to a lobby that resembled a backstage area. There was a curtained passage, and many conversations off in the distance could be heard.

The ladies who had spent so much time on Rhonda's hair earlier came to her and began to touch up her hair. The dark-faced lady with the salt-and-pepper hair said, "Don't be nervous, deary, you'll do just fine. If you are picked by the prime minister, you will have a life of luxury and the best the world offers."

Rhonda wanted to question her to find out more, but there was a sudden hush beyond the curtain, and she was rushed forward to be escorted through it into a large, open gymnasium-size room, lit by many candles and lanterns. She looked across the crowded room to see many men, primarily rough in appearance and possessing signs with strange symbols, all different, obviously a bidding identification device. She was led to a podium-like outcrop from the stage.

Rhonda could feel every eye in the place fixed upon her. An aura of breathtaking focus made her want to crawl under a rock and hide. She had never been gazed upon and wanted by men in small numbers, and nothing compared to a room with possibly 300 men who sought to buy her. She had been dolled up for auction and felt the color come to her cheeks as she thought of what these men wanted from her.

"Let the auction begin," said the man behind the podium with a hammer. "Do I hear one thousand Gold Emperors for this lovely bride-to-be?"

Several signs went up.

"Number four bids one thousand. Do I hear two?"

Several signs go up again.

"Number nine bids two thousand; do I hear three?"

This continued for several minutes.

"We have twenty-five thousand with number fourteen; do we have twenty-six thousand?"

One sign came up.

"We have twenty-six thousand from number four. Do we have twenty-seven thousand?"

There was a hush in the room, and many looked at the man who held number fourteen. He did not raise it this time.

There was disgust on his face as he got up and headed for the exit door.

"We still have twenty-six thousand. Going once? Going twice? Sold to number four, the prime minister himself. Congratulations, sir. You have chosen a lovely bride. Please come forward and claim your new companion."

Rhonda watched as the prime minister stood and moved down the aisle. The guards came to her, moved her away from the podium, removed her shackles, and directed her back onto the stage, then across and down a set of stairs. She was directed to stand and wait for the prime minister. He came to her with admiration in his eyes. She could feel the tremble of nervousness in her weak legs and hands. Her face even had a slight tremor, probably from the tension she felt in her neck.

In the distance, she heard the auctioneer start again. "Here we have our second noble purchase: the brother to the emperor's new bride. Do I hear one thousand Golden Emperors?"

Suddenly, the thoughts of the voice deep in Rhonda's soul revealed themselves. She looked at the man standing before her, well along in years, yet well dressed, and knew what she had to do. "Please, kind sir. That is my brother. I can't go with you without him. Please, sir, could you do me the honors and make him our servant that we never be parted?"

The emperor turned to the auctioneer to watch as the bid went up to five thousand. He asserted his voice, "Five thousand and ten!"

"The prime minister bids five thousand ten. Do I hear higher?"

The room was quiet. One bidding war with the prime minister was already a hefty profit for the auctioneer. There seemed to be a bit of fear to make the auctioneer any richer.

"Going once? Going twice? Sold to the prime minister, one yellow-haired boy," said the auctioneer.

Rhonda felt the tension reach its highest peak.

Her nervous state was suddenly accompanied by dizziness. Her vision became disoriented, and it faded into tunnel vision, and everything went dark. She felt hands try to catch her as she fell. The prime minister caught her with both hands as several others tried to prevent her fall, but she collapsed to her knees as everything went black.

---

Rhonda opened her eyes again to find that the auction room was gone. She was not on the island anymore. Rhonda was in a dimly lit room with several candles that flickered in the room's corners. She could feel the soft fabrics around her and the comfort of an actual pillow. It seemed like it had all been a dream if only this room were her home bedroom instead of another strange environment. She could make out someone who sat beside her bed. She looked at the figure and could make out the face. It was Wayne.

"Well, look who is waking up," said Wayne in a calm, peaceful voice.

"Where am I?" asked Rhonda, trying to raise herself in the bed.

"Hold your horses. You're at the prime minister's quarters. Everything is fine," he said to reassure her. "You gave us a scare back at the auction block. Don't you worry? Everything is going to be fine. The prime minister is cool, and he knows who we are."

"He knows who we are?" asked Rhonda as she rose up, supported by her elbows. "What did you do, tell him everything?"

"No, no, he already knew. He had a dream, and a heavenly being told him he would come and buy you as his bride because you carry the seed of the prophecy," said Wayne.

"What prophecy? What seed? What are you talking about?" she asked, rising up further from the bed, only to have the covers fall to reveal the slip she had pictured before putting on the wedding dress earlier. She quickly pulled the covers back over herself.

"Don't worry. You've got nothing to hide I have not seen already," said Wayne, "I'm the one who undressed you and tucked you into bed. Remember, I am now your hand-servant, by your request."

"You undressed me?" asked Rhonda with a more stressed voice, "You took my clothes off while I was unconscious?"

"Yes, and I'm sorry if that was wrong," he said with a tint of red on his face. "I did it without looking directly at you. You took care of me when we first arrived at the Wasamanee colony. Surely, my care for you now was no more than my return of the favor. I could never take advantage of you, even to peek at you when you were as vulnerable as you were. I respect you too much to do something like that. Besides, you still wear your special suit given to us before we were sent here, and I just don't want anyone doing examinations and for them to find more than we want them to know."

"Enough. Sounds like you were looking after me," Rhonda said. "You have explained your intentions well. I'm sorry, and thanks for looking after me."

"The prime minister's name is Josephus," said Wayne as he changed the subject, "He's nice and wants to see you. Shall I go get him?"

"Do you have to?" asked Rhonda with mixed feelings.

"Yes, he's done so much for us already. Let him talk to you, and you will feel better about him." Wayne left the room and was gone for a minute or two.

Josephus stepped into the bedroom. He appeared to be less impressive in dress in his own home.

He had a shirt, primitively made, and slacks of coarse material, but the first impression of him would be that he was of the age to be a grandfather to both of them.

"I'm glad to see you are feeling better, and I want to welcome you to my home," said Josephus with a nervous smile.

"I'm still confused about all of this," Rhonda said, trying to explain her feelings.

"Don't you fret any at all, my little one? I lost my wife, and in my grief, I'm sent an angel, as Wayne calls the heavenly being, that sends me to rescue you in your greatest need," Josephus said. "You two cost me a small fortune, but if you are worthy of bearing the seed of the promised hope, you are worth every piece of gold in the kingdom."

"The seed? What do you mean by the seed?" asked Rhonda.

"The prophecy says four will come from a faraway land, bringing hope and redemption to our terrible world. Two of the four will be warriors, and two will be servants. Of the two servants, one will bring the seed of change and return to the blessings of the God of the Most High."

"Still, that does not explain the seed," she said.

"Yes, it does," he said, "You are with child, and that child is the greatest hope of all our people."

"I'm not pregnant!" exclaimed Rhonda as she reached and felt her stomach. To her surprise and horror, there was obviously some growth in her stomach that she had never noticed. "How can this be? I've never? I can't be!"

"You've been chosen to bear the seed of hope. You are to bear a child in 89 days," Josephus said, "I'm called upon to be your husband and protector, but not to touch you in any way."

"I can't be six months pregnant. That's impossible," said Rhonda.

"Six months pregnant. No one can be six months pregnant. It only takes three months to bear a child," Josephus said.

She looked at him, totally puzzled again, and this revelation about the length of childbearing in this world added new questions she was afraid to ask. "This is all very confusing. I need to find a bathroom," Rhonda said as she rose to her feet and held her covering so no one could see her slip. As she stood, she felt an onslaught of nausea that surged to overwhelm her. Her eyes showed terror.

"The bathroom is right through this door. Let me get out of your way. You look mighty pale," said Wayne as he stepped to the side.

Rhonda ran for the door, threw it open, found what appeared to be the toilet, and lifted the lid, only to be hit with the smell of the sewer system below. She began to heave, but all that came up was a yellow liquid. Rhonda sat on the floor and closed the lid, hoping to avoid the smell and its potential to trigger further nausea. "My mama would kill me if she knew this," she said, as tears began to form in her eyes. "I am too young to be a mother. I've never even. It just cannot be. I am only seventeen." Her sobs came forth as the situation came to her in full force of reality.

Josephus took a square cloth, wet it in the basin that was filled with water, and gently wiped Rhonda's face. He wiped the tears from her cheeks and around her mouth. Josephus gazed into her tear-filled, blue eyes for the first time and said, "Our world has been in darkness from the emperor for hundreds of years. He never dies. That evil one reigns. He kills. He destroys. He has power even over the heavens. You carry within you the only hope of his power and reign ever coming to an end. You are a gift from heaven, and please bear this seed with joy. I'll provide all you need and keep you safe. I will die to protect you. You will remain in my house as my wife. Your child will be called my child. He will be raised as our offspring, but we will both know who He is."

"I am sorry. It must be all the hormone changes inside of me. This is just such a shock," Rhonda said, as if his words made her feel better.

"Is there water for a bath?" she said as she looked over at the wooden tub that had been whittled out of a log or stem.

"I'll have your hand-servant, Wayne, draw you a bath immediately. If you want, you will find his work easier if you can return to the bedroom. He will have to boil water and carry it into the bathing room. There is already a fire burning in the stove in the kitchen," said Josephus.

Wayne did not have to be told to get started. He left them and went straight to the kitchen. Metal pans could be heard as they rattled, and then the water flowed.

"Am I really your wife, now?" asked Rhonda, looking at the man for answers that frightened her.

"No, and yes. Regarding this community and those around us in government, you are my wife and are bearing my child. You are a child, between you and me, and I am an old man. It will be enough with the critical eyes of many who look down on this joining, but more so from my perspective. I feel more that you are like the daughter I never had. I am too old, wrinkled, and beyond my years to want a child as my true wife. This cruel world around us will be divided into two groups. Some will talk behind my back about me marrying too soon and to a young thing. The others will brag that I could snag a beauty in her youth with my money and power. I will bear it for you because of all you do and will do for my people."

"You say things in exceedingly kind ways. I am beginning to feel better about all of this. It just came at me so fast," said Rhonda.

"I would love to take you shopping for a nice wardrobe, but you can't exactly go anywhere dressed in a quilt," he said as he pointed to the covers she had just dragged into the bathroom in her haste.

"Don't worry. After my bath, I will find something you

hopefully will find pleasing," she said to him while she thought of some of the outfits the other girls at the auction house wore. "Do women here wear pants?"

"Pants?" he asked, "Women all wear gowns that reach their ankles. What are pants? Oh, you mean leggings like I have on?" He pointed toward his brown cotton slacks, split into smaller strips for weaving.

"I'll find a dress that you will find suitable and wear pants underneath it, just to be me," she said.

"I'm looking forward to seeing what you will come up with," he said, "I'm sorry that we don't have a good collection of gowns for you to select from. I got rid of my late wife's clothing, thinking I would be alone for the rest of my life. This place has been a dark and lonely torment until you arrived. You two are a blessing to this old man who never was able to have children with his late wife."

She looked at him and saw his eyes of admiration and affection. She moved from the bathroom but still carried the quilt for a covering into the bedroom. She moved toward him and reached out to hug him. She felt a sob, and then he released her and left the room. She was sure she saw a tear in his eye. As he left, Wayne came in carefully with a metal bucket suspended from a handle that appeared to be entirely aluminum. It steamed as he moved to the wooden tube, poured the hot liquid into it, and then turned a valve that let cold water flow. After a minute, he felt the water and quickly turned the valve off to stop the cold water from flowing into the mix.

"Your bath is ready, Your Majesty," Wayne said as he looked around at her, where she sat on the bed and still held the quilt.

"Thanks, my kind and loving servant. Go have breakfast on me," she said with a smile.

Wayne left the bathroom and closed the door behind him.

Rhonda found her way into the bathroom after dropping the quilt to the floor, then picked it up to toss it back onto the bed. After Rhonda closed the door to the bathroom, the young lady thought of being naked, and the slip disappeared. She also noted the mirror-like polished metal surface on the wall was rather significant, and she could see herself well. She looked back at the warm water, wanting to get into it quickly. To her surprise, the water's reflection of the candles around it was rather beautiful. As her foot reached for the water, it vanished before her. Her whole body disappeared. This scared her and puzzled her at the same time. She grabbed the wall and could feel it with her hand, but her hand was not there. With one foot in the tub, supposedly, even if she could not confirm it visually, other than the invisible penetration of the water's surface, she looked at where her legs were supposed to be. The other foot was still on the floor physically, but not visually, so she looked back at the mirror. She was almost totally invisible. There was a faint bend in the light as she moved from left to right and observed the mirror. She climbed into the tub to see the water displaced by her invisible presence, immersed, and thought of her skin again. To her surprise, she reappeared.

She looked at herself, amazed. She also realized her heart was racing. She now knew she could make herself invisible just by visualizing the apparent nature of water.

She bathed in total luxury. There was a liquid soap that quickly made bubbles when she ran her hands through it. She hoped it wasn't antibacterial soap, because getting a doctor's treatment for an infection caused by that kind of soap here might be impossible. She added liquid perfumes to the water. The soap was milder in form and, therefore, not as harsh to the skin as the soap of the Wasamanee. She lowered herself carefully into the water up to her neck, with the thought that the wooden tub might cause splinters, but realized the wood was polished and coated with something to make it smooth and waterproof. The warmth of the water offered a comfort she had not experienced in many days. There was even shampoo, or it appeared and worked like shampoo. The inscription on the bottle was unclear, or in a language she did not speak or understand. She remained in the water as the suds she created dissipated, and the water temperature dropped, causing a chill. A well-deserved bath was her only thought as she climbed out of the tub and found a rough towel to dry off carefully out of fear that it might scratch her with its rough surface. She stood and gazed at the mirror, still unclothed, to see her stomach in the mirror, but the table with the wash basin was too tall to allow her to see below her midsection. She did move her hand across her stomach with thoughts that surely she could not be pregnant.

Delivery in eighty-nine days seemed so impossible. Rhonda looked at her pale face in the mirror. There was something significantly different about her emotions, her body, and her vulnerability. She leaned forward and looked around, hoping to find a toothbrush and toothpaste.

She thought new inventions for this world were in order. She did find a comb and combed out the tangles.

She wished for a hair dryer, but maybe she could get her hand servant, Wayne, to fan her fast to speed up the drying process and give her hair that wind-blown look. She found the idea funny and thought no more about the possibility. She looked again at her still naked body; she thought of a long dress, perhaps from a prairie story on television, and looking around, she had puffed sleeves, an embroidered front on the dress, and it extended to the floor. She also thought of her favorite pair of jeans that appeared under the gown and felt sure they were on. She raised the long dress to reveal the jeans, just as she remembered them, and short socks and blue tennis shoes. She thought of getting ready for school and never missing the bus again by dressing this fast. She also thought of her mother and father. She truly missed them. She even missed her annoying little brother, Edward. Her home seemed so far away and almost a fairytale at this point.

She walked into the bedroom and looked around at the candlelit walls. The color was not gray like the cave's rocks. There were even a couple of paintings on the walls, with candleholders on either side. She opened the door at the departure from the bedroom to find a living room-like area. She looked around for a television or radio, but there was no such thing.

There were books, but they were much wider than most she remembered. The names on the side were in symbols she could not read. She knew she would appear quite illiterate in the social arena, being the prime minister's wife.

She found Josephus and Wayne in their leisure at the kitchen table, sipping a dark liquid that sat before them. Their chairs were equipped with backs, a design she was immediately impressed by the texture.

There were plates in front of them, but they were both already empty. Rhonda thought a bowl of cereal or perhaps some bacon and eggs would be in order, but with a glimpse at the cooking utensils next to the wood-burning stove, the food prepared resembled hard tack. It was beige in color and more of a whole bread substance than anything else. She had eaten that once in a demonstration of the type of food George Washington ate as a soldier of the Revolutionary War. Her queasiness seemed to make her have second thoughts about nourishment.

Her view of the kitchen was suddenly interrupted by, "Wow, you dress up nice. Did you make that dress out of the quilt or something? I've never seen it before."

She immediately focused on the dress that had mysteriously found her when the only clothes she had to wear were her slip and the wedding dress she arrived in and worn the night before. "I'll have to explain. It was inside the wedding dress. You know, something to change into on the wedding night?"

Josephus looked back at Wayne and said, "She's not really good at lying, is she?"

Wayne grinned back at him and said, "She does struggle when put on the spot. The dress does look a little better on her than that quilt."

"Well, I…" said Rhonda, trying to find words to explain.

"Wayne was just telling me that shopping for clothes will be quite cheap since all you have to do is think of the outfit you look at or think of as if it were on you, and it just happens," Josephus said.

"Wayne, you talk too much. Have you ever thought of that?" she asked with a bit of bother.

"Come on, Rhonda, your trust needs some improvement," he said, trying to assure her, "Our friend is part of an oppressed people. He was their leader but had to obey the emperor and follow his directives. Just because he represents an oppressed people does not mean he is an oppressor or agrees with the rule of the emperor. He was taught as a child of the promised prophecies, and now he is thrilled they came about in his lifetime and enabled him to be a part of it as a protector."

"Your dress is pretty, but we need to look around to find clothing similar to the other women in the area," Josephus said, "I don't want every man in the area sent here by their wives to inquire about where you got that lovely dress. I might have to develop a way to make dresses like that to quiet them," he said with a smile.

A sudden idea popped into her mind, and she smiled at Josephus and then Wayne. "How would this outfit look around town?" she asked, her thoughts on the bath water's transparency causing her to suddenly vanish before their eyes.

# CHAPTER 11

After several days of discomfort with her vast expanding size and frequent pains as if labor were starting, only to taper off, the day came with the breaking of water and the beginnings of contractions that grew steadily more frequent. Wayne ran for the doctor as if he feared the baby would be born before he was able to get back. He even outran the doctor on his return to the prime minister's home. Wayne was not allowed in the room. Rhonda had instructed earlier that only the doctor would be there for the delivery. Wayne had stressed he had some knowledge of Lamaze classes. Still, Rhonda felt highly uncomfortable with the presence of the prime minister, not to mention Wayne, as she endured that experience. Neither had seen her even partially clothed, and she would not change that any time soon.

Rhonda felt stressful pains with each contraction. At first, she felt like it would not be any trouble. Rhonda asked the doctor if he knew anything about epidurals, but was quickly disappointed that the medical establishment was not that advanced. She declined to explain the medical procedure due to the start of the next contraction. Rhonda heard Wayne and Seph yell through a cracked door that they loved her. She knew they probably hoped to reassure her in her struggle with childbirth and was grateful.

The doctor had her get off the bed and squat on the floor. He said the gravitational pull would help to speed the delivery. He had already covered the floor with clean sheets. With one hand, the doctor helped keep her stable and in position and reached under for the protruding head to help guide its delivery. After half an hour of contractions and stiff, painful pushes, the head was evident enough for the doctor to reach with both hands. Rhonda held onto the doctor's clothing for stability in the difficult-to-maintain squatting position. Once the head was grasped by the doctor, he instructed her to take another deep breath and push with all her might. She did so, and the baby came forth.

The doctor took the baby, held it by its legs, and gently patted it on the fanny to cause the mucus to dislodge from the baby's mouth, and the first sounds of the newborn rang forth. Rhonda hoped so much that Wayne and Seph would hear the little cry. The doctor cut the navel cord and wrapped the baby in a specially folded sheet. Rhonda followed her doctor's instructions and continued her push to pass the placenta that followed the baby. The doctor had her move back to the bed.

"Here is your little boy. Congratulations," he said as he smiled proudly, "He's perfect."

She beamed as she reached out and held him. Tears trickled down her cheeks as she held him for the first time. The doctor continued to clean and administer medical care, and she felt some pain, but her mind was with the newborn child, and nothing else mattered. After fifteen minutes of the doctor's assistance, Rhonda was able to fully cover herself and send for Wayne and Seph.

She held the baby beside her and admired its features and maturity. She watched the doctor open the door to allow the two who waited in the living room to come to see the newborn. She saw both of them as they stood at the door, excited and anticipating. They stepped into the bedroom and moved to her side to visually inspect the baby held by his mother.

"He's beautiful," said Seph. He smiled at her in a whisper so the doctor could not hear. "You did wonderfully. My people will be forever grateful for the suffering you endured to set us free."

Wayne was quieter and looked in amazement. "Are you okay?" he asked with a concerned look.

"I'm fine, Wayne, but thanks for asking," said Rhonda, returning her eyes to the tiny baby. "Would you like to hold Him, Wayne?"

"No, no, I'm afraid I might drop him or not hold him right," he said shyly.

"I'd be glad to hold him," said Seph, "And then I will show Wayne how to do so, also."

Rhonda gently handed the baby to Seph, with care to ensure the head was supported.

He took the baby ever so gently, and tears fell from his cheeks as he looked down at the most incredible visitation, and he said, "This is the most precious sight I have ever held in my arms. I bet he will be walking in a week."

"Let's not go that far," she said with the assumption of what she thought was his sarcasm. "It will be almost a year before he can do that."

"A year?" he said, "I was walking ten days after birth. You wait. He will have the wisdom of his father and his mother by birth. He does not have to learn to do anything. He already knows how. You must eat well because you will be nursing a fast-growing child."

"How fast can he grow?" asked Rhonda, as if she knew it would take eighteen years for him to grow up.

"He'll be fully grown in a couple of years, just like you," said Seph.

"It took me seventeen years to grow to my current size and age," she said, confusedly.

"Seventeen years?" Seph asked, "That is way too slow. Why did it take so long?"

"Seph, I'm seventeen years old, too, and I am not considered an adult, either, in our world," said Wayne.

"So long? Why? You are born with your parents' learning and skills?" he asked with a puzzled look, "Your body's growth took that long?"

"Sure," Rhonda said, "Maybe we take longer because we are of the giant populations you have seen above this cavern."

"You are one of those?" he asked, a bit taken aback by the expression on her face.

"Yes, before we were rescued and taken to another place to be prepared to join you, we were, in fact, of that giant world," she said with a look of flattery.

"Surely, you were prepared for this world to include childbearing in the spring, and by next spring, you are ready for another," Seph said. "To still have sixteen years to go after the first year, how does a mother handle more than one infant?"

"Some, not very well, but most survive and flourish," she said, "My mother raised three of us."

My mother raised two of us," said Wayne, "And that took the last twenty years because my brother is now twenty, and he's still not grown yet. He is in college but still a kid at heart and may never grow up."

"Wayne, don't confuse him," said Rhonda. "He needs to know your brother grew slowly like you did. Life may be tougher here, and growth may be different. If you think about it, most insects mature in far less than a year."

"Right, but we have the blessing of living beyond that first year, sometimes thirty or forty years if we are lucky," said Seph.

"The life expectancy where I am from is in the seventies and even higher for women," Wayne said, "Some even live to be a hundred."

"Of course, we take the first twenty years growing up," said Rhonda.

"Twenty years growing up?" Seph asked. "That is a long time for growth."

"By the way," said Wayne, "What are we going to name him?"

"How about Joshua? That name has special meaning," said Rhonda.

"Joshua is a beautiful name, and it does have special meaning," said Seph, with his voice indicating great approval and marvel at its magnitude. "It means He will free his people. He will be our deliverer."

"He seems so small and fragile," said Rhonda with a choking sound in her voice as she tried to hold back the tears. "What He is sent here to do makes me want to run away with Him and hide from the dangers that threaten His life right now."

"We must be prepared to flee at a moment's notice," said Wayne.

"If word gets out of His presence, surely those who seek to destroy the people's hope of deliverance will not rest without the spilling of blood."

"Surely, we will be safe here, but preparedness for a quick departure is a perfect and calculated safety measure," Seph said. "My status as prime minister will hold protection for Him for now. But, in the meantime, Rhonda, you need your rest and the pull on your body; feeding this fast-growing child will be tremendous. You must eat well. To run would be too much on your body with the nursing of the child and the wear of the journey. If we must flee, I have sanctuary in hidden places I cannot mention."

"Yes, rest, Rhonda. Regain your strength. We will prepare supper," said Wayne.

Rhonda went back to sleep, cuddling her child next to her, held closely. She feared His being taken to sleep in a crib or cradle. She wanted to be ready to run at a moment's notice. Her fears and the fragile state of her newborn Son would significantly change in the coming weeks.

Joshua grew at a tremendous pace. In one week, he

appeared to be a year old. Rhonda's weight was reduced by the pull, even when well-fed. At the end of that first week, he took his first steps and said his first word, "Mama." His growth accelerated even more at that point as he moved toward solid foods and reduced nursing. In two weeks, He was weaned from nursing and verbally advanced when compared to a two-year-old. Seph explained that it was the standard growth rate for children. It seemed that he was already born innate with the skills to walk and talk, and could sometimes recall events from his mother's childhood in detail. He knew His mother as well as she knew herself. Rhonda quickly regained her strength and became busy caring for her new toddler. She struggled with his knowledge of her written language, untaught, but swiftly realized that Seph would have to teach his own language because it was foreign to Rhonda. She also participated to reinforce the teachings, despite the busy life of Seph and his prime ministerial duties, which kept him away so much.

Joshua's mastery of His native tongue still exceeded anything Rhonda could muster. He ended up teaching Rhonda how to read the language. She was sure the youngster spoke His native language when reading the words, but she heard her own language. She was sometimes surprised that He could talk to her, and Seph could not understand. He knew her English language as well as the language of His people. It sounded the same to Rhonda because the suit provided an instant translator, enabling her to understand all languages.

One evening, Seph brought in a mess of fish. To Rhonda and Wayne's surprise, the fish began to talk once the stringers were removed from their mouths. They resembled giant minnows (even though they were new hatchlings), yet both could understand the fish language clearly as they begged for mercy. Seph indicated he could hear nothing but the whining of the fish out of the water. Joshua asked to be held up to see the fish in the sink. He spoke to them, and their begging ceased. They started, instead, with indications of honor in being their maker's meal of nourishment. Seph heard none of it, but Joshua's fish sounds, too, and supposed he mimicked the gurgling noises. Rhonda and Wayne looked at each other, knowing that this was one of many extraordinary abilities as this child grew rapidly.

Rhonda often discussed with Wayne whether Joshua must follow his destiny as their Savior did for humankind. She struggled with the thoughts of her Son suffering for this entire small world they were in to help free the people from the bondage of their fallen hearts. She even questioned if Seph would feel the same way about Him if he knew that instead of a conquest of the dreaded emperor, He would make Himself a "sin" sacrifice to redeem this world's people of their ungodliness. This must prove to be the more significant achievement.

While Wayne and Seph tried some late fishing after work one evening, Rhonda sat in her kitchen while Joshua played in the living room with his toys. She thought of how he would have to die. How He would have to suffer incredible pain. She thought so much of his being her child, offspring, and only child. How can this be? Before she knew it, her eyes were filled with tears, and her breath became involved with the emotional quiver of crying helplessly. She felt a small hand reach for hers and take it.

He spoke. "You show tears for things that have yet to be. Mom, don't cry. What you think of, I live to accomplish. It will not be as you think, but it will be to save you and all of the people of this great land," he said with a bit of mystery, "One day, you will thank Me for being your Savior twice in one lifetime."

Puzzled and observant, she sat as He walked back into the living room and returned to His toys. Did he even know her thoughts? He was incredibly unique. She pondered how Mary had felt many years before when she had raised her Son and tried to protect Him from natural dangers around them, such as their flight to Egypt to escape an evil ruler of that time. She thought of their escape plan now. The plans for escape to the boat dock. Sneaking onto Seph's smallest boat needed stealth. With further skill, they would paddle to the middle of the lake. Their hopes depended on their quest to find the white rock. All else would be explained later.

She thought of the butcher who complained of pulled muscles in his back one day, when Rhonda and Joshua came by to pick up cuts of meat from the livestock lizard population. The next time she saw him, he was much better and gave credit to the pain going away during their last visit. She knew why, but said nothing. The butcher's comments that perhaps it was due to the presence of such a lovely woman and her precious Son stood uncontested.

She also thought of the old dressmaker complaining about her rheumatism, which bothered her because she continued to complain, visit after visit. She figured she just liked to talk and complain rather than to acknowledge any actual ailments. She began to show a happier expression on her face with each visit. She even appeared to get around the shop much better, but still, she complained about the effects of aging and joints that seemed stiff and sore, even though not lately; she just knew they would start to act up again any day.

While walking along the cave lake's dark shores with Joshua one afternoon, she heard a scream from the balconies above. Down plunged a construction worker from one of the new cut-a-ways being hewn from the rocks above. He hit the edge of the rocks and bounced into the deep waters. He sank into the waters, and only bubbles came to the surface. Before she could grab Him, Joshua dived into the water after the construction worker. She took off her shoes, ready to dive in after both at that point, but a voice inside said all was fine, just to wait. In less than a minute, Joshua surfaced with the construction worker's neck wrapped in one arm and swam to the shore as He pulled the man behind.

There had already started a gathering of many to try to figure out where the fall victim had disappeared. Several assisted the small boy, who pulled a fully grown man toward the shore. The man was alive. He had no injuries beyond the sputter of a few mouthfuls of water. The spectators applauded as the man was helped to shore along with Joshua.

One lady asked the boy, "Where did you learn to swim like that, young man?"

He smiled back, "My mother taught me. She can do amazing things. That is why she is the ambassador's wife."

The lady said, "Your father will hear of this and be mighty proud."

Rhonda took Joshua, moved quickly through the commotion, and returned to quarters, fearing they had drawn too much attention. She knew that Joshua had done more than just pull that man from the water. Rhonda knew He had healed him of his severe injuries under those dark waters. She pondered these things to herself and told no one, fearing it would endanger them all.

While fishing, Wayne, out of frustration after failing to catch anything all night, called Joshua on shore the following day to find out where the fish were. He said to throw your nets to the other side of the boat. The boat's crew grumbled but, with Wayne's persuasion, did so and caught a boatload of fish that nearly sank their craft before they could get the full nets to the shore. A couple of the fishermen even asked Rhonda if Joshua could ride with them on their future fishing trips, but there was no way to persuade her to allow Him out of her sight for any time. Wayne did sneak around and ask Almanac for insights into when and where the best fishing opportunities were. Wayne grew up as a respected young fisherman who never seemed to grow up. He remained a late bloomer and a teenager longer than most of that land had ever seen.

Several times, toward the end of the day, when the local doctor was swamped with patients, Joshua would venture down to the office. His presence was enough. Suddenly, when He passed through to visit the doctor, He would invite him to look out in the lobby. To the doctor's surprise, the hall would suddenly be empty, and the nurse at the front desk would say, "They all suddenly rose, declared their sicknesses, injuries, and ailments vanished. Many felt it was just being in the doctor's office. Rhonda knew better. He took it upon himself to stand out on the balcony that served as an extended sidewalk that connected the many homes carved into the rock. His favorite spot was between the two oil lamps, which provided the only natural daylight in the cave, suggesting daytime hours. When darkness fell outside the mountain, the oil lamps were extinguished. The only lights that remained were the lanterns set up outside the individual homes for those who came in late from work.

One day, while perched on the balcony in observation, the boats that returned from fishing for hatchlings, or perhaps a larger boat, pulled in a large minnow that had been harpooned and towed back to shore. He stood there, just twelve months old, yet he was every bit of twelve years old in size. His home schooling had advanced him academically, but not nearly as much as Rhonda had advanced in her mastery of the written language of the people.

From the external opening of the cave came a flight of several of the emperor's soldiers. Instead of the normal veer toward the military complex built into the cave walls at the other end of the cavern, two soldiers flew higher instead. They passed Joshua and stared at Him as if suddenly aware of his presence and who He was. They vanished into thin air before He gathered some vital information.

Joshua rushed into the living quarters. He said, "Mom, Mom, they saw me! They know who I am!"

"Who? What are you talking about?" she asked as a small amount of panic started to rise in her voice.

"Two of the emperor's lieutenants were just outside! They flew by after becoming invisible. I could still see them, and they saw Me. I heard them say. That is the Promised One. We must tell the emperor He is here. They flew higher and then vanished into a dark area at the top of the cave. I think I have located the emperor's hiding place."

To figure out what He was talking about, Rhonda tried her suit's ability to make her transparent. "Did they look like this when they vanished?" She thought of the water and became as transparent as it.

"Yes, just like that, but I can still see you," He said, "You are transparent but with a red glow to your outline. The two Lieutenants looked like that, and then they passed through a dark, wavy opening and vanished along with the strange opening."

"They obviously have body suits like ours. That is why they can fly. It means they have the same abilities we do. Where did they get those suits?"

"They got them from the Tree People. Our version of the angels, common in your world," He said, enlightening her with revelation.

"How could Tree People or angelic beings give evil people such powerful outfits?" she asked.

"A thing called false peace," he said, "It is giving the enemy their powerful weapons so the enemy will be pacified. By so doing, they will not have to fight a war that could destroy their sanctuaries and secret existence."

"You said they saw You?" she asked, suddenly raising her voice in further panic, "How do You know they saw You?"

"They said, 'There is the Promised One.' They recognized

Me on the balcony even though I was in the darkest area; they saw Me anyway. I do not know how they knew, but they hurriedly went to the emperor. We must flee immediately."

"You are right. I will grab the backpacks, and you run to Seph's office and get him," she said, already moving toward the closet to fetch the required items. She moved quickly, wanting to return to the balcony and see Joshua in His run toward Seph's office. She did not wish Him out of her eyesight. She glanced to where her belt had once held her sword before it was tossed into the creek when they were captured by a couple of the emperor's scouts. She could faintly see the red outline of the sword as if it were still there. She felt the area where the red shape appeared and could feel the invisible sword. The danger was upon them, and her weapon had been returned to her, invisible to the naked eye but not to her. She knew she had to be ready to leap and learn to fly at a moment's notice to rescue Joshua if the emperor's lieutenants returned and began their search.

She could see Joshua in the distance as she stepped outside their home. He ran and was observed as he quickly turned into the office. Seph was out the door with Wayne in the time it took her to rush down the sidewalk/balcony to catch up. At the same time, she kept her eyes peeled toward the darkness, supposedly where Joshua had explained it in His observations.

They all met with Wayne, who grabbed the two backpacks from Rhonda's hands. Rhonda had failed to put the backpacks on her shoulders. She desired to be ready at a moment's notice to leap off the balcony and fly to fend off any approach of danger. To fight forces bent on capturing Joshua before He left the area. The backpacks looked like fishing kits, with many lures and fishing gear suspended from the sides for easy access on the fishing boat.

They boarded a smaller vessel. A tarp was spread over Rhonda and Joshua in the middle. Seph paddled at one end and Wayne at the other. They moved through the water as they had done many times before. The tarp was customarily used to cover fish when caught to keep them from flopping off the boat, so its presence was not unusual. Rhonda and Joshua sat on the ship's floor to give no impression of the tarp that they were underneath.

Out of the darkness above flew the two lieutenants, and in the distance, a large force was seen as it charged from the military fortress on the opposite end of the lake. Many flew right over the little boat as it approached the rock that extended from the water's surface.

After he gave the area a good look around, Seph tied a rope to the two backpacks, tossed them into the water, and then removed the tarp that concealed Joshua and Rhonda. "I want everybody to take in a good breath of air and dive into the cold water. Once under, swim for the bottom of the rock. Do you understand?" he asked, "We do not have a minute to spare." With a good hold on the rope, Seph fell backward, off the boat, and into the water. He still held the rope in his hand.

He vanished from the surface. Joshua dove next. Rhonda looked back at Wayne and did the same, but in the process gave the boat a shove into the distance.

Once Rhonda hit the ice-cold water, she struggled to keep her breath and not cry out. She veered in the direction of the rock, faintly able to make it out by the torch extending from the front of the boat sailing away. Rhonda worried it might reveal their escape plans, but the most significant thing now was finding out what was at the bottom of the rock. She swam quickly to take advantage of her dive to maintain the depth needed to reach the bottom of the fake rock. At the bottom was a flat line. Swimming under, she found several ropes extending downward from the rock's inside. She pulled herself up one rope to break the surface of the air pocket trapped in the cup-type hollow rock. It was still pitch dark, and the one light source above the water suddenly vanished. She felt around in the darkness. She knew she was inside some kind of air pocket.

Suddenly, behind her, she felt another person climb to the surface. It was pretty crowded inside the air chamber. Four people all floated in total darkness.

"Are we all here?" asked Seph.

"I'm here," said Wayne, as he poked him with the now extinguished torch as if perhaps it could be used to add some light to their hiding place.

Rhonda stated that she and Joshua were present.

"Wayne, I'm glad you thought to extinguish the torch, but we won't need it where we are going," he said, "But hang on to it just the same. Let me squeeze over to the edge. Wayne, you go for the opposite side. There is a foothold there, and we must turn a crank to pull this bubble device downward to our destination before we run out of oxygen and pass out. What good is an escape pod if it kills us before we reach safe harbor?"

Rhonda listened to the two climb up and felt the sudden movement and the rope's upward pull as their flotation device sank deeper into the dark waters. She heard many grunts and noticed the air temperature rise as the labor continued. She also knew the best air was closest to the water's surface.

"Joshua, how are you holding up?" she asked her Son.

"Having a great time, but I'm getting the shivers from the cold water," he said.

"Wayne, you and Seph doing all right up there?" she asked out of concern for their apparent exhaustive efforts and the heavy breathing from their labor and depleting oxygen.

"I'm fine, but a moment's rest would be nice," Wayne said.

"We cannot rest. We must keep going before our oxygen runs out," Seph said. "We must leave this bubble, take our last breath, and swim through a tunnel to another chamber. It is not a long swim, but it might seem to be as your lungs cry out for another breath of fresh air. There will be air pockets through the water tunnel, but we must not dwell long at each point."

Finally, the echo sound of the fake rock's collision with the lower surface of the lake also revealed a slippery decline in one direction.

"I feel with my feet, and it appears we are to follow the slope, right?" asked Wayne.

"Yes, take three deep breaths, hold the last, and move down that slope. You must watch your head as you slip under the overhang and enter the water tunnel to the next cave above," he explained in detail. "Does everybody understand?"

Everybody confirmed. Rhonda and Joshua went first.

Rhonda could constantly feel Joshua's feet in front of her. She wanted to hold on to Him and carry Him with her, but He was strongly independent and an excellent swimmer. Rhonda thought that was another of those innate traits that He had inherited from her. She began to feel the urge to breathe. The young lady felt like her lungs would burst following the tunnel's slanted wall to the water's surface in the next cave's chamber. She began to expel some of the air, knowing that variations in the water level made the atmosphere less compressed, and feared harm to herself if she held the air in. The tunnel was slanted upward, and avoiding an occasional head bump with the ceiling was a great challenge. The most significant point was minimizing the force of her head hitting the water as they continued to swim.

Finally, she broke the surface and felt cold, clammy air around her face. She took in a deep breath. She then felt for Joshua and found Him as he gasped heavily for fresh air. Wayne was next, and then Seph.

Still, in pitch darkness, the air was fresher. The humid smell was not the greatest, but the air was fresh, and breathing again was incredible after such a long swim underwater.

"We swam through the slanted passageway. We have one more passage to walk through in total darkness. This one is a little bit further than the last, but much drier. I will hold Rhonda's hand. Rhonda, you will lead with Joshua. Wayne, you bring up the rear.

"I will do that."

"Are we ready, Joshua?" she asked her Son.

"Let's walk, Mama," He said.

They both launched forth. The darkness was frightening. The tunnel through the rocks was neither straight nor had a constant ceiling elevation. It was a slow, clumsy effort, but after around ten minutes, they began to see light in the distance. Soon, the source of light proved to be a hole in the ceiling of the passageway.

Rhonda released Seph's hand as she observed him struggle to climb the wall, seeking leverage to reach the opening. She then assisted Joshua with Seph's request, and he was also pulled into the passage. Once His feet were out of the hole, she raised herself into the opening with Wayne's cupped hands to aid her reach and give her that first big step. He quickly noticed the fresh air was much cleaner. She felt her twelve-year-old Son, who was only one year old in human years, grab her hand and pull her out of the way as Seph then reached to assist Wayne in his attempt to climb the wet wall to the opening.

The new cavern was small, and the light came from the other end of the chamber. The group was still in recession and would need to climb to reach the lighted passage. "Give me a boost up, and I will look around to ensure the area is clear of intruders," Wayne said.

"Sure, my good man," Seph said, cupping his hands together, allowing Wayne to step into them and be boosted upward.

Wayne hesitated for a moment and then began to climb up. "Give me your hand, Joshua, and I will pull you up."

Joshua, Rhonda, and finally, Seph were quickly pulled up

to stand on the rock wall. Rhonda looked around at the new cave dwelling.

It was small but well-lit. In the distance, giant cave crickets lined the walls on the opposite end of the small cavern, but no hostiles were present now.

"We are on the Southeastern side of the mountain. Since you were captured on the mountain's opposite side or have allies there, most search parties will figure you will flee back in that direction. They know there are four of you and figure you will want to catch up with your comrades," he said, "Our best hope right now is to try to find a good group of Herdsmen and find sanctuary with them for the moment. Some Herdsmen groups hate the emperor as much as the Wasamanee. They will be red-complexioned, with shorter, rounder bodies when we find them."

"Some say they can squat on a branch filled with aphids and go unnoticed because they look so much like the aphids when they pose a certain way. We must hurry because, if you notice, the bright sun that bothers our eyes will soon slip beyond the mountain, and darkness will be our new enemy and its creatures that feed at night."

# CHAPTER 12

Carson and Roxie were famished when they entered the dining room of the Tree People's grand facility. A long table was spread with all the trimmings of a seven-course dinner. They were quickly guided to the head of the table and seated alongside Johannes and many others, who excitedly discussed the presence of their two special guests.

With his hunger pains still present because of the short-term effect of liquid diets and their flight's obvious pull on their energy levels, Carson waited impatiently as long as he could. When the host took the first bite, they dug in.

The smell of food was in the air, as was the excitement of their special status among the gathered people. He saw a messenger arrive, approach Johannes, whisper in his ear, and then take a seat at the table.

Johannes stood at the head of the table, and the room grew quiet with expectation as their leader was obviously about to either bring the blessing or introduce his guests. "May I speak to you at this moment?" he asked confidently.

They would agree, and the room grew silent.

"I have just received news that a force of the emperor's men is marching in this direction and is a four-day journey from reaching us. I am afraid they know where we are. I feel they also know of our special guests seated beside me. We have waited a long time for our deliverers. Now, we must train and defend them until they are fully trained to battle the forces of evil."

The crowd murmured among themselves, and some of the joy in the earlier conversation had diminished.

"We will feast well this morning and begin immediately to prepare for war. We will not sit idly by in our sanctuary and let the enemy march upon us. We will go out to meet them at our calling and time of choosing," he said confidently and assuredly. "I have a plan and feel that with our new warriors joining us, the victory is ours. We must win that victory. Nothing comes easy, nor will it be handed to us without dedication, initiative, or sacrifice. The days of weakness are over. We will be a mighty people again for the cause of good."

There was quiet in the group for the remainder of the meal. Carson felt that, in their old age, the Tree People feared going to war, fighting an enemy who could burn them out of their sanctuary and end their existence. They had to overcome the fear that had driven them to weakness, and change would not come easily.

The meal was served with green substances and a slice of meat on the menu. Carson looked at Roxie and said, "This stuff tastes great. What do you think it is? Roast beef?"

Roxie smirked back at him and said, "You eat, and do not ask what it is. Can't I enjoy a meal without thinking of what bug it came from?"

Carson smiled and said, "This came from no bug. It had to be an animal. Look at the meaty texture; it tastes like roast beef instead of chicken."

Roxie continued to eat and tried not to look at him. She said, "Yeah, but still, I do not want to know what it is until I eat it and it has settled on my stomach, please?"

Carson grinned and said, "I think you are right. It is good, and let us just pretend it is a fine Yankee Pot Roast until after the meal." He continued eating with a funny expression, noting the strange taste of the vegetables. There were two flavors. Each was somewhat mushy but significantly decent in taste if only some salt could be added.

The rest of the meal was uneventful, and Carson contained his desire to tease Roxie about his speculation of whether the meat was from a lizard or a small rodent captured by the Tree People for the feast.

—

After the meal, the two were guided to a room several floors below. Carson even suggested it was underground because of its broader capacity, which was more like a gymnasium instead of the limitations of the width of the tree trunk.

Looking around the room, Carson saw several obstacle courses and unique posts with a sword that extended from a spring-like mechanical arm. Carson quickly said, "Now that has to be a sword-fighting device. I hope it holds up better than the post we were provided by the Wasamanee."

"You are very insightful, Master Carson," said Johannes as if out of nowhere, "You will master sword fighting here and a few other details. This sword will counter your strength and reflexes and challenge you beyond anything you have ever confronted."

Carson stepped up to the post that dangled the sword before him. He pulled his weapon and struck the dangling blade. It was quickly knocked away, to his surprise, yet it circled the post to return with a dangerous slice toward him from a lower angle. He blocked again, and the blade spun back around the pole. The quicker his strikes against the approach of the edge, the faster it got, extending further as it passed by him. Instead of being able to block, its speed showed he must dodge those high-speed swings, too, to stay in the battle and catch the next slice toward him in retaliation.

Carson had to step away in ten minutes and let the blade spin around the post several times. He was wringing-wet with sweat and completely out of breath. He heard someone say, "Break!" Looking around, he saw some chairs lined up against the wall.

"Man, that thing can fight, can't it?" asked Roxie as she approached a chair beside Carson. "That blade hit me twice. This armor suit works great, but the force of the blow will knock you down."

"It has not hit me yet, but I guarantee you it came close a couple of times," he said, looking back at Roxie; she exhibited a lot of moisture about her hair and face, including drips from her wet hair as if coming out of a shower.

"Train with that for a few days, and we can be up to par with anybody," said Carson.

"Anybody but the emperor himself," said Johannes. "He is the greatest swordsman that has ever lived. He has been challenged by our best and, with his size, defeated the challenger in an exhaustive battle, and he hardly breaks a sweat."

"We will keep training until we get that good," said Carson.

"You do not have enough time to train to that capacity," said Johannes. "You will just have to find a way to beat him through your inner strength and cunning. He is considered invincible."

"There's got to be a way," said Carson, "What other reason would we be here?"

"That sounds promising, but your purpose is not for violence against evil; it's to conquer evil," Johannes said with a grin. "You will just have to trust me. Your time will come. We must, however, take on evil's hideous followers and their overconfidence at this point. It is there that we win the most significant victory of this time. Our first battle will set a precedent for the rest of our confrontations."

"Do we wait for them to get here, or do we take the battle to them quickly?" asked Roxie.

"We will strike this evening as they have marched for a considerable distance through rough terrain," said Johannes.

"We will fly out as a small party to catch them at dusk."

Looking around, the three observed other Tree People as they returned to their swordplay because they had perhaps taken up to three breaks since Roxie and Carson started their confrontation with the mechanical combatant.

"I have been pondering a question, and I hope you don't mind my asking," asked Roxie.

"Go ahead," said Johannes, "I'll give it my best effort, but take it for granted; I don't know everything."

"You said some of you were here at the beginning of time," said Roxie, "If you were here when the world was created, I have a deep question that has been asked many times, and I really want an answer." She looked at Johannes with a severe, perhaps embarrassed expression as she approached the question. "If Adam and Eve were the first people on earth, their son, Cain, found his wife in the land of Nod. How did he do that, or did he marry his sister?"

"That is an excellent question. I am surprised you do not already know the answer. Your scriptures state that the earth was created in seven periods or days, as several of your primitive translations call it. Man and woman were created in the sixth period, and the Lord rested on the seventh. Then, the scriptures speak of the creation of Adam and, later, Eve. If you look closely, they are not the same. Adam was created as a special, Godly-instructed messenger to carry God's message to an uncivilized race of men, to offer them God's culture and hope. Adam and his wife fell to sin to render their message of hope to all of mankind a blemish of shame because they no longer had the purity that a messenger of God would need to achieve the planned message. They became sinners at the level of those on the earth who needed hope to conquer their sinful nature. Their personal sin compromised their faith, and therefore, their witness was hindered from the start. Cain found his mate among the primitives that dwelled in the land of Nod. Adam instead became a messenger who struggled, with great difficulties, even with delivering the message to his own children, and Cain was a reflection of that struggle."

"That's pretty powerful stuff," said Carson. "I bet I know some Baptists who would contest that theory."

"Who said it was a theory," added Johannes.

"Remember, I was there. I thought Adam was hen-pecked, myself."

"He was the first Adam," said Roxie, "The Promised One is the second Adam, and He did not fail because He was the Son of the Most High, right?"

"Right you are, and that is who your friend in captivity carries in her," said Johannes.

"Rhonda is pregnant?" asked Roxie.

"No, like I said, she carries the seed. She will be by the end of next week," Johannes said, "Your purpose has a serious reality, and the hope is greatly achieved. It is in His birth and conquest that the emperor will meet his doom."

"If we are to battle this evening, should we not be up and back at practicing?" asked Carson.

"That is exactly the momentum we need, Carson, to become conquerors of evil in our lifetime," Johannes said, "Let us be the first to the battle simulators, shall we?"

The training continued for another hour or two, but always avoiding exhaustive workouts to avoid soreness that could hamper their efforts for the next four days.

The afternoon meal was served around four o'clock, as indicated by Carson's watch, which he kept under his sleeve. It went quietly and solemnly. It was as if some felt it might be their last meal. Soon, their forces would fly to meet the enemy beyond their tree refuge and boldly into their presence to take the battle to them.

---

The group gathered just beyond the opening at the top of the main chamber of the tree. The assembly of twenty-five Tree Men, Carson, Johannes, and Roxie, gathered for the flight from their vantage point to seek the advancement of the emperor's army. Early information stated that the force steadily advanced on them and was nearly a fourth of the way to the lake, where they prepared to stealthily swoop down on them from the air.

The team reviewed quick signals and tactics, including going invisible and methods to subdue their foes. Knowing their enemy's last location, it was agreed to advance by air to just above the valley the enemy was marching through and catch them as they set up camp for the night. They all took off quite effectively. Carson and Roxie observed the launch methods used by the Tree People and, for the first time, were able to take off flat-footed, eliminating the need for a drop-off to gain airborne status. The flight was uneventful. With the twenty-eight people's flight in a fortress-type formation, a signal was given upon approaching the mountain ridge above the valley where they were last seen to become invisible. Surprising to Carson was the fact that those who flew in the formation farther to his left and right were distinctly brighter to his vision than those closer to him. He observed that they had noticed the problem, too, and immediately flew closer to him to retain the advantage and, probably, to know where everybody was in his realm. He figured that those in it would become invisible to those outside it by stepping out of his coverage.

He made the decision to explain this problem upon arrival at their vantage point at the top of the ridge; he noticed in the distance that their two advance lookouts were dead and lay on the ground below. The two old Tree People were stripped of their protective suits and weapons. To their dismay, two of the emperor's soldiers stood beside the bodies as if they awaited their approach. The soldiers were invisible to the naked eye, but not to those cloaked in the same fashion as those in Carson and Roxie's realm of influence, as either the Promised Ones or because of the unique makeup of their suits. The outline of the two soldiers glowed with a reddish hue. Indeed, they were overconfident in their invisibility and unaware of the group's silent approach.

The landing around the two guards and the Tree People casualties caused noise on the leaves. The soldiers immediately moved to a defensive posture but, upon a quick glance around, appeared to assume the commotion was caused by the wind.

Carson reached for his sword and stood ready. He tried to figure out his next move, aware of the limitations of movement on the leaves and the noise he would make when he drew his sword; he hesitated, as several others did. Suddenly, to his left, Johannes stepped out of his protective realm and became visible to the two soldiers. They drew their swords and charged toward him. Suddenly, the sounds of many swords drawn simultaneously rang forth. The two, perhaps in fear that they were about to be charged from over the ridge, hesitated.

Two blows went forth to each of the victims. The Tree Persons struck the first blows to their heads to remove their helmets. The second blow struck with the blunt side of their swords, causing a double red line on the side of their heads, and knocking them out cold. Immediately, they were rolled onto their stomachs, and their suits were cut from them, leaving them in a naked, visible posture to await their discovery later or to awaken in need of fig leaves or something. Their suits and swords were seized by the Tree People for future use.

There was a moment of grief for the two fallen comrades who had done so well in their effort to keep tabs on the approach of this army that had marched forward like columns of ants from the Wasamanee tribe, where they had searched earlier for the four Promised Ones. Carson thought the two brave men who died appeared in their sixties, even though most Tree People seemed much older. Both had suffered broken necks, and with their swords still in their sheaths, they had to have been taken by surprise. Their suits were also removed, but there was clothing beneath them. Their bodies were moved to a more distant area, placed under the protection of a tree root, and covered with a special covering said to ward off ants and other insects seeking an easy meal.

The two unconscious soldiers of the emperor were left naked, tied up, gagged, and stretched out on their stomachs. Without their special suits and weapons, they were no more than standard Wasamanee guards, only more naked. They were also food for thought in the eyes of any predator that might pass by.

Their suits made them powerful. Now, they were useless to the emperor. The gathering around the two fallen comrades was solemn; there would probably be more before it ended. Many men with gray hair stood there in a circle with Carson and Roxie. Their red glow still indicated they maintained their invisibility to avoid further detection by other soldiers patrolling the area. The challenge before them was loaded with risks. The point was to advance on the camp as stealthily as possible and remove one of the emperor's soldiers at a time.

It was agreed that rather than send the whole group into battle, a small force of six would fly out and try to slip up on scouts and outer guards of the emperor's men. Carson took five of the youngest men to battle with the leaders of this large army. Knocking them out with the sword bluntly resulted in the successful incapacitation of four more soldiers. Most soldiers marched with their basic troops to maintain unit integrity and guide their advance.

They were expected to break for camp just before dark; Carson was surprised that they marched up several pine trees, climbed the bark, and spread out among the bark extensions and cracks. This facilitated further assaults on individual targets. Carson looked at one of the Tree People posted at a lookout point on a high limb of a Maple tree. "Why are they climbing the pine trees?" he asked curiously. It was then that loud thunder was heard in the distance.

"That sound should be a serious clue," said the Tree Man.

"We are about to be washed off the face of the earth. They intend to utilize the available shelter inside the bark cracks to avoid the deluge of rain about to fall. They obviously can predict the weather better than we can."

"Yeah, I thought I felt it in my bones, but with the knowledge of how much practice we put in today, I figured it was from that instead of a weather change," said the next Tree Man to the first.

"That means we are not only going to have to move fast, but we are going to have to find shelter of our own at a moment's notice as well."

Looking at the clouds, Carson could tell they had some time yet. "Let us fly around at close proximity and see who we can find among the pine trees currently loaded with foot soldiers," he said.

They all took off rather quickly. Often, they bumped into each other in their efforts to circle the trees, but could plainly see that most of the emperor's soldiers either buzzed around in observation of the movements or at the foot of the trees in provision of supervision of traffic. In conquering a ranking soldier, the group flew right into his position in front of the marching line. Two blows and the helmet bounced off, and the soldier fell forward, unconscious. Several foot soldiers chuckled, as if to avoid being heard, at the sight of their commander's sudden fall, and then his uniform was stripped and vanished before their eyes.

The clouds continued to darken. Carson got bold and

asked one of the foot soldiers, "Where's your lieutenant?"

The foot soldier looked surprised at the air that spoke to him. He either knew something was unique at this point or figured the invisible person was another emperor's soldier in an invisible state for some reason. He said, "He is setting up his poncho for rain just above that next piece of bark."

"Thanks, you're a good soldier," said Carson. He then pointed to let his comrades know which direction he headed next. They all flew up to find a heavy-set Lieutenant busy assembling a small tent-like structure, obviously preparing for the approach of weather problems.

Carson and his comrades lit quietly, only to cause a slight breeze. The lieutenant glanced around, saw nothing, and continued to try to hang the upper part of his weather protection device from a point just under the subsequent protrusion of bark. It took four blows and a commotion, and the soldier was out and stripped of his uniform.

They immediately evacuated the scene before any further aid could be rendered on the fallen lieutenant's behalf; the group flew out quickly, more spread out than usual. One of the Tree Men flew out of the protective realm of Carson and was sighted by one of the emperor's Dragon Guards. Suddenly, a shower of arrows flew in his direction before he vanished back into the realm of Carson's approach, but the arrows struck the invisible as effectively as the visible. The Tree Person was struck in the neck and began to fall right back out of the protective realm. He struck the ground hard, and several soldiers charged forward to capture him. Carson swooped to retrieve him, but the effort to hide him was further hampered by the fact that the wounded fellow had lost consciousness and had become visible to all. Carson grabbed him to remove him from the threat of capture, and arrows continued to fly their way. Carson flew with his head low as the strikes of the arrows were deflected off his suit of protection.

Their flight took them down toward the other ridge long enough to create interest in that direction. Quickly, they cut back toward the defense group that awaited them at the top of the hill. Carson veered over to crest that ridge and followed it up the back way, intending to evade another swarm of arrows on their quest for a safe haven. The wounded man was hidden under a large leaf there, and the rest prepared to take on their pursuers.

They maintained their invisibility, yet the rush of the emperor's flying forces upon them was quick. The group flew right past them, in pursuit, perhaps of the wind that might contain their next victims.

The group leaped into the air right behind them.

They could make out their invisibility glow as they got closer. They did not show any effect as they were overwhelmed by Carson and Roxie's advancement. The tail end of the group caught the worst. Several blows occurred, and down went the victim's sword. He, however, was grabbed before he could fall significantly far and immediately stripped of his protective suit. His naked body fell into the leaves below and alerted others that not only was the noise of a struggle behind them, but proof now tumbled to the grounds below. Because the group of five and one casualty had returned to the total group and the invisibility realm of being close to Carson and Roxie, the twenty-seven warriors took on the next advancement of the emperor's men. They felled four more while maintaining their invisible posture before the rest fled toward the trees that harbored their army.

The sudden end of the downpour caught them off guard, leaving them no time to find decent shelter. They flew toward the ground as quickly as possible. Their plunge ended only to try to avoid collision with the ground and lunge for quick cover as the heavy drops of rain pelted them viciously. They were wet, distracted, and seriously knocked around by the bucketfuls of water that hit them rapidly, causing their invisibility to diminish quickly.

With the knowledge that the weather was not fit for man or beast, there was little fear of further advancement of their enemy at that time. There was greater fear of the potential for torrential rains and high-speed currents. They were quick to find leaves, strong enough to offer protection, but the water washed under those leaves was strong enough to not only move them but also weigh them down, keeping them in waist-deep water. In the struggle, they found a root that offered an anchor; they all waded to grab hold. They hoped the downpour they continued to experience would dissipate before being weakened and washed down the hill by the current accelerating.

Carson looked around in hopes of seeing Roxie. She was nowhere to be seen. He suddenly wanted to run out from under the leaf and start an immediate search for her.

His heart pounded even more desperately in his throat. His face became flushed with the fear of this turn of events. He feared Roxie might be captured by the emperor's soldiers while he whiled away the hours, root-dangling in what seemed like a river's flow. He wanted to yell out for her, thinking that maybe the weather would carry his voice, but the knowledge that the group they pursued was not far ahead of them and was probably trapped in the downpour as well stopped him. To alert them of their location could bring their advancement their way before his friends were ready to undertake another confrontation with increased numbers this time.

The rain continued. The flow of the water around the group caused the need to move up further toward the tree that the root was attached to, to maintain their foothold and stay above the water flow that pulled firmly as it made its way past them from higher up the embankment, and also from the tree above whose roots anchored them. The heavy part of the shower was over quickly, but the drizzle continued for at least another hour.

Darkness overcame them earlier than planned with the dark, overcast rain clouds. Their advances seemed hampered further after the rain stopped because of continued drips from the trees.

When the rain finally stopped, it was soon followed by a cloud break. Summer showers are like that, and the chill comes along with it. Temperatures dropped, but the moon broke from the clouds, almost three-quarters full, to give enough light to allow them further advances on the enemy tree occupations or a flight back home for a fresher start the following day. The wounded Tree Man suffered from a neck injury where the arrow had punctured his neck on the right side, damaging muscle tissue. He was fortunate; it did not penetrate the left side, which could have severed the jugular vein. He was weak and unable to fly back. To carry him would only allow short hops, so four were sent with him to take turns on those leaps back toward the safe haven of the headquarters at the lake.

Carson located Roxie in the dark, under the next set of leaves, and had remained suspended from the roots of the same tree. There was great potential for a sudden ambush by the group of the emperor's men, so movement was quick and quiet. Quickly, they flew out of their holdout and circled around the force. They maintained invisibility and stayed in the group's tight circle, allowing only their own to see them. They posted their next position to the rear of the large army that would break camp in the morning and begin further advancement on their Tree Man headquarters, perhaps at sunrise. Their red patterns were clearly visible in the darkness, but they saw no further traces of the forces they had pursued earlier. There were thoughts about whether the pursuers could stop using invisibility and disappear into the night undetected.

Carson, Roxie, and his team of Tree People waited for the break of dawn to begin their continued harassment of the march, but deep in Carson's heart, a voice spoke. He listened, and it became clear that things were not going as planned.

The voice said, "You must withdraw immediately, return to your tree sanctuary, and continue to train. You have caused serious worry in the enemy's camps, but they have also sent word to the emperor, who is now en route to join them. He can see you no matter how effective your stealthy apparel appears to others. His guidance will render your mission a disaster. His arrival will alter their plans, too. It seems that more Wasamanee tribes have dared to stand up to his control because of the massacre that occurred at the cave where you escaped recently. The morale of his forces, though large in number, was held at bay outside the Wasamanee cave while the emperor's lieutenants caused much bloodshed among the leadership of the cave dwellers. With your attacks last night, many common soldiers could sneak up on the emperor's leaders, too, and relieve them of consciousness, strip them of their protective suits, and depart the area. The enemy is now considered to be going toward the rebellious Wasamanee villages to suppress the new outbreaks. Your attacks have sent waves of animosity through the emperor's leadership and brought him out of his power center to personally bring calm and assurance. You must leave in haste without being detected."

Carson looked at Roxie and Johannes. "Let's get out of here; they are on to us, and trouble is on the way, he explained briefly. "Do not question; just gather everybody, and let's head back to headquarters and train for our next mission. The threat of attack on the headquarters is temporarily halted to deal with the rebellion in the emperor's realm. We must now aid the rebellion to keep his forces busy."

The group quickly accounted for everything and fled back to their tree sanctuary. Their flight was further along the ridge to stay far from the emperor's arrival. Along the way, a group of Wasamanee troops, a couple wearing the emperor's uniforms with rips down their backs, were sighted and appeared to flee the main force. This altered their departure because the two who wore the emperor's uniforms also exhibited cuts similar to those used by the Tree People to disrobe the emperor's soldiers the night before.

The group quickly surrounded the small group, but remained invisible. All at once, the force appeared to the small band of soldiers, completely encircling them and presenting their arms to fight a battle if necessary. They quickly drew their weapons but did not move forward to attack. They saw the swords and suits of the ones who surrounded them; they remained at bay as if to await their punishment for their rebellion.

"Peace to you. We detect you are in desertion of the emperor as we are and wish our aid," said Johannes, "Can we be of some assistance?"

The soldier who wore the emperor's lieutenant uniform stepped forward and stated, "Yes, please, we wish to fight the emperor because of the blood bath brought to our people at the Wasamanee mining company a couple of days ago. Many of us lost dear family members, and now we cannot serve this evil who uses us in destructive ways or uses us to stand guard while his lieutenants do such horror to our people."

"How did you come by the two uniforms that once belonged to his lieutenants?" asked Carson, hoping to hear of goodwill in that possession.

"We saw the others who were knocked out by invisible forces and assumed it was a sign from the Most High that we must do the same thing to our captures so we could escape as the storm distracted our superiors," said the soldier.

"You know the emperor will track you down and punish you for what you have done?" asked Johannes.

"That is a risk we chose to take," said the soldier, "We would rather die than be a part of his killing machine anymore."

"Your escape will be aided," said Johannes, "We will fly

you back to our headquarters and equip all of you with suits to do battle to begin to aid your people."

"Who are you?" asked the soldier.

"We are those sent by the Most High to free His people," said Carson in a manner he felt would fit the soldier's current situation and still be faithful to the word.

The group immediately fell prostrate on the wet ground to honor the force surrounding them.

"No, don't bow before us," said Carson, "We are humble servants; worshiping us is not our purpose or goal. Besides, the ground is too soggy for such activities. All we ask is that you join our fight. Your knowledge of the army we fight should aid our movement in dealing with its strategies."

"You have our loyalty and trust," the soldier said as he and his comrades rose.

"We will have to carry you back to our headquarters blindfolded," said Johannes. "You will have a rough flight with constant stops and security problems, but we can use you."

"It would be an honor, sir," the soldier said, and with the looks on the faces of his comrades, the statement was mutual for the whole party.

The men were quickly distributed to the other Tree People and Carson, and their flights began again, with them as additional cargo, with several stops to breathe, gather strength, and nourishment, back to the tree near the lake below the mountain. For the first time, the Tree People would allow common Wasamanee into their sanctuary for special training and begin progressing toward thwarting the emperor's power over their realm.

Once they arrived at the headquarters, the soldiers were guided into the tree, still blindfolded, and kept in the dark about the actual location of the headquarters and its entrance. Once inside the secret quarters inside the tree's trunk, their blindfolds were removed. They were escorted to the lower quarters, where visual avenues that would have allowed sight outside the tree realm were not an option. The captured uniforms and swords were distributed, but not enough for all of them, so to train in the use of weapons and protective suits would require them to train in shifts. The most significant advantage was that this brought some youth into the force who would eventually have to fight the battle with the enemy.

While they trained and worked with the many Tree People, age greatly limited their strength and battle-worthiness. The soldiers added physical fitness to the training, and many old men gained strength through activities that would tenfold improve endurance and fighting ability. What age and lack of use had done to the Tree People's stamina, the physical fitness training gave back in many ways, despite the soreness that came with such efforts.

The new soldiers also gained many advantages in stealth by developing the ability to use the newly acquired uniforms. They continued to refine their hit-and-run tactics against the emperor's army, taking more of the emperor's soldiers by surprise and acquiring their protective gear as well. Often, the lieutenants were caught in the trust of their own Wasamanee soldiers to maintain their security. Notes were passed to soldiers who were known to be trustworthy to the rebellion against the emperor, and the army's strength and confidence began to weaken. The emperor saw his own numbers diminish, and the number of lieutenants also declined as more were caught alone and stripped of their uniforms and left naked to explain not only their lack of apparel but the missing soldiers who fled with his uniform and weapons.

Carson and Roxie led bold penetrations into the emperor's army with small accompaniments. Most of the adventures of the Tree People were to patrol and pick up deserters from the emperor's army who had followed the instructions given by those still in the ranks. They also sought those who wished to return home, join the growing forces, and train additional troops to battle the emperor's rule.

# CHAPTER 13

Their arrival in March had been uneventful for the park. However, as summer progressed toward its end with its heat and humidity, the fact that the area was a park became evident daily. On a cool evening in late August, Carson and Roxie agreed to go up to the end of one of the branches to observe the crowd of visitors to the park as they swam in the lake in the cooler part of the afternoon. With the heat of the dog days of August in the usual exhibition as unbearably high and humid, the chance of sunburn increased. Many brought their children to the park's swimming hole as the sun progressed toward the eclipse of the foothills to reduce sunburn.

Carson led the way to the top floor of the Tree People sanctuary. The glow and brightness of the upper chamber still amazed him as if he were on a visit again to the streets of heaven, or at least rooms and buildings that had that style of design. He opened the doorway leading to the main chamber's branch extension. There was a hallway that extended up the branch, with woodcarvings on each side that displayed many of the historical events of the people of the area. The passageway ran up the branch, too narrow as they ascended, sometimes even stairs, to reach the narrowest end of a glass-domed hall with strange wood-like designs painted on the glass above. To see the tree from a distance, no one could distinguish this tree from any other. The fact that the glass top was almost entirely transparent from the inside yet looked like any other tree branch from the outside gave Carson a unique sense of amazement at this tree's splendor.

At the end of the hall, a little hatch offered access beyond the threshold that extended almost to the end of the branch. It narrowed to the point that no one could pass that way, and it would also weaken the branch if made wide enough to continue. Carson opened the hatch, looked out, and then offered to aid Roxie in climbing onto the branch's top surface.

Roxie climbed out of the hatch and offered aid to Carson as he climbed up to join her. She had already started to scan the area for any risk of insects or small animals that might catch them unaware. She had already developed a keen sense of her surroundings and could almost feel danger, even before she could see it or hear its approach. Perhaps it was another benefit of the particular suit she was given and trained to use.

"Thanks," said Carson as he climbed out of the hatch to join her, "Let's carefully move toward the end of the branch. A nice fork in the branch at the end has a perfect lake view."

"You've been out here before," said Roxie, with a suspicious tone in her voice. "Been out here checking out the girls and the bikinis?"

"Oh, yeah. Nothing like looking at giant babes, stretched out on the beach, catching some rays," said Carson, "I would much rather see you in a bikini, but situations prevent such incredible opportunities."

"I've never worn a bikini," she said sheepishly. "I'm just a bit too modest to run around in something smaller than my underwear."

"That would not be a problem," Carson said, "You would look great in a one-piece swimsuit just as well." He looked at her as her eyes stared back into his.

He was so caught up in her silent gaze that the change in clothing went unnoticed. She was sitting next to him on the fork of the branch, and suddenly wore a lovely blue swimsuit with cute yellow flowers and green leaves.

"Well, what do you think?" she asked inquiringly. "I bought it on sale at the end of the summer last year with hopes to wear it when it gets warm enough this year."

Carson felt suddenly shy and breathless. "You…look amazing," he said as if struck for the moment with awe and intimidation. "It looks great on you."

"Thank you," she said with a smile on her face. "Care to join me in your swim trunks as well?"

"Now, that will take some thought," Carson said, changing his gaze from her to the beach in the distance. He noted that on the pier in the middle of the lake stood a guy close to his size, wearing a pair of swim trunks. Carson felt a little timid about wearing the more petite swimming pants. He thought of the black swimming pants, and almost instantly, he sat beside Roxie in black swimming shorts and wore a Red Cross blood donor's T-shirt.

"Cool, but where did the T-shirt come from?" asked Roxie with a smile, "Afraid you might get sunburn?"

"Yeah! That is it," he said immediately to avoid the feeling of his own consciousness of youthfulness. "I am light-complexioned and have always worn a T-shirt to go swimming. Tell you what. I'll lose the T-shirt if you switch to a bikini."

"Now you are pushing it, buster," Roxie said as the tone of voice changed, "Maybe you, in that T-shirt, will be just fine."

"Thanks. I was hoping you would say that," Carson said, "I'm a little modest myself, and the T-shirt has always been my mom's remedy for sunburn, and I don't remember ever swimming without it."

Roxie reached for his left hand and held it tightly, then gently raised his arm to move to where her head would rest on his thigh. She scooted to a more comfortable position.

Carson felt a little tense with her closeness, but felt more secure as she held his hand in both of hers. His eyes diverted from too much of an indulgence.

"It is so beautiful out here, don't you think?" Roxie asked, feeling more aware of their aloneness than she was familiar with in their relationship.

"We do have a marvelous, bird's-eye view of the whole lake and the beach inhabitants."

"If all we had before involved evenings like this together, this would be the life," Carson said.

"Thanks. I see there is so much about you and your perception that I find fascinating," Roxie said.

"Well, I work at it, with all of this modesty stuff we young men struggle with."

"I'm glad," she said, "I've grown to appreciate you a lot since we came here. I first thought you were shy and hopeless, but you have been so brave and daring in showing me how to be stronger, too."

Feeling embarrassed again, he looked her in the eyes to see her admiration in ways he never imagined. "I would love to say I was just showing off for you, but I would be lying," he said, being honest. "What we are doing instills confidence because it is our only hope in combination with faith. There is nothing greater than hearing that voice that says, "Do it."

"Yeah, I know what you mean. Like when we were pinned down under the leaves, chasing the emperor's soldiers that night, and we got separated. I wanted to scream out your name so I would know where you were and feel safe," she said, "That voice inside said you were just a leaf away, and a greater hand was upon you and the fellow fighters that would protect you and me."

"I know inner voices much better here than I ever have," he said, "I hear another inner voice that says I love you, Roxie." The words came out as if he were out of breath.

"I know," she said as she gazed up at him with a grin, "I've known for some time. I felt the same when you grabbed my hand as we flew across the woods before the first storm. I felt it even more when you let me lead, and you took over the watch of the storm approaching and dodging the huge drops of water coming our way. In my heart, I said I wanted you for the rest of my life. Is that wrong to think or feel?"

"Oh, no, it's the greatest thing I have ever heard someone say. We make a great team," Carson said with the same breathtaking zeal. "I hope we will make it through this and go home, knowing each other compassionately."

Looking at Roxie, he knew she wanted him to kiss her. He took his hand from her, and she leaned toward him with her eyes closed, and their lips met.

The touch was wet and wonderful. Carson's heart pounded as she reached to embrace him, and he held her shoulders.

"Hope you two are keeping a good eye on things up this way," said Johannes, catching both of them totally by surprise and causing visible redness on both faces.

"It's a good thing you came along," said Roxie.

"Yeah, we were just enjoying the setting sun and the view of the beach on the lake," said Carson with a smile.

"Sure, I could tell. Your senses were in full swing and in total control," Johannes said with a greater insight than they had hoped.

"Okay, you saved us from enjoying the outdoors too much," said Roxie, "We were definitely getting carried away."

"Sorry to lose my mission focus, but I love Roxie, and I know she loves me," said Carson, "I just feel so strongly for her."

"Carson," said Roxie with a bit of hesitation, "I love you, too, and I feel just as responsible for our endeavor as you."

"Well, we have that out of the way and out in the open," said Johannes, "You will have to keep your emotions a little under control and let that love grow between you. You want to have a lifetime to enjoy your hope of a relationship, but first, you must be victorious here and earn that opportunity to have a life together. Your control now will strengthen your leadership and confidence later when your togetherness is right and planned beyond hormones and the moment."

"We weren't that involved, were we?" asked Roxie.

"No, but your minds and hearts were heading into new territory, and thoughts lead to adventures," said Johannes, "Your love for each other must grow, and by doing so, it will mature and become something even more beautiful that will last you your whole lifetime."

"Now you are starting to sound like my mother," said Roxie, "Thanks for looking after us. It is nice to know we are well chaperoned."

"I'm not your chaperone," said Johannes, "I just understand teenagers. I have watched them for years. In this world, they mature faster than in your world, but they do know their parents' experiences through heredity. You must depend on instruction, guidance, intervention, and making your own mistakes to understand life and its temptations and challenges."

"If the people here inherit their parents' knowledge of life, why are they not smarter than they are?" asked Carson.

"The shorter life and suppression keep them at bay," Johannes said, "The world here is much more dangerous, and survival is paramount. To wipe out the dangers as your world has done would also damage the ecosystem and create more problems than we eliminate. Besides, if several generations are oppressed and ruled by the emperor, the trend is to stay in that tradition and not question it. Oppressing the prior knowledge of a people that was once free, self-governing, and faithful to their creator becomes the norm."

"If we can defeat the emperor," said Roxie, "The people will be able to think and remember what their forefathers knew and regain the relationship lost to oppression, right?"

"Yes, and with that renewed relationship comes the Tree People's return to the people's lives and the protective realm of our presence," Johannes said, "The world returns for our people to again enjoy hope, peace, and a strong relationship with the creator for all of us."

"The world we have here now is a lot like that of the Tribulation Period mentioned in our Book of Revelation, it seems," said Carson, "A people without the angelic and God's spiritual intervention must depend on individuals with certain gifts to defy the enemy and bring a message of hope to overcome the oppressors of evil nature."

"That's close," said Johannes, "The difference is there was no evacuation day before the veil of darkness that cut off the light. Our decision and compromise brought it upon our people. The Tree People's leadership, seeking peace with evil that appeared set to destroy all, allowed fear to dominate and eliminate faith."

"I hope we can be the examples of the incredible strength you need to turn things back to what you once had," said Roxie with a serious tone.

"You alone will never be enough," said Johannes, "The emperor cannot be defeated by you. His power must be broken by a greater power. You are just the vessel that brings the ray of hope. The greatest hope of our deliverer was born a month ago and is in the care of your two friends, Rhonda and Wayne."

"You know about them and how they are doing?" asked Roxie, excited and suddenly curious.

"We know of them, but not directly," said Johannes, "Rhonda was with child and bore a Son within three months of her arrival at Bald Rock Cavern."

"Let's go and get her or them," said Carson, "We can slip in there and have them out quickly."

"No. We fear that the emperor will know and move upon us so fast that all hope will be destroyed, and he will rule forever.

We even feel he knows of the newborn and awaits an opportunity to make an example of all by their capture and execution," said Johannes, "We also know who they are protected by, and their escape arrangements are already organized and well planned."

"How can she have a baby in three months?" asked Roxie as if she suddenly realized how short the birth was. "Was she pregnant before she came here?"

"No. Rhonda carried the child to term in only three months," said Johannes, "This world is different here, and you have many of the characteristics of our people, purely with your presence and modifications for survival in this environment."

"How did Rhonda handle going through a pregnancy? That must have been frightening," said Roxie, "It would terrify me. All I could think of was how my mother would handle it."

"I'm sure she crossed those lines, but hope has a way of showing the greater importance of what she was chosen to do," said Johannes, "Not only is the pregnancy only three months; the child is fully grown in only two years, as compared to your world and the two decades of growth to reach full maturity."

"Is it safe to have the baby and Rhonda under the emperor's nose?" asked Carson, "I would be scared to death he would find out and destroy all hope like that of King Herod's efforts in 3 B. C. in our Biblical history."

"Oh, he would if he knew, but there are protective measures in place that he doesn't know about or fails to recognize. If dangers get too great, we will be called upon to advance to rescue and assist. I thought you might like to know that, amid unrest across many of the Wasamanee tribes, the emperor's security has been spread far beyond his traditional modes of massing armies to attack individual outposts that may flare up. He has lost many of his lieutenants because of the spread of his forces. We have even liberated a couple of his armies from all of their leadership. Our people enjoyed seeing the forces break up and the men returning to their villages to defend their homes, rather than retreating to their headquarters to regroup and face punishment for failure. As we regain more and more of the suits that enable us to equip young recruits to go back out and apply their own training in scouting and military strategy, the enemy feels the heat. The emperor has also burned several Oak trees, hoping to destroy our headquarters, so we seem much safer than we once thought. Still, care must be taken to prevent any revelation of our hidden sanctuary's location."

"We are making progress with our training of new recruits and are not as dependent on the aging Tree People to do battle," said Carson.

"Maybe, but the training you brought to us is a serious part of equipping new recruits, and also gave many of our Tree People enough physical fitness improvement to start building their own stamina to fight. Their confidence has long established the ability to attack without your stealth protection. They work so much better by surprise and in numbers that overwhelm the leadership of many moving forces."

"Soon, we will have defeated his whole army?" asked Carson.

"No, it will only mean we must meet force on force. He defends Bald Rock Cavern as if he lives there. We hope we will one day learn where he resides and corner him and cut him off from ever harming others again."

"When will we be strong enough to march on Bald Rock?" asked Carson.

"Maybe after another year or two of tactics like we are currently using, we can move on to his main army headquarters. We must continue to achieve surgical hits that take out the emperor's leadership; he will be weakened and unable to maintain control over such a vast army. We must build our numbers by taking him and recruiting Wasamanee people to step up and take arms with us. Either way, we will need a mighty force to assume a defensive posture at the Bald Rock fortifications due to their height and limited avenues of approach. It could take years to nibble away at their forces until they are reduced to a strength we can conquer. If the emperor joined the battle, we would struggle to win under any circumstances. With your presence and confidence enhancement, I hope that will not be the case, but only time will tell."

"Sounds like we are here for a while," said Roxie.

"It sounds like a long while. It will take a miracle to break this power we struggle with," said Carson.

"A miracle indeed, yes, and you will be here to see it happen," said Johannes, "Now let me leave you two love birds alone and slip back down the tunnel before it gets dark. Do not tarry here too long, or I will come up looking for you again," he said with a smile.

"We get a few minutes together even after we were caught necking?" asked Carson.

"Necking? No, you two were being affectionate. I just want you to remember to be careful and trustworthy. Your time together alone will always have to be limited. Certain things you must save for the future when you can safely coexist and grow a lifetime of commitment," said Johannes as he headed for the hatch that led down the tunnel back into the main headquarters.

In order to take in the few moments they have, Carson looked at Roxie, who began to scoot over next to him on the tree branch. He felt her warmth as she got close to him, and he reached his arm over her shoulder to pull her closer.

"Hey, look, the swimmers are gathering their things and leaving. The cool of the sunset is coming, along with a swarm of mosquitoes, and I suppose it is time to head back to the campsites," said Roxie.

Carson continued to look at Roxie, soaking up the

closeness. "I see. Soon, they will be putting on their shirts and clothing to ward off those mosquitoes," he said without looking at them.

"You seem to be a little distracted from the view," she said, looking more toward him as he moved closer to her lips. She remained ready as if she knew he was going to kiss her again.

"I'm still amazed by the lovely swimmer next to me; that has my heart and my fascination," he said just before their lips touched again. They released after a few moments, and their breathing grew much faster as their heartbeats beat in time together.

"Let's go before we bring Johannes back up here to rescue us again," she said, climbing to her feet with a sympathetic look that told Carson she felt the same way he did but knew what was right and just.

Carson rose to his feet, gently placed his arm around her, and escorted her back to the hatch that led into the passageway down the limb. He held her hands as she stepped into the opening and gently lowered her into the tunnel. Carson jumped down, but first, the young man sat on the edge, dangled his legs, then lowered himself into the opening and dropped the last few feet to land beside her. He closed the hatch quickly. They again held each other as they walked down the passageway. Before they entered the central area, they kissed at the door and agreed not to show affection beyond that point or in front of anyone else, unless an opportunity arose that gave them some privacy to appreciate each other's love, closeness, and comfort.

# CHAPTER 14

Continuing to make hit-and-run attacks on the emperor's forces, one unit of Wasamanee people, protected by Tree People leadership and stealth, was ambushed by three of the emperor's lieutenants who utilized a new weapon system. The Tree Person had suffered severe injuries but returned to the headquarters by the lake to receive medical help and warn his allies of the new danger.

Johannes approached Roxie and Carson with the news of an interruption of their sword drills with fellow soldiers.

"Carson, Roxie, you need to come with me. I have some grave news to discuss with you," he said with an urgent tone.

"Sounds like trouble," said Carson, "Roxie, guess the fun is over for today. Let us get down to business with things that want to get complicated."

"OK, I was getting to the point with that Wasamanee recruit where he was starting to get the best of me. I need a break. I hope the news is good or at least interesting enough to spoil getting stomped by my trainee," said Roxie in relief.

"It is dire. We have a wounded warrior you need to see," said Johannes, "He's been through a lot, and it is nothing we have ever seen, done, or used."

They walked up two flights of stairs and entered the medical section of the facility. They located a room that appeared to be a wing of several hospital rooms. Entering, they found a black-haired Tree Person with casts on his arm and both legs, bandages on both hands, and stitches to his face in several places. There were also swollen areas on his face from the injuries.

"Joekeea, I'm sorry to have to disturb you again, but our special warriors need to hear your story to figure out our strategies to counter the new weapons," Johannes said to the now awake victim.

Joekeea looked their way with swollen eyes that were also very bloodshot, as if there had been scratches to the surfaces of both of them. "They have a new weapon, and it kills. My squad was hit hard, and with one flash, bodies were thrown everywhere. I saw them and became invisible, hoping to avert their attention when the three emperors' lieutenants raised black, triangular devices and aimed at me. From the end of the device came a red object at high speed. It hit the middle of my squad and bounced around a little, and then a very loud flash occurred, and my men flew in every direction. I had already moved away from them and averted much of the blast. It was still so strong that I was thrown away with a force I had never experienced. Even with this protective suit, I received broken ribs and may have injured my back severely."

"How many were injured in the attack?" asked Carson with grave concern for the struggle of this man with his injuries, trying to tell this story.

"All of my fellow warriors were killed. All of them," he said with an emotion that suggested he may want to cry over his love for the soldiers he trained and led. "I managed to move toward the attackers invisibly but was blown from the air by the force of a second flash. I landed beyond their obvious search realm. I awoke hours later in the leaves, hurting in ways I never imagined possible. Both of my legs were broken, and one of my arms. I did manage to sit up and concentrate on flying and got off the ground, enduring terrible pain. I flew over the area where I had left my squad, and all of them were dead. Parts of some of them were seen. This attack is more terrible than anything I have ever seen. We have no weapons to fight such advancements.

With these weapons, they can wipe us out in no time."

"That sounds like an explosive device, perhaps a grenade or a rocket launcher," said Roxie.

"I would think so," said Carson, "That is pretty advanced. How are we going to counter it?"

"It looks like you are going to have to go out there and take one away from them to examine and give our guys a chance to make replicas to counter their use against us. We must do it quickly, or they could wipe our moving forces out," Johannes said, "We have reports of several Wasamanee villages that were also attacked by these. The devices bounced into the caverns and exploded, not only killing many but causing cave-ins."

"Let us get started with locating them right now. We need scouts out and should not put our ground troops at risk until we can counter this new threat," said Carson.

"Our scouts are already out there, and we have them located. We need you to organize a party to confront this force head-on and try to neutralize its capability, or the battle is in their hands from this point on," said Johannes. "I suggest taking your four best-trained Wasamanee soldiers who are suited and ready. Roxie should go with you, too. I know this is risky, but by bringing her, your party can split in two directions, go invisible, and remain unseen by the emperor's lieutenants, giving you time to counter their attacks."

"I have heard that when attacked by grenades, you should leap to the ground away from where the grenade is or where it is going and fall to the ground as flat as possible or behind an obstacle. By doing so, you avoid the damage to a certain extent. Your back should be to the potential blast, since your blood vessels run along the front of your body. Injuries to your backside are less likely to cause you to bleed to death. Trying to fly would only damage your wings, making you immobile," said Carson.

"Sounds like you already know some things. Let us get

moving!" said Johannes.

They all left the hospital wing and gathered what they felt was needed for this incursion. The additional personnel were selected, briefed, and issued Tree Person gloves and masks as additional armament to lessen injuries in the event of another explosive confrontation. The masks and gloves provided additional protection and could become transparent to help the party identify who they were with during the mission. Though uncomfortable, visually, they appeared normal, except for the hair being pressed closer to the scalp.

With the final preparations, the force flew to the reported area near the Park's hotel complex. They flew up the mountain based on the latest reports indicating that the three weapon-carrying lieutenants were using the restaurant complex and its observation post to detect and monitor signals from scouts in the area. They were ready to immediately launch their attacks toward the spot where flares were sent. They arrived by flight before sunrise, used the moonlit night to gain altitude, and followed the facility's lights to reach it before any giant troop movements beyond park security could start the new day.

The group landed on the hotel roof. Three of the Lieutenants were sighted as they sat on the handrail of the observation area and used a looking glass to scan the areas below. In the distance, a small flare was sighted, and one of the lieutenants pointed in that direction to alert the other two.

They knew the situation was about to change, and their advantage of observing their activities would not be beneficial if they left the area before they could move on. "Roxie, you take the other four and stay invisible while I attract their attention and try to use this roof as a target to draw their fire. We can test their range and see what happens to the gutters when their explosives ignite. I will duck down and flee through the drain system over there," said Carson as they pointed to the drain on their left. "I just hope the "Bouncing Betties" do not bounce down it along with me."

Roxie and her comrades went invisible and flew over to the patio furniture to take up new positions to observe the three enemy personnel from their flank.

"Hey! You nimrods down there," yelled Carson, "We have you surrounded. Throw down your weapons and give up, and we will not have to hurt you."

The three lieutenants turned and acted as if they could see him on the ledge of the gutter. They raised their triangular weapons that appeared to have two handles in the back, and a point at the end was now pointed in Carson's direction. There was no hole for projectiles to fly out of, like a barrel or cannon-type launching device. All three fired at the same time. The three projectiles flew, not as bullets at high speed, but as tumbling red capsules.

Carson leaped from the gutter's edge and flew straight for the drain's opening. He was just in time to hear two of the canisters hit the side of the drainage system with an explosion on impact, while the other bounced up to the roof shingles, rolled back into the gutter, and ignited. Carson was out of the gutter drain exit before realizing his failure to go invisible as planned. He became invisible but noted that projectiles were already headed his way. With his invisible state, his maneuver veered upward to avert the explosion of the red canisters that landed in the path of the direction he had flown from a split second earlier. The force from the blast still affected his flight, but he maintained airborne status to maneuver up and over the handrails to approach from behind the lieutenant on the right flank. He drew his sword and struck with full force, with a blow to the flat side of his blade. The victim fell to the patio surface unconscious, but not before losing his weapon.

Carson could see the other two lieutenants who took aim

with their weapons toward him as if they saw where he was headed. With a glimpse at his hands, he was still invisible, but the gun he had taken was glaringly visible and a seriously moving target. He took both handles and aimed them back toward the other two when the first two projectiles flew his way. He changed directions, flying upward. The blast from their explosions still shook him as he moved out of harm's way, gaining acceleration as a byproduct. They continued to track and aimed their weapons to fire again. He thought to himself, "How do you fire this thing?" after he pulled what he thought was the trigger, only to have nothing happen.

The voice inside Carson's heart spoke in that still small voice, saying, "You have to will the device to fire and imagine the projectile to its target."

Carson again changed directions as two more projectiles were fired, as if to give a lead and intersect his direction of travel. Making a 180-degree turn, he aimed the device again, pulled the trigger, and thought to will the projectile toward one of the lieutenants. It actually fired a red canister. It traveled toward them but faded before it reached them and vanished to bring laughter from the armed lieutenants, who now fired back with actual canisters. Carson dived downward, this time to land behind some rocks below.

The lieutenants aimed at his now-hidden location in the rocks; he aimed the weapon back at them, pulled the trigger again, and willed forth another canister. It sailed upward as two canisters sailed back toward him. He faded out as Carson ducked to avoid the blast and darted to his right, attempting to dive into the subsequent rock formation to prevent the explosive impact of the approach of the projectiles. They both exploded, sending debris flying at him. Fortunately, he had stopped his flight earlier, and his wings were not deployed. The rocks and debris hurt, but not nearly as much as losing flight potential at that point. He rolled over to knock off the debris around him. He also looked back to see that the two lieutenants were no longer at their vantage point but had flown to overtake him before he could regroup.

He had left the weapon behind when his last attempt to fire it had failed to do any harm. He assumed the gun had been destroyed by the previous explosion. He stood up and prepared to fly, but with the falling rocks and pebbles, his invisible position was easy to detect, and both Lieutenants stood on the rocks above him and aimed to make one final attack on his position.

Suddenly, both weapons flashed in a heavy amount of sparks, and both became two pieces as invisible swords cut through them before another set of canisters could fly Carson's way. With their weapons suddenly exhibiting a desire to explode in their hands, they dropped them and tried to draw their own swords.

Two Wasamanee warriors suddenly appeared before them with their own swords ready. As the two lieutenants drew back their swords to charge at the warriors, two invisible blades dismembered their weapons at their hilts, and that rendered both of them weaponless except for a dagger hidden at their sides. Roxie appeared in front of them. The two other warriors, who had just disarmed the two lieutenants, appeared with their blades pointed at point-blank range at the small of the backs of the now weaponless prisoners. They were immediately searched, disrobed, and left with their third partner, who was still unconscious, naked, and defenseless.

I hope your emperor sends someone looking for you soon. It gets cold here when you are not properly dressed. We will take what is left of your weapons back to study and make duplicates. Tell your captain thanks for this generous donation of such new technology to fight this war.

Carson quickly thanked his comrades for their amazing

arrival to squelch the situation in the nick of time. They took what was left of the weapons and the three captured uniforms and flew back toward headquarters. Their second thoughts about abandoning the three former lieutenants there to tell the enemy about the potential of the weapons suddenly stopped them. Inclinations suggested they needed to be held as prisoners of war. They turned around to recapture the naked lieutenants, only to gain the ability to see the tragic situation before they could intervene and retrieve them. Two sparrows were busy with the naked lieutenants in preparation for their morning meal.

All three weapons were so severely damaged that there was no way to duplicate or repair them. The guns' firepower was incredible. Carson eventually realized that the red canisters were more like sticks of dynamite instead of military weapons. He was still puzzled about why his efforts to send projectiles faded and failed to explode. Perhaps Carson was unable to imagine the device utilizing a lit fuse with explosive potential. Maybe he did not want to blow up his enemy as much as they did him. His auditory perception was limited for a few days, with the ringing in his ears that he feared would never go away.

Johannes worried that more of those weapons would be developed and used. Later, it was assumed they were prototypes, and since no reports of their successful use were made, the emperor advanced no further development based on what was observed. The three abandoned, disrobed Lieutenants were greatly challenged by several sparrows shortly after Carson and company took flight. Possibly, the further developments of weapons of that potential were considered too significant a contribution to the resistance when captured, and that was the end of their use in combat.

The challenges continued for the forces. As the emperor's forces decreased, his lieutenants became more protective of each other. The armies sent forth were more destructive and oppressive, intending to let the word out that all would be subjected to the emperor's wrath for the scattered rebellions. Roxie and Carson became less mobile because of the increased chances of ambushes that could be overwhelmed by the emperor's men in search of the cause of their problems. Soon, armies of their own carried out many missions and were headquartered and trained in friendly Wasamanee villages eager to join the struggle to free their communities from the attacks and bloodshed brought by the random visits of the emperor's armies.

Carson and Roxie's presence gave the Tree People special suits and powers. Still, with the growth of their own force with new recruits and rescued suits from incapacitated lieutenants, they felt equal, if not superior, to the troops they challenged. Hit-and-run missions became more and more successful. Observation positions were developed in most of the region, and constant awareness of the emperor's armies kept his movements and attacks in disarray and confusion. It had reached the point through winter that the enemy's armies remained isolated in the Bald Rock Caverns with no ventures forth. Spring came early, and activity increased. Some forces had shifted toward Bald Rock Cavern throughout the winter months when ice, rain, and snow were less restrictive. With the knowledge that the enemy was massed at one location, self-assurance led them to believe they could be more easily controlled and restricted with large counterforces that waited near their exits from the Bald Rock stronghold, their last bastion of strength.

---

One afternoon in mid-summer, after a challenging workout with several warriors, Carson and Roxie stole a few moments alone at the top of the stairs. Their visibility of the central area was much brighter, and the temptation of a couch in the lobby offered a moment of relaxation. They shared a couch, side-by-side. The two sat close together, relaxed with the intent to enjoy the precious moments alone.

Roxie leaned into Carson's shoulder, and he held her with his arm around her and held her right upper arm with his right hand. "Do you realize we have been here for a year?" she asked suddenly, "This is the second summer that has passed, and the giant leaves will be turning again soon.

"I have observed my watch closely, and time has ticked away. Sometimes, it is hard to keep up with the month since we are the only ones who know about months here. You know, we missed the football, basketball, and baseball seasons, too. Our classmates who graduated last spring are probably married, going to college, or hitting life head-on. I wonder how our parents are doing?" he said.

"I'm curious about whether they assumed we died in the blaze or declared us missing because no bodies were found," said Roxie, staring off into the distance, resting comfortably on Carson's shoulder. "You would miss football."

"Yeah, but I miss my mother more. My mother must be climbing the walls, or maybe coming close to getting over the loss. It takes a year or two of grief before you start making some kind of headway in dealing with life and picking up the pieces, I have heard," Carson said.

"I think our never being found makes them think we are still alive somewhere. Who knows? We may be on some milk carton somewhere," she said. "I imagine they are all stressed out, looking everywhere for us. Do you suppose two boys and two girls missing might correlate?"

"Do you think we will go back in time to the very point of our rescue, or maybe earlier?" asked Carson, "Could you imagine our just showing up after missing for over a year and trying to explain why we were gone so long and where?"

"I'm sure we would return to before the explosion and keep us from entering the building," she said, "That would be the least we could ask."

"I would think you two would want to go back and stop the fuel truck from reaching the building in the first place," said a voice that caught both of them by surprise. Before them appeared the angel, Gabriel, as sharp-looking as he appeared at their briefing before their arrival.

"Wow, you caught me by surprise," said Roxie as she suddenly rose from her comfortable position, embarrassed by the moment. "How long have you been there?"

"I have been here watching since you arrived from the staircase," said Gabriel, "You two make a lovely couple. I visit often just to look in on you, and sometimes I speak to you in that small voice you hear."

"You said you would visit us often," said Carson, "I figured you would come by for meetings and stuff."

"Oh, I have had a few meetings. I meet regularly with Johannes; he speaks highly of you and your work, training new warriors for battle. My halo, if I had one, goes off to you."

"Well, Gabe, did you come by to tell us how and when we are going to go back home and rejoin the world we left behind?" asked Carson with hope of some news.

"Your parents are fine. I have even visited them to rest their hearts," said Gabriel with his words.

"When do we go home?" asked Roxie.

"You will go home soon, but not real soon. We have some serious trouble developing involving Rhonda, Wayne, and Rhonda's Son.

They have been discovered and have had to flee their hiding place," said Gabriel, "They are not in grave danger yet, but to prevent a serious search for them, you must draw attention with your armies by marching toward Bald Rock."

"How are they, and will we be able to rescue them?" asked Roxie excitedly. "I would so love to see Rhonda."

"I know you would, but you two are the warriors and fine warriors you have become," Gabriel said, "It has come when your leadership and cunning will make the difference in this struggle."

"How soon do we need to deploy our forces, and where?" asked Carson.

"Move everything you have toward Bald Rock and wait without going in. Your army, in total force, is still not as huge as the emperor's stronghold. His forces, being in a defensive posture, also have the advantage. To get to Bald Rock, it is all uphill. Meeting an enemy rested at the top would be a disaster in the making. You must draw his forces out and maneuver to control and use your strengths. You must deal with his height advantage and his archers. Making shields to block the arrows will protect your men from heavy losses. The mountain's steepness will also add advantages to his archers' reach and surprise. You must double your Wasamanee soldiers' armor at the shoulder and chest. While you prepare, start some forces moving on the front toward the cavern to give them something to think about, but not close enough for their arrows to be accurate. The further your forces can be seen moving down the mountain, the more air currents will affect those falling arrows."

"We'll get things rolling as soon as we are finished here," Carson said, climbing to his feet. "Will we be able to find Rhonda and Wayne and offer them our army's protection?"

"No, they have escaped to the other side of the mountain and will try to buy time and find refuge there until your forces can access the Cavern and break the morale of the emperor's remaining army."

"Where will they go, or have they already gone there?" asked Roxie.

"They have traveled a reasonable distance at this point.

The disadvantage on that side of the mountain is that your

movement has not crested the top to reach the people that live there and work their domains," said Gabriel.

"Could you send word to them that we know and are trying to pull danger off of them?" asked Roxie.

"I will speak some comfort to their hearts, but their lives are in serious danger," said Gabriel, "Now, I must be going, and you have a lot of work to do, and it may mean very little sleep for a few days and a lot of flying. Use your messengers when you can. You cannot be everywhere." Instantly, he vanished before their eyes.

They immediately rushed from the room to find Johannes and organize forces to prepare for a mass movement to Bald Rock. Soon, messengers were on the way toward many posts to advise on armor preparations and forced movements of troops advancing on the emperor's central and perhaps his final line of defense. They had to send an army toward their enemy before it was strong enough to conquer the larger adversary, to ward off or deplete forces in search of three people. A lot would need to be invested in a massive diversion for the safety of those three.

# CHAPTER 15

Seph, Wayne, Rhonda, and Joshua followed the flat rocks out of the opening on the Northeastern side of Cheaha Mountain. By any means, the gap they exited looked like another mighty cave opening, when it was a crack in a rock extension, among many that outlined the side of the mountain.

"The trees here look small and beat up compared to the trees located where we were originally captured," said Wayne, "Why are they so small here?"

"They have always been small in this area," said Seph, "This is the highest mountain in Alabama, and we are near the top."

"I figure the wind is pretty rough, as it is forced over the top and, therefore, causes severe wear on the trees that protrude here with no fellow tree protection that you find in the valleys and glens," said Rhonda.

"That does sound pretty logical," said Wayne, "Does that mean we may have trouble finding Herdsmen up this high?"

"No, they are here," said Seph, "The plants are more weather-worn but smaller and present an opportune place for the Herdsmen and ants to exploit new growth in herding aphids for their milk products."

"Now I could totally indulge in an ice-cold glass of milk," Wayne said, "How about you, Joshua?"

"I doubt you will find the kind of milk you are thinking of," said Joshua, "The aphid milk is red and more of a sweet juice. It is not milked; it is deposited by the aphids. Besides, most of what you call milking is fermented for alcoholic use instead of a cool glass to drink."

To his surprise, Seph looked at Joshua as if a twelve-year-old could not know that much but said nothing. Changing the subject, he said, "I sure hope we find the aphid Herdsmen first before we are found by the ants that own the aphids."

"Do you think they would treat us differently from the aphid Herdsmen?" asked Wayne.

"No, they would figure we were an additional meal of protein to enjoy in their march to wherever they were going at the time," said Seph, "That is what I figure, but I don't get out often. Cave life is so much safer with its population.

"The sun is going down pretty fast, and I don't see a moon tonight," said Joshua, "I think that tree over there with the woodpecker holes would offer us a good place out of the wind this evening."

They all looked at each other with amazement at the child's knowledge of the world around them that He had never seen.

"That old, dying tree sounds like a great place to spend the night," said Rhonda, "I'm a bit tired, anyway. This heat is tough after we've spent so long in the cavern with all of the coolness and moisture around."

"Joshua, you have picked a great spot, and if you look down a little further, you can see several plants growing with wrinkled leaves," added Seph, "The woodpecker holes can give us the vantage point of checking out the area in the morning to plan a bypass around any ant movements and go directly to any Herdsmen there."

Soon, they were all climbing the tree bark, which offered much better handholds than a rock climb. The rough surface had so many handholds and places to gain leverage to pull yourself up the side of the tree. The woodpecker holes and their climb presented a greater challenge to them, which proved more of a struggle than anticipated, with so much rotten bark to grab while climbing. With constant adjustments to the bark and its best access point, they finally found a series of woodpecker holes running side by side. Two of the holes were selected based on their depth into the tree. Rhonda and Joshua chose to sleep in one, and Wayne and Seph would have to fend for themselves in the next hole. Rhonda wished for privacy to use some of the water she had hauled along in her bags, which were so heavy from all the moisture they had gained while swimming up through the tunnels. That weight might have been the reason for so much fatigue now, but to have a few things along would make life somewhat bearable in the wilderness of the cold evening of the mountainside and its winds.

Rhonda helped Joshua to sponge-bathe, too. They both felt much better after a cool-down with the small amount of water available for such activities, with an effort to avoid cutting too deeply into their water supply for future hydration. The sunset in the West, and the temperature either started to drop rapidly, or their bath had lowered their temperatures excessively. Soon, Joshua and Rhonda were snuggled close together, with Rhonda holding her son close to him to keep him warm and safe, as any mother would do when alone in the dark in a small hole in a tree in the middle of a vast national forest. She had never visited here before, but now had grown to appreciate its beauty and amazement.

The night was cold and very chilly by morning, and haunting with the wind whistling through their sanctuary in the tree opening. Sunrise was slow, with daylight and long shadows appearing much earlier than the actual sunrise. They peered out from their woodpecker hole. They spied several ant trails in steady marches. Some slowed in traffic at points where they could soak up some energy from the rising sun's brightness shining through the trees. Their probable plant destinies were also visible in the distance. The four plotted a course that would take them through several thick areas of brush, but avoided the soon-to-be busy ant paths that they feared would bring a sudden charge of the creatures seeking a quick meal for their queen. The visible ants were much smaller than the carpenter ants of their past experiences. Their numbers and speed made up for their size, but they could still be intimidated by their pinchers, stingers, and aggressive numbers. They were of the type known as sugar ants. Black and smaller, they were exceptionally good at ascending up the sides of bushes and perhaps even moving aphids around from old leaf growth to new leaf growth to allow the ant cows to suck fluids from the new leaves that provided soft surfaces for punctures and feasts by the aphids.

The activities of the ants were sluggish early in the morning, with the chill still in the air. Cold-blooded creatures struggle with that issue in the mornings and cold snaps. But let the sun warm them, and they have excellent speed and agility. Their movements were still active, but much slower than their movements toward their many food sources. The visibility of several short plants in the distance indicated trends among them and seemed to be ant activity. Seph clarified that the early morning harvest of the honeydew from the aphids was a common characteristic of the Herdsmen. They were warm-blooded and could move to the plants in the cold morning, way ahead of the ants, gaining an advantage by hiding and waiting for them.

"We need to move out toward the plants over there with the shriveled leaves if we want to beat the ants," said Seph, pointing toward the undergrowth below, which had new growth and leaves that were wrinkled and curled at the ends. "We need to be there before the morning scrapes are completed."

"Scrapes?" asked Wayne as he started his climb down the bark of the tree from their woodpecker holes, sleeping quarters from the night before. They scrape the aphids to milk them of their honeydew?"

"No, they scrape the excrement left behind by the aphids," said Seph, who also started his descent down the steep bark of the tree.

"Ew! Gross! The honeydew that is so popular for making alcohol is actually aphid poop?"

"Yes, actually, of a sort," said Seph, "The food is processed by the aphid, and the chemical change makes the sweet byproduct, once the nutrients the aphid needs are removed."

"Give me a pooper scooper, but don't expect me to eat any of it," said Rhonda, "I've eaten enough bugs already to last a lifetime and to stoop low enough to start consuming insect droppings; no way."

"Ah, Rhonda, you're such a stick in the mud, but I like you anyway," Wayne said, "You make being here so much fun."

"If I were not focusing on getting Joshua down this tree right now, I'd try to help you down much faster, Wayne," she said with a smirk toward Wayne.

"I'm fine, Mom," said Joshua with a smile, "If you want to help Wayne down the tree, I'll be safe alone."

"Joshua, don't encourage her; she might take you up on it," said Wayne as he tried to humor back a response. "Once we get to the Herdsmen, we may find that our hunger will grow to the point that anything will be better than starving."

Their continuation down the tree was uneventful, and all made the climb carefully and safely. They quickly scurried toward the closest shrub they had identified earlier in hopes of reaching it before the ants and the Herdsmen who visited the tree for the morning harvest. They arrived at the bush, or what appeared to be a green tree with no natural bark, as seen on most trees. With a close-up visual of the plant, it was smaller than several others in the distance, and only a couple of small patches of aphids could be identified more in their approach than right under the bush.

"There have been no Herdsmen in this bush. The herd of aphids has only just started," said Seph.

"How do you figure?" asked Wayne.

"There are no climbing spikes on the side of the stem or trunk," said Seph, "They have to have some means of getting up the tree, and the smooth stem does not offer good climbing abilities on this particular plant. Let's look at that bush down that way."

"Sure, but I see trails to and from this bush," Wayne said, "Something has been by to visit this bush."

"The trails are probably made by heavy ant traffic," said Seph, "Let's get moving before we prove that probability."

They moved further down the hill toward the next plant. Soon, they were under a much larger bush, and to their pleasure, the plant's stem or trunk had wooden spikes driven into the sides, randomly placed to allow someone to climb. With a gaze up the bush into the foliage, leaf movements were noticed. Voices could be heard faintly, also. They waited for several minutes, with no one indicating a desire to climb up the bush and greet the Herdsmen by surprise. Soon, a fat red man climbed down through the lower foliage but stopped after he visually swept the ground below and spied out their presence from his higher vantage point.

"Who goes there, and are you friend or foe?" asked the Herdsman as he continued to hold to the top branch, he had just climbed out of with his dangling scrapper, bucket, and a small brush that decorated his belt.

"We are friends seeking assistance," said Seph with a pleasant voice that would hardly scare anyone.

"Joe Bob, we got company," said the Herdsman back up the plant to his friends.

Another voice came from up in the foliage, "Do they have any gold, Travis?"

"Don't know, but hurry down, and let's find out," said the Herdsman, who had to be Travis. He carefully used the spikes and reached the ground quickly.

"Mighty fine scrapes this morning," said Seph as he gazed into the bucket of red jelly substance that filled about two-thirds of the swinging bucket.

"Yeah, thanks," Travis said, "We have done well with this tree, but the aphids are overpopulating the plant and are starting to grow into winged critters. They will be flying to another tree when they are grown."

"That future bush over there will probably be your next destination. There are no spikes there, and aphids have started," said Rhonda.

"That bush won't last long enough for the work it takes to drive all of the spikes. Chances are, the spikes would kill it. Give it about thirty days and a couple of good rains, and we will go to work there," said the Herdsman, "You, cave people?"

"Yes, we are cave people, and we are tired of being cooped up and missing all the warm weather," said Seph.

"You're not here for business?" asked Travis.

"We might do some business, but not over honeydew products," said Seph, "We are looking for food and temporary shelter as well. We are on an adventure, looking for special herbs that grow this time of year for medical purposes."

"Tell me what plants you look for, and I'll help you find them for a small fee," said Travis with sudden bright eyes as if this interested him very much.

"Now, if I tell you which plants, we will have to buy them from you, too, like we do the honeydew byproducts."

"We are always ready to help, and making a profit is part of it, Sir," said Travis, "We all have to make a living. Aphids don't produce gold, but what they make brings it. With gold, we buy more spikes to climb more bushes and gather more honeydew to sell for more gold. It's a vicious cycle, but we survive."

Wayne continued to watch the conversation and allowed Seph to dominate because he knew the people they were dealing with and how to talk to them in a manner that seemed non-threatening.

"It's unusual to see people travel with their family," said Travis.

"Usually, but this time of year, the whole family out to see the sights is a fine adventure and educational."

"Are you sure you are not running from someone?" Travis asked.

"Oh, yeah! We are running from the emperor," said Seph as if to joke right along, "We found his hideout, and he does not want us to tell anyone."

"Now that information would be worth a lot of gold," said Travis, glancing up at a couple of the other Herdsmen who now descended the stem. "We need to keep you, people, around. You seem to know something."

The first of the two stepped off the spikes, turned to the group, and said, "I'm Joe Bob, and that coming down there is Corky. I think you've met Travis."

"Since we are introducing ourselves, I'm Seph, and this is my wife, Rhonda, my son Joshua, and our servant, Wayne. We are glad to meet you and hope you can be of some help," said Seph, and reached to bump fists together in a type of greeting that was a tradition among these people. They looked at Wayne and Rhonda, then touched them with the same fist.

"You brought a pretty wife. Is she for trade?" said Corky with a grin that revealed a few missing teeth and a good bit of decay.

"She's a keeper, so don't get your hopes up," said Seph.

"You must have money to get a young thing like that," said Joe Bob, "What can we do for you before the ants arrive and decide we are their next meal?"

"I do have money, so your help will be rewarded," said Seph, "Now, if you would, let's move to a safer place to parley."

"Walk this way," said Joe Bob as he took the bucket from his belt to carry in his hand instead of weighing heavily and being unbalanced on his belt.

They moved quickly down a well-trodden path. Soon, they came to an old, half-crushed tin can. The trail led right up to the opening at the other end. Joe Bob gestured for them to enter, and they proceeded into the tin house and found a gathering of females and children waiting upon their fathers' return. The buckets were handed to the women, who moved to the area that appeared to be the kitchen and began making a rich liquid from the contents of the buckets.

"I hope you will join us for breakfast; the old lady will have it ready in a few minutes. " It will be made from the morning scrapings, and the rest will be blister bagged for aging and fermenting," said Joe Bob. "We run a small business, but it keeps us fed." What brings you here?"

"We are searching for rare herbs that are said to grow among the ferns in these parts. I want to teach my family how to find them for future generations," said Seph, If my wife knows, all her children will be born with that knowledge, so you see how significant this investment and search is."

"You have a smart way about yourself," said Joe Bob. "I would never bring the wife out like that, but you have people who are strange."

"We do have our customs," said Wayne, who had been relatively silent through most conversations until now.

"The youth speak, also," said Joe Bob, "It sounds like he knows a good bit, too, and rightly from his parents."

"He is my servant, and his parents were very bright," said Rhonda as she indicated she wanted to be in on the conversation.

"You are wealthy to have servants," said Joe Bob, "Why do you not just send out your servants to gather your desired herbs?"

"Because I, and I alone, know where they are to be found, and it will take several to bring back a quantity of the findings. The herb is used to add flavor to our foods and will soon be in great demand among my people, and making agreements with you for safe passage seems in order," said Seph.

"Perhaps we could trade some of our drinks for samples of what this herb will do to food to make it better," said Joe Bob.

"Soon, we will have lizards passing through here hauling great quantities, and we will be glad to trade portions for your Honeydew drinks to help us relax after the long journeys," said Seph, as he appeared to try to gain their confidence.

The wife came to them with warm wooden bowls and distributed them to the hungry travelers. In observation, Rhonda concluded that a spoon was unnecessary, and the Herdsmen quickly began to sip the concoction like coffee. She sipped hers to find it was sweet, like a blend between tea and sour appleKool-Aid. She could tell by its richness why the Herdsmen's teeth were well decayed. Perhaps a trade of food items would improve your people's diets. She hoped that Seph would live up to his promises and bring better food to these people who seemed to live in poverty.

As she sipped her warm drink, she could see around the large tin can home; the provisions were minimal. Much was made of twisted straws, which had the look of a primitive wicker design. The beds were scattered across the large area with woven walls that could not be seen, offering some privacy. The three men seemed to have many children with their five wives who were present. She pondered if perhaps a couple of the women were widows who lost their spouses in ant confrontations in the past. Many children indicated that they were born about every three or four months. Her observation of the three concluded that the environment, the consumption of their own brew, and the limited diet took a toll on their health and aged them quickly.

Seph and two men left through the day's heat and returned with cuttings from a fern bush that appeared to be the curly portion of the new growth or perhaps the spore-producing area from the plant. A piece was cut for each to carry between the four: Wayne, Seph, Joe Bob, and Corky.

Looking around, Rhonda noticed that Travis was not there. It was assumed he was about the other chores; it did not become apparent that he had left them to see someone else until he arrived late that evening and was not equipped, as the four men were with further findings of Aphid harvesting. It was a while before Wayne and Seph could explain their efforts on the bushes to Rhonda. They spoke of a walk out into the foliage to cut holes in the leaves, and how they hung through the holes and used the long-handled scraper to reach red piles of excrement that the aphids scattered on the bottom surfaces of the plants. Some of the honeydew even had molds that started to grow on them, but Joe Bob said to bring them, too, and they would eat them for supper. The moldy honeydew had protein benefits, making it a unique flavor for meals. They found that out to be true the hard way.

Seph did know things about herbs, and the early and late harvests of honeydew gave plenty of time, even through the heat of the day, to skip a siesta and gather fern sprouts and vegetables to bring back to the small clan's table. Soon, he taught them how to dry the plant collections in the sun for storage and use when the cold months arrived. Dry goods were quickly stored in several hollow tree limbs, free from moisture and lasting through the winter. Plus, they still use raw plants for meals. He continued to talk a lot about their departure to get the lizards for transportation as soon as the quantity was substantial enough to justify and cover the expense of the lizards' employment.

# CHAPTER 16

A couple of months passed as the four fugitives worked in aid of the Herdsmen and taught them the use of many plants in the area to improve their food quality and help their children grow up healthy. With all the contributions given, it would seem to mean something that would prevent the day the lizards arrived. The long, scaly creatures were not there to transport vegetables back to the cavern. They were there, loaded with soldiers arriving even before the morning harvest of the honeydew. The ten lizards carried twenty soldiers apiece, providing two legions of men. They arrived early, but had arrived the evening before because the lizards did not travel well at night or in the cool of the morning. They advanced on the little can hut without warning, surrounded the place, stepped in with drawn swords, and captured Seph, Joshua, Wayne, and Rhonda. Resistance was futile. The surprise was too overwhelming. With a look around to see the reaction of the Herdsmen, the whole tin hut had been abandoned during the night. They were set up to be captured, and perhaps for a fee. They were all disarmed, tied, and carried to the lizards.

After a time delay that Rhonda figured was related to the cold nature of the lizard transportation, they were each placed in front of an individual lizard. She knew she would not have any further contact with Joshua or the others until nightfall. She recalled that Seph had told her lizards were telepathic and could communicate through thought patterns, so she decided to imagine a conversation with the lizard she was assigned as transportation.

*"Hey, nice lizard, can you hear me?"* she thought in a manner directed toward the lizard.

*"Yeah, I hear you, little lady,"* the voice said to her inside her mind beyond her ears. *"I would not speak to you, but you are a prisoner of theirs, too."*

*"It sure looks that way,"* Rhonda thought back, *"Are you captive, as well?"*

*"Yes and no. The oppressors have my eggs, which were buried to hatch in freedom next spring, but they caught me burying them, and they hold them to get me to work harder and longer for them. I don't want them to be their steaks for dinner or slaves either."*

*"Where are they taking us?"* she thought toward the lizard to change the subject.

The voice came back as if she was thinking the words in her mind, yet had no control: *"You are being carried back to Bald Rock Cavern to meet with the emperor himself,"* said the voice in Rhonda's head. *"I'm sorry, dear. No one has ever returned alive from meeting the emperor at his quarters."*

*"Where is his abode?"* asked Rhonda.

*"All I know is that it is somewhere high in the cavern because captives who meet with him for torture and death are flown to that location,"* said the lizard's voice in her mind. *"It is too dark in the cavern to see enough to know where. When I am in the cavern, I am terribly weak because of the cold. My reward for work is to be taken out and sunned. If I can't work, they keep me in the cold. They have no understanding that I must be in the sun to be able to work my best."*

*"What do they use you for?"* asked Rhonda in her thoughts again.

*"They use me for moving heavy objects and supplies through the cold, slimy cave,"* the voice said. *"When I am in the cave, that is."*

*"They use you outside the cave, too?"* asked Rhonda.

*"Yes, I am part of a large force of lizards, utilized for quick movement of soldiers for battle,"* said the voice, *"The emperor is*

*massing a large army to move at high speed by lizards and has drawn the rebellious forces to Bald Rock for a great battle, but little do they know, the main force will go forth and destroy all of the homes of the rebellious forces to lower their morale with word that their families are dead."*

*"Is there a way we can get word to them?"* asked Rhonda.

*"No, by the time we get there, I will join them, and the movement will begin,"* said the lizard's voice, *"The emperor's army has tunneled through a new exit from the cavern and will move his forces by lizard out of it totally undetected by the rebellion's leadership and defenses."*

"We've *got to do something,"* said Rhonda.

*"I'll tell them when I get there, but unfortunately, I'll have the invading Emperor's army on my back, and there will be no time to regroup and defend the rebellion."*

*"This is terrible,"* said Rhonda, *"I have friends out there, and chances are they are leading this rebellion."*

*"I'm sorry. Even if the rebels are a part of this uprising that is poised to attack the old entrance at Bald Rock, the avenue is steep and extremely well defended with the emperor's best archers and heavy quantities of arrows to shoot at them for weeks."*

*"Can any of the other lizards hear what we are saying and tell my other companions and my Son?"* she asked in hopes of some avenue of comfort in this desperate worry.

*"The other lizards can only hear what I tell them, and they can only speak to the other prisoners if they speak first, as you have,"* said the lizard.

Rhonda looked at the other lizards carrying Seph, Wayne, and Joshua. Her hands were tied, so she could only mouth her words, use head motions, and hope they would understand. Wayne was confused and had no clue, but Seph knew and smiled back. So did Joshua. *"Do any of the lizards speak to the soldiers?"* she asked.

*"No way! Those brutes bored holes in the scales on our backs to*

*mount their saddles and hooks to carry their supplies. We hate them, and they gave up communicating effectively with us long ago. All we recognize from them is the one-word commands they use, and only because they torture us if we fail to comply. They have special hooks mounted that cut deep into our scales and reach into our flesh, and stubbornness on our parts can bring the use of those embedded hooks to drag us around and cause terrible pain,"* the voice said.

*"Is there any way the lizard people could suddenly join us in the rebellion, catching the emperor's soldiers off guard and throwing the movement of forces completely out of their plan?"* asked Rhonda with great hope.

*"Perhaps you may have a great idea there, but if the rebellion fails, we all will die,"* said the voice.

*"Think of your eggs and eventually your children. Can you see them living as free lizards and not slaves to this mad emperor who holds this terrible grip?"* she asked.

*"I will give this some thought. Many of us fear pain so much that it will be hard to accomplish, but I will think and hope this idea, passed among my fellow lizards, will plant the idea of hope in them,"* he said, *"If we were to carry the soldiers far out over the steep edge of the mountain and then all, in unison, throw the soldiers in one sudden rage, we might get lucky.*

*Dear you, you inspire me. I hope we all live to see you alive after this and be able to thank you if it works."*

*"Don't praise me; praise the God of the Most High, who sent me. If we win, it is because it won't happen without His help,"* said Rhonda.

*"You are from the God of the Most High?"* said the voice, *"You four are the Promised Ones we have waited many years to see. This is the blessed appearance. We must do what you wish because you are the blessed hope. Maybe we should throw the soldiers now and free you to escape before we even load up for the forced march back to the cavern."*

Rhonda pondered this idea and quickly thought of their

escape with the four in command and six additional lizards that would follow and defend them. In her heart, another voice spoke, *"Rhonda, you could do this, but your mission would fail. You must be carried before the emperor in his domain and face him. That is this world's only hope of victory."*

*"You must carry us back to the cavern to meet the emperor. It is part of our plan,"* said Rhonda as the idea made her heart race.

*"You are a brave young woman. Death is waiting for you. Are you sure?"* asked the voice of the lizard.

*"I'm sure, dead sure,"* she said, *"Defeat the emperor, and the war will be over other than some minor clean-up activities."*

*"How can four people, tied up with ropes, defeat the mightiest warrior that ever lived?"* asked the voice.

*"I don't know, but my Child knows. He is our greatest hope,"* said Rhonda.

*"How can one of you be the Blessed Hope and still be the four Promised Ones?"* asked the voice.

*"Well, two of us are of the Promised Four. One is the former prime minister of the cavern, and the Child is the Blessed One,"* said Rhonda.

*"Where, then, are the other two?"* asked the lizard's voice in her head.

*"They are the warriors that march on Bald Rock Cavern to rescue us or take on the emperor in his final battle,"* said Rhonda.

*"Then the lizards must carry the forces off to attack the undefended, while your forces take on only the archers. If they can get past them, and that is a big if, they will have the run of the whole cavern because the rest of the force is off to attack their homes using lizard transports,"* said the voice in her head.

*"Sounds like I will be going home soon; either way, it goes,"* Rhonda said.

*"How can you be going home by going to the emperor?"* asked the lizard's voice.

*"It's a long story, but the challenge seems to still be ahead of us,"* said Rhonda, *"Hey, looks like they are motioning for you to move out. Apparently, they think you have sunned enough, and it is time to get rolling."*

*"So be it; I'm not going to move until they make me,"* said the lizard's voice, *"Don't want to draw attention by being different now."*

Soon, the ten lizards, with ten warriors mounted on each and four additional people tied at the front of four lizards, began their movement across the valley. The train of transports began with three advanced lizards, then the four that carried the captives, and finally the rear guard, as if they anticipated an ambush intended to rescue the prisoners.

The warriors were ready with their bows and arrows, watching the flanks as they traveled in spurts across the terrain.

Soon, the sun's heat energized the lizards for fast spurts across open terrain to bunch up at cover points.

Traveling along the mountain's side was difficult, always with the fear of a fall. Still, the lizards were well equipped for the rocks and scooted across many areas with little trouble, other than the cargo of soldiers who leaned to one side in their saddles as they traveled sideways. Soon, the surface leveled off. In the distance, a great, long-running, red bridge could be seen, and many giants walked back and forth on it.

Several kids stopped and pointed at the lizards as they trailed up the hill and under the massive bridge. A couple of boys seemed to have mouthed the idea of an effort to run and catch one of the lizards, but with the warm air and heat of the day, the lizards were way out of sight before they could find a set of stairs that let them come down to the ground level.

As they ran along the other side of the giant bridge for what seemed like a couple of hours, the lizards reached the end of the mountain and its rock formation that extended from it. Rhonda thought perhaps it was the Bald Rock formation that she had seen the day she was taken prisoner and carried to the slave auction. She had hardly noticed the redwood extension that gave the giants a vantage point for observation on top of the rock formation. Rhonda held on as the ten lizards crested the rock mass and, before many pointing parents and children, started down the steep rock protrusion to descend toward the crack that led into the cavern opening. She looked desperately for rebel forces; her vision was not able to pick out much in the distance, so she knew her hope of rescue was about to fade quickly. Rhonda uttered a long scream as the lizard reached the entrance and turned inward. She looked to see the edge of the rock covered with many, many archers, bows ready to await any advancement of a rescue attempt.

With the movement into the passageway and the descent into the darkness, she felt the cold, damp air hit her face. In a way, the cold felt good, but a chill set in quickly. The lizard force moved quickly into the cave and descended toward the lake bottom.

When they reached the shoreline, they turned right and moved toward the military fortress on the other side of the lake. About halfway around the lake, the lizards stopped; a group of lieutenants walked up, had the prisoners released, and lowered them to the ground. The lizards quickly scurried off into the distance. Rhonda could see in the distance a mass of many lizards, all boarded by warriors dressed for battle. As soon as the ten lizards reached them, they began to progress in large quantities through a dark hole that appeared more of a log jam with the forward lizards, which still suffered from the cold nature of the cave's limit on their energy levels.

Her gaze was suddenly interrupted by two higher authority lieutenants who flew to the bank to join them. She had hardly noticed Seph, Joshua, and Wayne, even though she had her arm around Joshua as soon as they were on the ground; if she reached around as far as you could with her hands tied behind her, it was called doing so. At least she could touch Him as she gazed into the distance at the massed lizard army, which marched to war on the undefended homes of the military rebel force below Bald Rock with faint hopes to rescue her before it was too late.

One of the two ranking warriors spoke to the others by saying, "Take the old man and throw him into the city jail. He must be made an example for his efforts to not only harbor the enemies of the emperor but also keep them right under our noses and then flee with them when we come to capture them. He will be executed in the morning. He will be tied to a post and roasted over an open fire, slowly dying in pain tomorrow, to warn all who dare follow him of their futures if they fail to remain loyal to the emperor.

Seph was dragged away without a word. His quiet nature made chill bumps climb Rhonda's back as she thought about what would come next. She feared the worst but still wondered where the emperor was and thought perhaps he was underwater in a submarine or something that kept him so well hidden from the eyes of all who looked for him day and night in these dark caverns. Suddenly, there was a slight rumble, and the two leaders looked up. Deep in the darkness, a wave of distortion appeared in a large circle. Rhonda felt the rough arms of the eldest warrior leader grab her and grip her hard. She also felt his lurch forward and reach into the air. She looked back to see the same thing happen to Wayne and Joshua. All three were being flown toward the dark spot with the quiver of night's looks.

Passing through the dark veil, they entered a well-lit, very luxurious room. There were marble walls, and the floor was covered with the finest wool tapestries. There were mirrors on the walls and curtains pulled to reveal mirrors, paintings, and wood carvings. All three were placed in the middle of the room to await their fate after one of the emperor's warriors stepped away through a passageway behind one of the curtains at the far end of the large room.

The emperor's leading warrior soon returned and instructed that the Child would be chained to the floor while the other two were tied to the pillars on each side of the Child. The chains seemed to have just appeared, attached to the bottom. Two short and two longer, that would just reach his hands. His feet were chained with the shorter two. Joshua stood between His mother and His mother's servant, Wayne.

Rhonda felt her arms stretched around the column, and chains were added to her wrists. She looked across the room at Joshua. Rhonda could also see Wayne chained to the pillar beyond Joshua. She looked around the room at the three emperors' soldiers as they went to their knees and bowed before the curtain. Suddenly, the curtain pulled away, and the most hideous man Rhonda had ever seen stepped out. His face was cratered and scarred as if it had once been crushed, yet he lived. He was robed in the finest uniform, with a beautiful sword attached to a golden belt and black leather boots. His hands were equally as revolting and pitted. He smiled as he stepped through the curtain into the room and caused a chill up Rhonda's back. She felt fear in ways she had never been afraid.

"My warriors, you have business elsewhere. Be gone!" he exclaimed, with hate in his voice. I want to deal with my little toys on my own.

The three soldiers jumped and fled from the black passageway they had arrived through earlier. It vanished, revealing only another wall, decorated with a painting of a tree, two naked people with fig leaves, and a serpent wrapped around it.

"So, we meet again, my fool," the creature laughed as he approached Joshua, "You come as Your little people's redeemer, but far from it this time. I have taken you out of Your world this time and into mine. Your death here will save no one. This is my own world, my own creation. I've gained on your Father. One small world for me, but a giant step toward world conquest beyond and out of your protective realm. My power will live on forever."

Joshua stood silent before this creature. Rhonda watched in hopes he would speak and bridle the creature's tongue. Yet He stood brave and humble as a child who does not understand.

"My, you are such a brave child. It's too bad you will never preach a sermon on a mount. You will never heal the sick, and people know who you are. You will die here, separate from the world you came to save, all in my plan to conquer and destroy. While you die here, my men march forth to destroy all the women and children. Then, they will return to finish off the men who challenge my best archers at the mouth of the cave. Your whole society will be in ruin, and you will be dead here, beyond the hope you would have been to them had they known you had come. Two of your Promised Ones are here to die beside you, while your other two Promised Ones are fighting my three best swordsmen right outside the passageway and to the death for them. So we must get down to business."

"You wouldn't kill a little child?" asked Rhonda, "Why do you think you can gain anything by killing Him or us?"

"Actually, I only have to kill Him. You are already dead. I killed you with one of my servants back at your hotel a while back," he said with a jeer on his ugly face, "They just didn't want to tell you so you would be good boys and girls and do what they want you to do here. The only thing is, you failed. All you could do is birth this mortal presence of God so I could destroy Him right here in my world and free the universe of His presence and my conquest forever."

He stepped over to a curtain. He reached in and pulled out a long, sharp spear. Its metal point was half the spear's length, leaving the second half as the wooden handle and grip. It was double-edged and came to a very sharp point. He walked over to Wayne. "You think that suit is powerful enough to defeat and protect you from my weapons. This sword was held by the angels appointed to guard the entrance of the garden that was forbidden to man, once I defeated them. I took those swords and made that land a vast desert. Now, these mighty swords will destroy His servants."

Wayne looked him in the eyes with contempt and courage. His suit appeared to be breast plated with steel, and Wayne gave his best defiant challenge that can be given when wrapped around a marble pillar the size of a fuel truck.

"Let me see how tough your steel is against the mighty weapons of the ancient angelic beings of your primitive history," the emperor said as he walked up to Wayne and swung back to drive the sword into Wayne's midsection.

Rhonda watched as Wayne screamed out in pain and passed out from the sudden thrust of the spear. Rather than pull the blade back out, he yanked it to the left, and the sword cut away out of his stomach and dripped blood to the floor. "No, how could you!" she screamed.

"Mother, it's all right," Joshua said, "Look, his cuts are healed. He is not dead. Trust Me."

Rhonda looked to see where the cuts were and the blood that had spilled just moments ago, and she could see that it was so, but Wayne was still unconscious.

"What good is healing a dead man? You want to raise him from the dead right quick, while I do in Your mother?" said the emperor as he walked across the floor to Rhonda. "She looks so terrified. I think her faith is dwindling. You, mortals, are like that. Have the Messiah in front of you, and voila, you doubt at the first sight of blood. Oh, where is your faith now?"

Rhonda looked at Joshua and tried to let Him know she

still believed. "I love you, Son," she mused in a whisper. She quickly turned her eyes to the approach of the creature of hate. The sword was pointed toward a victim again. This time, it was her.

She heard his voice as he laughably said, "Want to feel my blade? It cuts through the thickest steel vest that Wayne could conjure up. Let's see what you will think of to stop the blade. His blade did not jab swiftly toward her midsection as she had seen him do to Wayne. It instead approached, so intimidatingly, toward her right shoulder. She felt the searing pain as it slowly punctured her flesh, forced its way through her shoulder, and then collided with the marble pillar behind her. "It hurts, doesn't it?"

Rhonda screamed out as if she had been holding her breath and trying not to. Her voice filled the room with the anguish of her pain.

"Shall I twist it and see if it hurts you more?" asked the emperor, "I like to see you lose your faith and die with your so-called Savior chained right there in front of you to spend eternity haunting my palace." He took the sword and twisted it, not once, but three times; each time, he appeared to smile with joy at the pain he was causing.

"Don't you think it is time to stop toying with me and get on with what you plan to do?" asked Joshua as boldly as a full-grown man instead of the Child, looking fourteen years old, yet being born only thirteen months ago.

Rhonda, still reeling from the painful intrusion into her shoulder, suddenly felt the wound disappear and also the painful throb of its deep cut. Before her stood the emperor, who held the blade that had once pointed straight and sharp but now drooped as if it were made of melted plastic. She looked at where the bleeding wound and pain had been and could see nothing, not even a cut into her clothing. All the massive pain was gone.

She looked at the puzzled emperor.

"Well, easy come, easy go. At least I have two of them. Excuse me while I re-arm myself," he said as he returned to the curtain and brought out yet another spear, equally as foreboding as the last. "I see you want to protect your mother from pain. Perhaps she would like to be awake and alive when her little boy meets His tragic death, far from the world He was sent to redeem.

Rhonda looked at Joshua and knew what He had to do, but questioned if this should be the place or the time. She hoped, just maybe, he would melt away the new spear as the emperor walked toward him and grinned down at Him. His height was menacing.

"Can you melt this blade as fast as I can stab you with it, my little man?"

She watched him raise the spear and aim downward at his chest. She noted the hesitation and the knowing grin back at her. Then, the creature looked down again at his victim. "Any last words, young Master?"

She looked at Joshua as if He would say something to stop this. He stood brave before the taller figure of a man who wielded His death instrument just above Him, ready for the plunge. Their eyes met, and, momentarily, gazed as if to say goodbye, fearing the worst.

The sword plunged quickly through the young fellow, quickly piercing his chest, to come out of his lower back and also penetrate the very floor behind him, and mounted His suddenly lifeless body, to sag only slightly due to the angle of the blade that held Him. His head rose, but for a moment it dropped to the sword's handle, his gaze fixed on His mother as his eyes dilated. His life was over quickly.

Rhonda screamed, "Noooooo!" as she watched in horror as her firstborn Child, her only Son, her Infant, raised as a Gift from God, was murdered right before her eyes. She, instead of hate for his murderer, thought more of those He died for and the hope He was bringing. Indeed, it could not have been taken from them.

The emperor walked around for a few moments. He danced. He cheered himself. "I've won. I've pulled off the very obvious. I've defeated the One and Only. I've become God," he said as he danced and skipped around the room.

Rhonda tried not to look at him and his joy. All she could see was Joshua and His lifeless body, impaled to the ground by the colossal spear blade. She asked the question, "Where's the hope?" Louder, she yelled, "WHERE'S THE HOPE?"

Then, there was a dimmed effect of the lights. There was a sudden vibration of the floor and the pillar Rhonda was tied to. The beat got more robust, and the whole place shook. The walls crumbled in several positions before her and around her. Several openings appeared in the walls around the room, but all she could see was darkness beyond them. Then she heard the creature say, "No! NOO! NOOOO!" She could see his eyes fixated on the spot where the passageway had been earlier. The wall painting of the two naked people holding fig leaves in the garden was replaced by another hole in the wall. Now, there was a gaping hole. She could not see what was beyond, but hoped beyond all hope. Why was the emperor afraid?

# CHAPTER 17

Carson and Roxie followed the advance of their forces as they steadily climbed the steep mountain slope leading up to Bald Rock. After a month of movement and shifts in troops, their massed forces now looked up the mountain at Bald Rock and the well-defended entrance to the cavern. Defensively, the fighters had been equipped with shields made from plastic drink bottles, aluminum, and more complex alloys to counter the archers who awaited them. They used every tree, bush, limb, stick, leaf, and root to slowly advance their army up the mountainside.

Johannes slipped up on them with his camouflage-strapped branches and leaf cuttings. Obviously, one leaf was way too large to use as camouflage, so pieces were cut and tied on to provide concealment. The leaves had also been peeled to separate the top layers from the bottom to lighten the weight that the added foliage would add to the individuals and their mobility. Johannes was the general of generals. He led the advancement and kept Roxie and Carson far to the rear to take advantage of their unique abilities to overcome obstacles that might hamper the advancement. They could intervene by changing the invisible to deliver severe distractions to the defending archers if the advancing party encountered difficulties. Little recon could be done in the area, so advancement was trial-and-error. The forces had to feel their way among the foliage and trees, to move swiftly yet stealthily to get as close as possible in their gradual climb up the steep mountainside without being noticed. The underbrush and fallen leaves offered much of their advantage as they advanced, like ants cutting paths as they moved.

Scouts were positioned in many of the trees and to the front to observe archer activity to warn of the approach of attacks by the many archers posted at the cavern's opening above. They carried shields made from plastic, 20-ounce drink bottles. By using them, they could observe the enemy while having a thick, protective device in front of them, offering a possible means of survival against an archer attack if they were detected in their well-concealed positions.

"Carson, our men have taken on the first arrow attacks from above," said Johannes, who appeared to have run a considerable distance under cover before he flew to them from a safe point. "We found the emperor's forces deployed beyond the cave entrance. They've set up a parameter of defense below the rock formation, just beyond the footpaths of the giants. They are trying to pick us off as we advance with heavy barrages of arrow attacks. The arrows are much swifter than ours and seem tipped with extremely sharp metals, penetrating our shields. Not only do they penetrate them, but the closer we get, the deeper the arrows puncture."

"I thought I had heard screams. I assume those were the first victims of their defensive efforts," said Carson.

"Look, we are going to lose a lot of men and end up failing no matter what we do," Johannes said with severe frustration. "We can't fight a well-defended army with inferior weapons and, to boot, inferior shields that won't protect our soldiers. If we get to the top, through their first line of defense, we are sitting ducks, even with shields, when we try to scale the rock formation to reach the cave's opening. Their best archers are in reserve and will pick us off as we crest the perimeter and charge across the opening. Our plan is falling apart."

"Should I fly up and see what kind of mischief we can cause by being invisible and cause a diversion?" asked Carson.

"No! We should withdraw and regroup, trying an attack

from above next, and rappel down upon their defenses instead of climbing. Our forces have taken the first barrage of arrows before we even reached the launch point for our night attack," Johannes said, "I think we should keep a small force moving just beyond their range and keep them watching and taking potshots at them while our main force withdraws and redeploys from above, even if it means risking an overland battle just to get to the top of the rock to rappel downward. There will be no surprise. They will know we are advancing, and chances are, in a direct battle, we are the ones with the inferior weapons, but it is all we have. Maybe we can just hit or miss, each time trying to reach the top of the rock formation, but pull back and take a day or two between to let them get comfortable and hit them again."

Suddenly, from the rock formation above, a faint scream from a woman rang out. Looking up at the rock formation, ten lizards were seen moving down the steep slope, entering what appeared to be a crack in the rock, and disappearing.

Roxie spoke up first, stating with terror, "That was Rhonda. I know her shrill voice anywhere. One of those lizards had her!"

"No, those are intelligent lizards. They were probably transporting Rhonda into the cavern. Now, things are dire. She's been captured and will be taken to the emperor for execution. And, too, if the emperor is present, he can also see us when we are invisible, so even an advancement of invisible warriors would only be met by his lieutenants, and we have already proven that to take them out, we must catch them unaware. I'm at wit's end," said Johannes. "What do you think we can do at this point? Getting in that cavern to rescue your friend before she is taken to the emperor seems to be in serious jeopardy."

Carson looked up at the rock formation, the observation deck built above it, and the giant visitors who observed the incredible view from that vantage point, saying, "I've got an idea. Wait here." He vanished before their eyes and flew into the air before there could be a second debate about what he was about to do.

Carson flew high into the air, way beyond the reach of arrows and above the entire rock formation with its observation deck. Looking downward, he observed the emperor's defensive forces at two fronts: one below the rock basin and the other along the opening of the crack leading into the cavern. He had to do something, but what? "Where's the inner voice when I need it?" asked Carson with a desperate desire for answers.

*"I'm always here, but you rarely call on me. You are such an independent thinker. I would have thought you would have looked at those two teenage boys standing at the edge of the observation deck, drinking their sodas,"* said the inner voice, *"Have you given some thought to flying into their ear and telling them to reach into that cement cigarette butt container with its large quantity of sand and telling them to try bombing all of those ants they can see below them?"*

"Wow, what an idea," said Carson excitedly, "I think I can better that." He flew directly toward the youngster on his right, veered around, and entered the left ear to stop his entry, colliding with hair, earwax, and the smell.

It got suddenly dark, and Carson knew his presence had been detected. He had to think quickly, or that finger might push enough wax to make it his permanent home.

"Hey, you with the big finger," Carson yelled toward the direction he figured the eardrum was in the dark, "Want to have some fun? Try pouring your soda off the cliff onto those thick ant lines along the basin and rocks. Imagine what falling cola would do on impact from this distance."

The movement was felt, and Carson's footing was very questionable as the head leaned forward to look, and then suddenly turned to the kid next to him to jerk Carson around even more. He felt glad his wings were not deployed at this point, or they would be so waxed he would never fly again. The ear opening suddenly allowed light in again. He heard a voice like one heard in a barrel. "Hey, Billy, want to play Bomb the Ants with soda pop? I see two lines of ants and lots of them.

"I bet they will never know what hit them when my drink rains down."

Another faint voice said, "That's cool, man. You take out the big line along the outer edge, and I'll do the line on the rocks behind them. I'll finish them and come back and help you further below, and then we will climb down and see the damage."

Carson could still feel movements as the two boys hung over the edge of the observation deck and poured their drinks on the unsuspecting victims below. He heard the voice in the barrel again, and it said, "That's all of my soda pop. Now let's go below and see what happened."

"Dude, what about all of that sand in that big cigarette butt device. You can rain sand down on the ants to stick to the soda, and then the ants will never escape your wonderful touch," said Carson, as he again focused his yell at the eardrum.

"Wait, let's give the soda something to stick to besides ants," Carson felt again the ear canal move sideways as the young man bent forward to scoop up, hopefully, a good-sized handful of sand and cigarette butts.

"This is an even better idea. Bombs away," said the distant voice.

"Well, my work here is done. You two did an awesome job," said Carson as he quickly shot out of the ear. he tried to avoid collisions, mainly hair follicles inside the ear, as he buzzed toward and out of the opening. The teenager made two or three more attempts to pour sand from the container, and then the two boys started back up the stairs to climb down and see what kind of damage they had caused to the ants below. Carson watched for a moment.

Another voice was heard almost immediately, and it

screamed, "You two get back up here. That's all I need, to have my two sons fall off the side of the mountain while your daddy is over here spending quarters trying to see if he can see Anniston through the "Pay-Per-View." She hit her husband, who continued to look.

"My quarter is not up yet," he said, continuing his visual search of the distance.

"You are just like one of the boys," she said, glaring at the boys who were re-climbing the stairs. "Scoot over and let me look before your time runs out, and you watch the boys before they get themselves killed."

Carson's train of thought quickly shifted to Rhonda and the turn of the tide of battle below. Yells of the advancing soldiers could be heard as they crested the edge of the footpath. They charged into chaos and had to avoid the sticky mess themselves as they advanced past the overwhelmed defense, which now had super-sticky liquids and sand boulders that stuck to them and around them. Swords flew forth, and many emperors' soldiers were disarmed quickly without resistance. Many of the salvageable bows and arrows were taken. The advance up the rock formation followed the now sticky but undefended rock path to the opening. He knew now that Rhonda had hope.

"Well, don't fly there and soak up all the glory. The battle is won, but we must win the war. Let's enter the cave and see what is waiting next," said Johannes, who had flown to meet him along with Roxie.

They all three flew into the opening. They turned invisible out of fear of a reception from the next advancement of foot soldiers who would replace the front lines that had been incapacitated with the stickiness of the soda poured on them, the acid effects on their bodies, and the boulder attacks that prevented the soda from dissipation quickly. Their flight veered downward into the dark cavern and reached the entrance into the great open area above the dark waters. Carson, Roxie, and Johannes continued their careful flight for a few minutes to allow their eyes to adjust to the darkness. The torches along the walls to their left were their only significant light, besides the cracks in the walls that let in light only at certain times of day.

"Where are the reinforcements?" asked Johannes, "This can't be all of the emperor's army."

"Look, three men are on the shore's footpath below."

"Yeah, I see them," said Johannes, "They appear to be coming from the military complex at the far end of the cavern."

"Let's make ourselves visible. I don't see any threats at this point," said Carson.

All three, visible and with swords drawn, flew toward the three who walked along the shore. Two men turned and ran like they had seen a vast army move upon them. The other stood there with his hands behind his back, and he even appeared to greet them with a grin.

Carson touched down first and asked, "What are you hiding behind you?"

Seph smiled at him and turned to reveal the twisted ropes that were wound heavily around his wrists.

"Hold very still, and I will remove them from you," said Carson as he cut away the rope easily, and they fell to the path below them. "Who are you?"

"I'm Josephus, former prime minister for this province before I ticked off the emperor. I was just on my way to my execution when you came to my rescue. I assume you are Carson, and this young lady is Roxie, but I don't know who your friend is."

"My friend here is Johannes, Leader of the Tree People, and how did you know who we were?" asked Carson.

"I know a couple of your friends, and they are up there, beyond that black wavy thing that leads to the emperor. Their names are Rhonda and Wayne," Seph said, pointing toward the top of the cave, with the dark, wavy spot still visible. "It's going to be dangerous, but your only chance to save them is to go through that pass, too. Good luck, my friends, and may the power of the Most High go with you."

They realized the lack of any other danger and the hope and urgency of the task to rescue their friends. The three flew toward the dark portal of darkness. They pulled their swords, ready, as they approached the strange phenomenon. Just as they reached it to try to fly through it, out charged three of the emperor's warriors, suddenly catching them with surprise, but not totally unexpected, and their reception greeted them with swords ready. Collisions were avoided, but their swords were pulled faster than the startled Carson, Roxie, and Johannes could strike. The air battle began with sword-to-sword action that altered the flights of both sword fighters with each blade's impact.

Carson felt the strength of his dueling partner with each blow thrown toward him. His blade took the blows, and sparks flew. The swordsman he dueled with was amazingly talented and used his strength to strike Carson's sword and push him further toward the water with each blow. He knew he had to stop this descent, or he would soon be swimming and fighting. His thoughts focused on his sword and its power; he shifted from defense to offense, striking faster than his assailant. Soon, his blows began to cut away at his opponent's blade. Pieces of the assailant's sword began to cut away. When his last slice cut the dueler's blade off at the handle, it was thrown at Carson, and the assailant quickly became a fugitive from justice.

Carson pursued the warrior and caught him from behind to grasp his lower clothing as the man's wings buzzed in his face. He ran his sword through the handful of clothing and cut upward to slice the dress between the branches. Carson put his sword back in its sheath, grabbed the ripped sides with both hands, lodged a foot to the back side of the man in the suit, and shoved with all of his might. The man's wings stopped working, and the case came off: first the legs, then the arms, and his flight ended as he plunged into the waters below.

With a quick look around toward Roxie, he could see her as she struggled against her foe's effort to pound her into the water. Her wings were mighty close to treading water, but Carson would have none of that; he raced forward to the situation and grabbed the swordsman by the seat of the pants.

Roxie flew up from the water that had already reached her waist and kept the dueler busy while Carson inserted his blade and ripped the back of this fighter's flight suit. With a foot forcefully applied, another of the emperor's warriors plunged naked into the dark, cold waters. Roxie had realized her strength and began to slice away at the warrior's weapon as effectively as Carson had done the first to keep him busy while his suit was cut.

They moved next to assist Johannes, already submerged and forced underwater by the emperor's highest-ranked lieutenant's sword strikes. With the knowledge that Johannes was much older than dirt, his aged status was no match for the assault of this mighty warrior. He was in a desperate fight for his life and an effort to keep from drowning as well. The warrior's blade sliced at him with each of his efforts to come to the surface to breathe. With one step to come up for air, the warrior drew his blade back for a fatal blow to Johannes, but instead felt a collision of Carson's blade at the handle that cut clean through, and the edge tumbled to the water. This time, Roxie had the seat of his pants while Carson distracted him with his flight in front of the weaponless warrior. Removing the suit was not as easy for Roxie, and Carson grabbed a leg and inserted it into a foot. The slice of the back of this leader's suit and the previous example of Carson's fancy footwork, and the man trod water with his two cohorts in a matter of seconds.

Their next pursuit was the old man who swam for his life among three angry, naked former warriors of the emperor. They grabbed his outstretched hands, then his slippery arms, and flew Johannes to the shore while he insisted they forget about him and fly to the entrance of the emperor's hall. They did precisely that. Only when they reached the portal did they encounter another battle with more warriors in surprise. The dark, wavy spot vanished before they could get within ten feet of it. They flew over its location and made several passes through the area where they thought it had been, then flew beyond where it was last seen and waited, midair, for some time, hoping it would open again soon.

Suddenly, there was a rumble. Instead of the dark, black, wavy patch in its reappearance, a giant stalactite appeared this time. Then, some holes crumbled away, revealing a lighted room inside the stalactite. Where the dark spot had seemed to be at one point was now a gaping hole, just large enough for a French door, but access was finally theirs. What lay beyond, Carson and Roxie knew, was their destiny.

As they flew into the new opening, they heard the screams, "No! Nooo! NOOOO!" From the other side of the glare that affected their eyes after they entered from the almost total darkness of the cave, visualization became an incredible revelation. Their eyes focused on a dark figure on the other side of the room, with a sword raised to do battle.

# CHAPTER 18

Carson felt his feet touch down as he advanced into the lighted room. The figure that stood at the other end of the room stood with his sword drawn to match Carson's for battle. He glanced to his left and saw a young teenager who stooped, impaled to the floor by a long spear that had penetrated his chest and extended further out of his back to penetrate the floor. A puddle of blood formed under the lifeless body.

With a quick visualization further to his left, he saw an emotionally upset Rhonda. He also heard her efforts for words, "My baby! My Baby!" in sobs of grief.

He looked over to his right, and his heart skipped another beat with the sight of his friend, Wayne, slumped and dangling from the marble pillar he was tied to, and he knew he was already dead. He knew immediately who the killer was.

The tall, colossal figure at the other end of the room, ready with his sword, exclaimed, "Two more have come to die. Are you the first to take my challenge, young coward?"

"To do battle is my purpose, for what else is there?" asked Carson. "I feel no truce or parlay will solve our issues. This is for Wayne and the Child you have murdered and for what you have done to Rhonda."

"Oh, let's not rush this," said the emperor, "Allow me to make a wager. If you win this sword fight, you toss me in this, and vice versa."

Against the wall, another mysterious passage appeared.

"The loser gets tossed in the distorted black hole and vanishes forever?"

"Close, it is a convenient portal that sends the loser a half million miles into outer space, and when you exit the other end of the portal, you become a comet, and you will be named by your Earth's scientists as a newly discovered comet at that."

"What makes you think I will be the one tossed into the portal for losing this sword fight?"

"Because I cannot be defeated. I am superior to you, a mere mortal. Prepare to be the solar system's next comet.

"Not under my watch. You are on."

Carson charged forth to swing his sword with all his might. The blades made great sparks but did not cut through the metal as they had with the conflicts with other members of the emperor's force of lieutenants.

"Wow, Gabriel gave you his sword. He claims the Most High gave it to him. Do you think the Most High would give Gabriel a weapon as powerful as mine after I almost defeated Him and tried to take His throne?" asked the emperor, "Gabriel's best weapon is hardly a weapon against mine. I'm sure you've been told you can't defeat me in a sword fight. He knew your sword would be destroyed if you took me on."

"Well, it appears I have no choice," said Carson, who would not cower to his threats. "Your sword will at least have a challenge it will never forget. Shall we start again?" He glanced to see that Rhonda had already been cut loose by Roxie. He could hear the emotional sobs of Rhonda to his direct rear and knew she clung to the impaled Child behind him. Carson turned to his right to see that Wayne had been cut free, and Roxie patted his face to wake him up. Perhaps he was not dead and would awaken to join him in the battle.

Suddenly, he felt the thrust of the emperor's sword that charged forth while he appeared distracted. The blow was deflected, and Carson moved beyond his reach to the other end of the room but quickly shifted to the right to move counterclockwise around the room in hopes of getting the emperor to follow and move away from his friends, who were wide open for him to strike with his sword.

Carson charged again. The two swords met in midair. The sparks flew, and Carson fell against the force of the blow; even if his sword could take the impact, the weight behind it pushed Carson back, causing him to lose his foothold, and he stumbled. He rolled quickly once he saw the thrust of the next swing of the emperor's blade. He blocked it as it cut toward him and regained his battle stance.

Over and over, the emperor charged and sliced with his blade. Every time Carson blocked, he fell backward from the force of the emperor's mighty blows. He averted sudden stabs at him while he regained his posture and scurried back to his feet each time. Carson, however, felt his energy draining, and fear rose inside him. How much longer could he hold up? Perhaps his friends would at least escape, but the sobs behind him told him that Rhonda was still there, and the others would not leave her. Wayne was no longer beside the pillar, but was not alert enough to join in the battle either.

After another twenty minutes of deflections of the emperor's blows, he felt he had almost failed to stop the last attempt to slice him. He got to his feet as quickly as his exhausted body would allow. He glared across the room. He was all that stood between his friends and the emperor's wrath, and he struggled with total exhaustion.

He thought in his heart and asked, *"Where's that still, small voice when I need it most?"*

*"About time you got around to talking to me,"* said the voice, a much younger voice, but still his Shepherd's voice, as if it had waited all day. *"Of course, I see you have been rather busy. You're doing a great job protecting your friends. Now, while he allows you to catch your breath, you need to work on your fear. He is not as big as he*

*appears; that is your fear and your fear only. He has you fooled. You are much bigger and stronger than he is. It is time for your second wind."*

"Shall we dance another round?" asked Carson aloud.

"You are ready for the next and perhaps your final round?" asked the emperor with a grin. "You can die a painful but swift death by giving up and letting me toss you into the portal, or I can cut you up, piece by piece. Which would you prefer?"

"Let's do this," Carson said with newfound energy.

Carson moved around the open area with greater movement, eyeing his opponent with more confidence. Waiting for the next blow no longer seemed strategic. A moving target required more planning and quicker, less forceful blows. The next blow proved that fact. Suddenly, the intimidating challenger did not stand as intimidating. He grew smaller as Carson made a forceful strike.

"So, you have found your second wind? You are still no match for me, weakling."

Carson struck again, and again. The strikes put the emperor into a greater and greater posture. With a moment's hesitation, the emperor rose to challenge again with greater strength, but strikes missed more than they met Carson's blade.

"I gave you a breather last, it is my time. You are a formidable opponent. This next round should be our tiebreaker."

"If you wish, but only as short a breather as you gave me," Carson said. *"He is not as small as I would like him to be. What am I doing wrong?"*

*"You are giving him a challenge he has never experienced. You must continue with constant offense and wear him down. Then you will gain strength he's never seen before, and you will know what to do then."*

"Let's begin the final round," Carson said, noting the emperor still breathed heavily as he did when the second began.

Carson changed the emperor, swinging eight quick

blows, all blocked, but noticed his opponent shrank in stature. The emperor shifted counterclockwise, and Carson struck six more times, but the blocks diminished, and the emperor moved defensively, shrinking even more.

"How are you growing in size?" as the emperor shifted and blocked the next two blows, becoming seriously winded.

"I am not growing; you are becoming weaker in this battle," said Carson, making six more quick blows to the now-cowering emperor.

*"Now slice at his sword instead of striking with great force,"* said the young voice in his head.

Carson advanced and sliced at the sword held defensively. The blade was cut in half, and the emperor held up a half-sword, moving quickly in the continued counterclockwise manner. His posture questioned the whole situation as another slice cut the remaining blade in half.

Another slice, and all the emperor held was the handle. The emperor now stood one-fourth the height of Carson and threw the hilt at Carson.

Carson easily dodged the thrown object and pursued the emperor like a parent chasing a rebellious child. Catching the defeated emperor, Carson picked him up by his collar and the seat of his pants, holding him in a fashion that ensured his hands could not draw a hidden dagger and render injury to his capture.

"Send my lieutenants! Send my soldiers, now!" the former emperor yelled.

Carson hesitantly looked at the port. Observing the former emperor's gaze at the portal, he realized he had moments before this defeated monster could easily cancel the portal, rendering him only a prisoner to be freed later. Charging forward with all his strength, Carson tossed the emperor, kicking and screaming, through the awaiting portal before it could be canceled.

Carson's heart pounded as he looked around the room.

He was overjoyed to see his friends had not been harmed any worse than they had been during the battle that had occurred. He also felt the deepest of sorrows, gazing at the teenager, impaled with the spear.

"Carson, you are amazing. How did you do that?" asked Roxie.

"I did not do it alone," Carson said, feeling the sudden surge of exhaustion. He pulled a juice packet from his belt and drank some energy juice to replenish his exhausted state.

A sound of a slosh-type walk appeared in the passageway. An old man, still wet to the bone, walked in.

He said, "Looks like I missed the whole thing." His voice stopped suddenly as he saw the Child, Joshua, impaled to the floor by the spear. His emotions brought him to immediate tears. He lowered himself to his knees, then prostrate before the body, to weep in sobs, and everybody knew why the power of the emperor had been broken. The last prophecy was that the blood of a little child would remove the impossible might of the mightiest conqueror. The emperor's created mini world had ceased with the incredible sacrifice made by Joshua's willful surrender of His own life in exchange for His friends.

"What day is it, Carson?" asked Rhonda.

"It's Friday, why do you ask?" questioned Carson.

"We must hurry and bury the Child because it is almost evening. If He is to have three days in a grave, we must move swiftly.

It took Carson and Johannes, with a mighty pull at the spear, to remove it from the floor and free Joshua's body from its hold. Wayne watched from his dazed yet growing alertness to what had transpired before him and what had happened. His injuries had healed entirely, leaving no scar. They gathered around the fallen Child, and Rhonda explained that she had the Child and carried the Seed that saved the world. She was still ripped apart by the very nature and horror of His death. It was nothing like she had imagined. She was so pleased to see Him removed from the spear and laid to rest in a proper position. She had stared at his open and dilated eyes; his head rested earlier on the very blade handle that had taken His life, and she could not get that picture out of her mind. Had He died of His own free will to conquer this mini world of the emperor and break his power? Could He have stopped the spear as He had done for His mother? Had He allowed His own life to be taken as a bounty required to destroy the power hold that the former emperor had on this world?

Johannes flew away to seek burial garments. Soon, Joshua's body was taken from Rhonda's arms for burial. The body was wrapped and flown to a burial site, selected on short notice, and placed there. He received a hero's burial, even if word had not yet spread to everyone; Seph had many friends who rushed to the scene to see this mighty hero who had conquered the emperor's power, which opened the door to final access and defeat.

---

The four walked to the cavern's edge the next day after an evening meal and final night with Seph. The voice in Carson's heart said they were to leave on Saturday. They walked to the edge of the rock formation, protected by the upper portion of the crack. They looked out toward the foggy appearances and a few breaks that allowed thunderstorms to be visible in the distance. In a way, the shock of its conclusion and the traumatic experience left them restless and in emotional pain with those who grieved the significant loss, particularly Rhonda, who had lost her only Child.

Carson looked at the four. "Johannes, it is time for us to return home, right?" he asked.

"Unfortunately, you are correct. The power of the Most High has been restored over our failures and compromises. The gifts of God have all been returned or restored, even though some are damaged by acids from a soft drink. They will be worn only by those who answer the call and are appointed and provided for by the Most High.

"We will even require those we armed and clothed with those special suits to fight on our side, to return them until provisions are made to refill them with worthy appointees, and even so, those individuals may qualify to do so. Do I look younger today, or am I just getting my hopes up?"

"You do look younger, Johannes, and where did all of your gray hair go? I'm going to miss you," Rhonda said as she moved forward and hugged his neck. "But I am going to miss Joshua more than anything."

"Rhonda, He will be with you always. You knew Him before you came here. You were sent by Him, and yet, now you grieve for his dying to free this world from a terrible menace. He will walk this world again and bring His message of hope to these people, a message that will last throughout eternity, but before that begins, you must go back. You must decrease that He might increase," said Johannes.

"Could I at least be here in the morning for the third day?" asked Rhonda.

"No, that day is already yours at another time and another place. You will know only that gift and its example. You will see Him again, in person, one day, and until then, you know how to keep in touch," said Johannes, "By the way, Rhonda, I spoke with your friend this morning."

"A friend of mine?" asked Rhonda, somewhat puzzled.

"Yes, a lizard named Plaudia," said Johannes, "It appears she is very proud of the courage you gave her. She passed word to almost five hundred lizards, each transporting twenty of the emperor's men to battle against undefended homes. She said that, with your encouragement, after leaving the new cave opening, when their movement across a mountain rock formation was the steepest, she began to buck her passengers. All the lizards threw their passengers from their backs. The only resistance came from the emperor's lieutenants; from what I hear, they caused serious indigestion. Still, their suits should be recovered today, and care in their recovery and a good cleaning are both in order. You helped end the war. Plaudia, by the way, is now a part of the humanitarian efforts of the community to go, at this very moment, to medically assist many of the injured soldiers with their broken bones and lacerations from the ordeal, but their fighting days are over. Even the military quarters in the cave will be converted into a hospital. You are a strong woman, and the lizard people will always hold you in honor."

"Thanks, Johannes. You've done a mighty work yourself, worthy of the angels in Heaven, but even you must return to your duties in your appointed manner," said a mighty voice.

Carson turned to see the Angel Gabriel, who stood before them all in white. "Aw, do we have to go?" Carson asked. "I was just starting to like it here."

"Yes, you need to go back in time and change history. You recall your hotel exploded from the impact of a fuel truck that plowed through the front of the building you were in. You must now go back and try to stop that from happening, or you will be trapped between worlds forever," said Gabriel. "It's up to you. Your passage back is now, or you will remain this size and your livelihood for eternity, and be limited to working for Johannes and staying invisible. He would be glad to have you on his team any day."

"You are so right. Hate to see you leave; please stick around. There's nothing finer than being angelic and living to the end of time," said Johannes.

"Never die?" said Wayne, "It sounds tempting, and I have felt the pain and come so close, I thought I was dead. However,

Johannes, I must go home and be with my family. I want to have and see my own children and make a life of my own that I once started. I can't see myself abandoning my parents and their great hopes for their young man. I want to graduate with my class. You know?"

Roxie said, "I feel the same way, and besides, I want to see what happens with this wonderful relationship I have found with Carson, who only lives ten miles away from me. Will we know each other and remember any of this when we return?"

"Yes, I will leave that memory because you want me to do so," said Gabriel. "Remember never to tell anyone, or they will think you are nuts."

"I think that would be something we can be careful of, Gabriel," said Carson.

"How do we get back?" asked Rhonda.

They all exchanged handshakes and neck hugs as they prepared for their departure. Johannes vanished before their eyes, and the five began to rise into the air, this time without winged flight. They passed beyond the observation podium mounted on Bald Rock.

On the rock was a young, black-haired girl. She stared out at them. She became suddenly excited. She ran to her mother, and all could just make out her voice in the distance.

"I've just seen angels flying. We must really be high up in the mountains. Come and look for yourselves."

The group of five people ran to the edge, and she pointed up toward them, but their size and distance had already made them oblivious.

"Looks like you won't be the only ones wishing to visit Bald Rock on Cheaha Mountain with a new perspective in the coming months," said Gabriel.

# CHAPTER 19

The four came out of the fog to discover they were in downtown Birmingham's alley next to Richard Arrington Boulevard. Automobiles zoomed past on the road at the entrance. They rushed forward. They quickly glanced left and right; the hotel was nowhere to be seen. A fuel truck slowed past them toward a red light ahead. His air brakes made a noise as he coasted to a stop. Seeing the vehicle made them rush to the street to see more. Suddenly, two men rushed from both sidewalk corners. They leaped up the truck's steps, pulled the handles, and the doors flew open from both sides.

The trucker turned in surprise and tried to grab the open swinging door. The man on the left swung a short club, and the trucker's resistance ceased. He was then dragged from the vehicle and rolled out into the street. Both men got into the truck, the light changed, and they pulled out, with sounds indicating the driver struggled with the gears but moved forward.

"Do you realize what just happened? We missed our chance to prevent our own deaths! We could have stopped them!" said Carson as he rushed forward and cut into traffic to chase the truck down the street.

Wayne, Rhonda, and Roxie were right behind him. "We can't catch that truck on foot. Do you think our suits still work?" asked Roxie with a look at her pink shirt and faded denim skirt, which she had not seen since meeting Johannes.

"Let's try it, but first, let's turn invisible so we won't be noticed," said Rhonda.

All four disappeared as the injured truck driver rose up

to ask them for help. He passed out immediately upon their disappearance before his eyes. They flew forth and could still see the fuel truck far ahead, and their speed enabled them to catch it in a few moments. Carson took the left side of the 18-wheeler with Roxie in flight as backup. Wayne took the right side, with Rhonda directly behind him to assist.

"We will both go in simultaneously, and you get to the emergency air brakes, and I'll wrestle the new driver," said Carson.

"Let's do this," said Wayne.

Carson flew up to the left side of the door, with a visual of the fact that the truck had run a red light, and several cars slammed on their brakes with no desire to prove they were in the right of way against a fuel truck. He looked through the glass window of the truck's cab to see Wayne's red outline on the other side.

He pulled the doorknob, and the door swung open. He reached for the driver, yanked him out, and struggled with releasing the wheel. He looked across and saw Wayne. He was upset that the other passenger had jumped and locked the door on the way out.

Roxie raced forward to kick the man holding the steering wheel, and the grip was released. She climbed in, and Carson watched the man hit the ground and roll, just able to miss the reels and possibly a severe road pizza effect from contact with the pavement and all the tires that passed by his final tumble. Carson looked back inside the cab at Roxie as she regained control of the truck. They both looked ahead to see the hotel building race right at them.

"Red! Air brakes! Pull it now!" yelled Carson.

Roxie's hand reached and pulled. The air sounded forth instantly. Both were thrown forward as the vehicle suddenly locked all eighteen wheels, and the front of the cab crashed into the entranceway. The engine lurched a couple of times and went dead. It was over. There was no big boom.

The fuel cell was intact and not an inferno as before.

Carson could feel hands reaching under him, pulling him away from the truck. He watched as Rhonda reached in and grabbed an unconscious Roxie, who had bounced off the steering wheel pretty hard, and pulled her out as well. They were both dragged to the grass area next to the sidewalk and entrance. When it became apparent that no one was looking their way, they became visible again. They watched as people rushed to see what had happened. Some even suggested the truck might explode, and then people started to back off. Soon, Roxie became conscious and looked at her friends, regaining her vision.

Several people who worked at the hotel came around the building from an emergency door. All four watched; Roxie nursed several bruises but became aware of where they were now. Things calmed down soon, and the fire department checked the vehicle for fire risk and finally backed it out of the doorway. A clean-up crew went to work to ready it for repairs.

They waited, and as they relaxed in the grass for a while, Roxie recovered from her trauma, and the clean-up crew began allowing hotel guests to enter and leave the building again. They got to their feet, entered through the now-huge front opening, and headed toward the elevator again.

"Let us take the stairs this time," said Roxie, "I am a bit leery of that elevator right now after what I saw come out of it last time."

"Hey, it's only two stories up, why not?" said Carson.

They entered the stairway and quickly climbed it to admire the white walls and the vastness of the passageway compared to what they had become accustomed to. They entered the second floor. The emergency doorway opened just as they entered the hall and turned toward their rooms at the other end. Out stepped a girl from Rhonda's school.

She whispered to get all four of them to listen. She said to them, "That's Candice Whaley. She buys all her clothes at the high-price uppity stores uptown. All of you look at what Candice is wearing and think seriously about her outfit, and you know where I am going," she said sheepishly as she led the way down the hall.

Rhonda glanced at her outfit, which had suddenly changed to look just like that of Candice, and rushed to catch up with the classmate. "Hey, girlfriend, I love your new outfit. I got one at Wal-Mart, too. The whole outfit cost me twenty-five bucks," she said with a big grin.

Candice glared at her, even more so as she looked at Roxie, who wore the same outfit. She got bug-eyed when she saw Carson and Wayne and what they wore.

"I just love the selections at Wal-Mart, don't you?" added Wayne with a warm smile toward her.

Candice steamed off to her room, swiped her card, opened the door, entered in a huffy fashion, and pushed hard to slam it, but the hydraulics of the door frustrated her in that attempt.

"That was so mean, Rhonda, but I loved every minute of it," said Roxie, "You guys look weird in dresses. How about a change back to guy wear? The joke is over."

"Aw, spoil the fun of being cool. What was I wearing when I left here?" asked Wayne. He suddenly changed into a pair of blue jeans and a T-shirt. "Wayne, you looked better in that dress, but your old outfit looks fine. What do you think, girls?"

They both looked back and gave a smile in agreement.

"How much Pizza do you have in the fridge?" asked Roxie. "It sounds a lot better than fifteen-month-old soggy Subway sandwiches. Pizza keeps better overnight."

Carson reached into his pocket and found his swipe card for the boys' hotel room door. We bought one pizza last night and got another one free. We could only eat one, so come on in. I hope you like green olives and Canadian bacon."

"Oh, that sounds so much better than bug soup and roast salamander tail," said Rhonda.

The door opened, and the wet towels, the upturned mattress, and the chair near the window decorated the traumatized room. "Well, at least we beat the maid service and can clean this up a bit," said Carson as all four entered the room.

"You know, Rhonda? That was the first time we actually got to fly back there. Wasn't it awesome? Isn't it a shame we did not try earlier?" said Wayne as he was the last to enter the passageway into the room.

"Do you think we will get to keep the suits?" asked Roxie as the door closed.

A couple of days later, they all learned that a mysterious red comet had appeared. Not so oddly, it was named the Devil's Comet because of its unusually red tail.

# CHAPTER 20

Of the four that remained true to each other, Roxie and Carson were an item. Their homes were near each other, and they continued to see and date each other as much as possible. Soon, graduation was upon them, and both enrolled at Jacksonville State University for the fall. It was as if they were meant for each other. No one else would believe their story. They continued to wear their suits, thinking perhaps they might need them or the powers they contained. They knew that the powers that went with them were on a "when needed" basis, so they remained ready.

Rhonda and Wayne had contacted them by July about a trip to Cheaha Mountain. They decided not to take the express route to the top of the mountain. They drove up the scenic road, and the 157 curves offered plenty of interesting insights and conversation along the way, but at a certain speed, there was a lot of beauty to admire. When the lake appeared on their left, they immediately pulled over to see the old swimming hole. They looked across the lake, and the old oak tree could be picked out in the wood line beyond the small lake.

The concession stand was open and busy, with a continuous supply of soft drinks and hot dogs. The four made purchases, though not swimming, and they got permission to check out the place for future visits. After a walk around, they admired the concession stand. Roxie and Carson reflected on memories of that rainy night and where they hid from the harsh weather. People thought it was odd that they tried to see the top of the stand's roof. Many tried to stretch their necks to see what was so interesting to them as the four moved on. The group descended the road again on foot to reach the other end of the lake. Getting to the old oak tree was difficult because it was well-secluded. By the time they reached it, their shoes were covered with the mud on the ground around it.

The tree itself did not look the same. It had deteriorated. The four looked up at the center portion, where there was once a dome. To their great disappointment, there was a hollow place as if it had rotted out. They figured to see little green men the size of pieces of rice, but instead, they were only bothered by the constant bugs that flew around them. Many questions went through their minds as they struggled through the thick vines and muck to reach the road again. What had happened to the tree holding the Tree People? Had they moved to a better location since they were on the job again? Were they moved to another dimension, like that of heaven? The place had to always be a secret, so they figured it had to move to be secure. Did they suspect Carson and his friends would come in search of the tree? Those were questions they would have to save for later because wisdom was not available to explain the changes.

After the struggle back to their automobile, they followed the road up to the top of the mountain. Still, on a slow cruise, they tried to pick out the curb where they first arrived to help the Wasamanee. There were three or four places where they thought it actually happened. The graffiti on the rocks was a good clue to the most probable spot. When they reached the hotel, they had to pay a dollar apiece to enter the park's main tourist sites through the gate. They sacrificed the money together and got through the gate. They stopped at the hotel to look at where they battled the most powerful weapons the enemy had at their disposal, yet won by defeating the prototype triangular weapons firsthand. Carson found the whole blown into the gutter near the drainpipe. It could easily be explained as evidence of someone who had thrown some kind of fireworks into it. The weapons destroyed there were probably the most significant loss to the enemy. Even the captured weapon proved useless because of the damage inflicted during the acquisition, and no one ever figured out how to make them send a projectile that would explode like a grenade.

Their last stop was the long walk out to Bald Rock on the wooden walkway. They spent some time at the observation deck at the end. Carson told of the victory where he got the two boys to pour their soft drinks on the emperor's warriors below. Roxie talked of the effect from her point of view. She said their own forces had to take some evasive measures to avoid hits from the soda foam attack, too, and later, the pieces of sand, about a fifth of their size at the time, came down like a landslide. Being in cover for protection from the many arrows that flew their way, they were in good shape. Their charge up the mountain after the enemy was overwhelmed was amazing. The sticky soda and foaming effects had made the enemy's movement impossible. Their burial in the sand was even more restrictive. The charge up to the entrance to the cave offered little to no resistance. They spent more time in rescue and disarmament of the enemy than in battle against armed resistance. Much ammunition was gathered before they entered the cavern.

Their charge into the cave was met with cheers from the people's homes. The whole army charged in, totally out of breath, but instead of another battle, they were shocked by the welcome.

The four even went down to the foot of Bald Rock.

The cave they remembered was by a small crack. Who would even think there was a chamber just beyond it, which held so many memories, and that small body of water? When they finished their walk around the base of the enormous rock formation, they moved back to the deck above, which had better footing, and no one cared to put a quarter into the viewing device. Their fascination lay in the place rather than in what could be seen in the distance.

While they stood on the deck, gazing off into the distance to figure out where the many Wasamanee tribes were located, Carson knelt on one knee. He pulled at Roxie's hand to look around. He held a small diamond ring in its ring holder and said, "Roxie, will you marry me?" He said it, embarrassed but determined to make it incredible that day.

Roxie blushed a little, yet knew what her answer was to be immediately, and answered, "Yes, I'll marry you. I would never want to spend the rest of my life with anyone else. You're my hero and my first and only love."

Carson was speechless, and tears formed in his eyes. He put the ring on her finger and then stood to hug her for ever so long. He eventually became aware of Rhonda and Wayne again. They were both still there, baffled by the event occurring before them, but they knew it was an eventual proposition, but not this quick. They all discussed that it needed to be a long engagement. Roxie insisted that they had already known each other for over two years, in what most people thought were just two months.

Rhonda and Wayne were not as close or even given commitment thoughts. Rhonda had talked seriously of a quest to become a Nun. Being from an Independent Church, she found that she did have a few conflicts along the way. Wayne remained supportive and encouraging. She called him often and spoke of enrollment at Notre Dame in the fall, the opportunities to convert to Catholicism, not to mention the classes that concerned her. Wayne attended them also. Wayne even considered the priesthood, but both found that the more they spent together, the greater the determination to continue the fellowship.

A year later, all four finished their freshman year of college and had a double wedding at the hotel. Both couples rented rooms with promises to not bother each other as they planned their private weekends for the first time as individual couples.

They said later they felt like they were at home. All four were fortunate to remain in college, get educational degrees, and be employed locally to stay near their beloved mountain.

Their parents often reflected on how clean their clothes stayed in the closet and how they began to take care of washing their own clothes. The clothing lasted so much longer, also. The only reason to buy new clothes was when their parents forced them to, and they felt they needed new stuff. To try on dresses was super easy. You just step into the booth, look at the clothes before you, and step back out wearing them.

All their parents often noted how much more mature they had become after that Beta Club/Honor Society convention in their senior year. Their maturity was most noted in faith. The four knew their walk had to be right because they dreamed of being on a team for another adventure to bring hope again to another lost and dying world. Carson pointed out that they needed to look locally for opportunities to bring hope.

There was so much need all around them. They still wore special suits and would not part with them unless requested.

It was not like being heroes or anything. Things did not happen, so you could turn into a suit and save the day. The real world and real hope were the greatest of combinations. Those living, walking believers who possessed the power had seen the glory and knew it dwelled inside; they knew they could do anything.

They all met the following year and, through prayer and supplication, surrendered their suits for the greater need of the world around them.

That awareness of the greater need grew more with that still small voice that said, "Feed my sheep."

The End

The Author: G. E. Dabbs, better known as Glenn E. Dabbs, Sr., is a retired school teacher who taught in Lowndes County, Troy City, Bibb County, Jefferson County, and lastly, Shelby County Schools at Linda Nolen Learning Center. He served as a Special Education teacher and also director of the Alternative School in Bibb County. He is a graduate of Munford High School, Jacksonville State University with a BS, and Troy University with a double master's degree in Education. He has served as a homebound instructor since retiring, providing educational pursuits for students who can't attend public school. He also retired from the Army Reserve with 38 years of military service, including three years in Germany and three combat tours in Iraq, where his highest decoration was the Meritorious Service Medal, the Bronze Star equivalent for desk jockeys. He retired as a Senior Chaplain Assistant. He has published three novels: *Lucy's Treasure*, a historical novel based on a true story; *Captive of Circumstances*, a fantasy novel written after his late son's request that he write a story about him; and *Three Dabbs Boys and the American Revolution*. He has written for Chicken Soup for the

Soul and two other anthologies. He also published articles in the syndicated news column, "The Front Porch," and contributed frequently to the monthly newspaper at Camp Victory Complex in Baghdad in 2008, the "Chaplain's Corner."

www.ingramcontent.com/pod-product-compliance
Lightning Source LLC
LaVergne TN
LVHW090600110826
845146LV00001B/205

* 9 7 9 8 8 9 1 2 6 5 1 4 1 *